RED CITY RUNESMITH

Red City Runesmith - A Wolf Shifter Urban Fantasy
Book 0 - Runing With The Wolves* - Fall 2025
Book 1 - Road to Rune - June 24, 2025
Book 2 - On The Rune Again* - 2025
Book 3 - Runing On Empty*
Book 4 - Runing Wild*

*Forthcoming
Titles and release dates may be subject to change.

ROAD TO RUNE

RED CITY RUNESMITH
BOOK 1

C. THOMAS LAFOLLETTE

ROAD TO RUNE
C. Thomas Lafollette

A Broken World Publication
13820 NE Airport Way
Suite #K395495
Portland, OR 97251-1158
Ancient Sword Shattering
Copyright © 2025 by C. Thomas Lafollette
ISBN 978-1-960766-23-6 (ebook);
ISBN 978-1-960766-24-3 (paperback)

Cover Design: Ravven
Editing & Proofreading: Amy Cissell

CONTENTS

Chapter 1	1
Chapter 2	7
Chapter 3	11
Chapter 4	15
Chapter 5	19
Chapter 6	25
Chapter 7	29
Chapter 8	33
Chapter 9	37
Chapter 10	43
Chapter 11	47
Chapter 12	53
Chapter 13	55
Chapter 14	61
Chapter 15	67
Chapter 16	71
Chapter 17	75
Chapter 18	79
Chapter 19	87
Chapter 20	93
Chapter 21	99
Chapter 22	103
Chapter 23	107
Chapter 24	111
Chapter 25	117
Chapter 26	121
Chapter 27	127
Chapter 28	131
Chapter 29	135
Chapter 30	139
Chapter 31	147
Chapter 32	151
Chapter 33	157
Chapter 34	165
Chapter 35	167
Chapter 36	173

Chapter 37   179
Chapter 38   185
Chapter 39   187
Chapter 40   191
Chapter 41   197
Chapter 42   203
Chapter 43   207
Chapter 44   213
Chapter 45   217
Chapter 46   223
Chapter 47   229
Chapter 48   235
Chapter 49   239
Chapter 50   243
Chapter 51   247
Chapter 52   253
Epilogue   259

The Red City Reaper Rides For The First Time In...   265
Acknowledgments   271
About the Author   273
Also By C. Thomas Lafollette   275

ONE

Ragnar squinted against the heat of the fire as he worked the bellows. "Just a little hotter," he mumbled to himself.

The coals needed to be just the right shade of red to heat the metal. Smithing was about fire and fire management. If the metal wasn't treated properly, you could bang on it all you wanted, but you'd never get the right results or even good results. His father had taught him that.

His father…

Ragnar felt burning at the corners of his eyes, which had nothing to do with the heat of the forge. Now that he was back in Red City, there'd been times when he'd wanted to call his dad to get his opinion. Once he'd had to stop himself as his finger hovered over his father's number on his phone.

His father would never pick up again. There'd be no advice. Or fatherly teasing. Or any more arguments. Sure, they'd been spirited, but they'd never been malicious. They'd loved each other too much to disrespect each other. Now Gunnar was dead.

Murdered.

There'd only been one time Ragnar had seen his dad truly angry

—when Ragnar had tangled with some members of the local chapter of the Black Suns, a white supremacist, wolf-shifter, outlaw biker gang. His father had worked to keep the bikers from harassing the people he protected and feared Ragnar's interference would tip the fragile balance.

There. The fire looked just right. With his tongs, Ragnar grabbed the piece of steel he'd selected for his project and plunged it into the hot coals. He had to put aside thoughts of his father to keep a close eye on the heat and maintaining it with the bellows. Pulling the metal from the fire, he checked it and returned it to the coals. Not quite ready.

Since he'd returned from his band's tour of the southwest, he'd spent a lot of time in his father's forge. Mostly because he didn't have one of his own. He'd given up the small one-room apartment when his lease had come up just before the tour so he wouldn't have to pay rent for a shithole he wasn't interested in returning to.

The forge was also the only place he found a bit of peace and respite, surrounded by his dad's tools—the tools Gunnar had taught Ragnar with. Sure, Ragnar had his own tools. But gripping the tools his father had handled felt like the last way to be close to him.

Ragnar pulled the metal from the coals. It was ready. As he put hammer to metal, the vibrations of the impact running up his arm felt like an embrace. When he'd been too small to do more than the most basic of tasks in the forge, he'd sat in the little nest of blankets he'd made and watch his dad work. The steady rhythm of bellows and the hammer on metal. The heat of the forge. The soothing voice of his father.

Gunnar had liked to keep up a running commentary as he worked, teaching and guiding. Most of the time it'd been about the practicalities and philosophies of smithing. Other times it was about their ancestral religion and their Norse paganism. Sometimes, his dad had spoken about other things like life and family.

The combination of heat, rhythm, and his dad's voice worked to put the young Ragnar to sleep almost every time. When his father was done in the forge for the evening, he carried the boy in and put him in his bed.

At the moment, Ragnar had the heat and the rhythm, but he'd never hear the words of his father again. They only existed in his memories and in his heart now.

When he had finished the second of the two halves, he prepared to forge weld them together. He could use the welding machine in the back corner, but this project demanded the respect of the old ways—the ways his father had taught him.

Ragnar, learn to forge weld properly, then I'll teach you the newer ways, his father had said.

But the welder is faster, dad.

I know. But learning how to do it the old way is important.

Ragnar had rolled his eyes but did as has father taught. Now all those lessons flowed through his arms and hands into the project in front of him. Once the two halves were joined, he plunged the piece into the quenching bath, raising a hissing plume of steam that seemed to carry away with it a bit of his numbness.

The emotional numbness had been a defense mechanism to allow him to help his friends being hunted by the Black Suns to escape. But it hadn't gone away once they'd made it home to Red City. Fortunately, this project had allowed him to work through some of his grief. While he was hammering at metal, he also pounded through the walls of his emotional detachment, creating cracks. The hiss of hot metal in water opened those cracks a bit wider.

Once the metal was cool enough to touch, he inspected the weld and the rest of the project for any imperfections. When he found none, he smiled softly.

A less fastidious smith would call the project done. His father's words from another lesson drifted through his thoughts. *It's functional. It'll do its intended* job. *But it looks unfinished. And even though everything below the surface is adequate for the* task, *the eye of the beholder will perceive weakness. And perception is reality.*

Satisfied that the piece was ready for the next stage, he filed off all the rough edges and buffed it until it shined. There wasn't a single rough spot or spur anywhere. He ran his hand over its length. Smooth as silk.

Next came the engraving tools. Once the metal was securely

clamped in a rubber-padded vice and all the tools were set out, he took a few moments to center himself. Like the visually unfinished project, he could create adequate runes do the needed job with only half his focus. He'd learned that early. He had a way with the rune magic. Even his half-assed runes were often more powerful than the work of people who'd put their full focus on the project. But this project deserved nothing but his absolute best.

Though he sat and meditated for a while before starting, he couldn't find the clinical detachment he sought. Focused intention led to powerful runes. But the detachment he wanted was much different than the emotional numbness dominating his core at the moment.

Sighing, he stood up and passed through the wandering stream of moving air generated by the fan he'd turned on to help mitigate the forge's heat. His cheeks felt cool. He wiped the back of his hand across one of his cheeks. Tears.

This project had started the process of breaking the shell of numbness. He'd let it continue its work. This wasn't a project for clean, professional focus. The piece demanded more.

With each line he engraved, with each rune pattern he finished, the cracks were forced wider until his detachment could no longer hold together, and it crumbled. Through blurry, tear-filled eyes, he worked with a tight, emotional focus. When he could barely see, his fingers and the magic guided him as he poured his heart and soul through his hands into the piece.

When he etched the final rune, something inside him settled. He felt empty as he hunched over the glowing metal hull. Placing one hand on each side of his creation, he leaned down and breathed over it. Then with the last puff of his breath, he kissed it.

"I love you, Dad."

Something inside him clicked. He felt just as empty, but now it was a clean, pure emptiness—a place of profound awareness and wholeness with himself and his surroundings.

A soft knock on the door behind him alerted him to someone else's presence. Without looking up, he knew it was his Uncle Roy.

Ragnar felt the older man's aura through his connection to the forge and smithy.

Roy cleared his throat quietly. "It's time."

TWO

"Are you finished?" Uncle Roy asked.

Ragnar, still hunched over the vice holding his project —his back to the man who'd once been a dear friend of his dad's—nodded. "I am."

He unclamped the piece and stood. Handing it to his uncle, he turned away and found a box of tissues so he could dry his cheeks and blow his nose. After he dropped the tissues into the fire and watched them flare to nothing, he faced his uncle. Roy inspected the hull of the two-foot long, steel longboat with a look of profound awe on his face.

"Boy, this is some of the finest... I've never seen anything quite like it before." He finally tore his eyes away, his brow furrowing. "But there are no attachments points for the mast or for securing the lines."

A sad smile spread across Ragnar's face. "There are."

From a nearby shelf, Ragnar picked up the wooden mast and cloth sail Roy had made earlier. His uncle had requested the honor of making them in memory of the man who'd once been as close as a brother to him. The mast and yardarm felt rough from the runes carved into them. The runes representing his father's name—Gunnar

—along with a prayer, had been carefully written on the material of the sailcloth.

Roy handed the hull back to Ragnar. Shaking out the threads that were to act as the ropes for the sail, he placed the base of the mast into the longship. A golden glow spread from where the mast touched the steel of the hull up the mast, out the yardarm, and down the lines and sail.

When the glow receded, the pieces—steel, wood, line, and cloth—were one.

Roy exhaled with an appreciative whistle. "I stand corrected." He reached out and grasped Ragnar's shoulders. "Your father would have been so proud to see what you've done with this. It's magnificent."

The sad smile returned to Ragnar's lips. While his father had always been a demanding teacher, he'd also always been effusive in his praise and pride, even when making suggestions or pointing out areas for improvement.

"Thank you." Ragnar blinked hard to stave off another bout of tears.

Roy nodded and a faint smile disturbed the line of his thick, steely gray mustache. "It's time to go get cleaned up."

Ragnar followed his uncle out of the forge, through the backyard, and into the house and set the finished steel longboat in a cradle that had been designed for such projects. His father had made more than his share of them for local Scandinavian immigrants and their descendants, and anyone else in the community he looked after who wanted them. This was the first time it had been Ragnar's turn to make a funerary longship. He wished with everything he had that it hadn't been because his father was the one who the ship was for.

Ragnar gathered the bath robe from his childhood bedroom where he'd been staying since his return to Red City and crossed the hall to the second bathroom for a shower. After he finished, he dressed and headed downstairs. His mother, wearing a conservative black dress and a pillbox hat, sat in her favorite chair across from Roy, who sat on the couch. His mother's red hair, which Ragnar had inherited from her, had been recently cut shorter so it brushed her shoulders instead of cascading down her back. She almost looked like a throwback to a previous decade thanks to her outfit.

Ragnar walked over and kissed his mother on the forehead. "Are you ready?"

She nodded.

Roy, having found a store with western-style clothes, wore a black western-cut shirt with pearl snaps, black jeans, a pair of black cowboy boots, and a bolo tie. He'd been forced to abandon all his clothes in Colorado when he'd helped Ragnar and his friends flee from the Black Suns Motorcycle Club. There weren't many stores that carried western-style clothes, Roy's preferred style, in Red City. His medium-long steely-gray hair was swept back and nearly touched his shoulders.

"I'll drive," Roy said, standing up.

Ragnar helped his mother to her feet, even though she was perfectly healthy and didn't need it. He just wanted to be there for her in any way he could. On the way to the door, he picked up the longship and its cradle, holding them carefully so as not to damage the delicate thread lines and woodwork of the mast.

After the heat and metallic smells of the forge and the stuffiness of the house, the fresh late-summer air felt refreshing, and contained a hint of the coming autumn. He looked up and down the street. A few of the earlier turning tree varieties had already started shifting colors. Movement under one of the trees caught his attention—only someone sitting on a sport motorcycle, either getting ready to leave or having arrived.

Once they got to the family sedan, Ragnar set the longship and its cradle in the back seat behind the driver, then helped his mother into the car. He climbed into the back behind his mother. She was a short lady and had slid the seat forward to accommodate Ragnar's long legs.

Uncle Roy drove them out of Red City into the hills and left the radio off; no one seemed to want the silence broken. Ragnar stared out the window. The city changed to suburbs and then hills as they climbed out of the basin Red City sat in. The day had been a been a bright, sunny end-of-summer, early-autumn day. The fresh air streaming into the car from the vents felt cleansing after the stinky, polluted air of Red City. He inhaled it deeply, holding it in his lungs so his body could purge the ugliness of the city he called home.

They turned off the highway and passed by the reservoir. While it was the nearest large body of water to Red City, there was no way anyone would hold a funeral there. Sure, the lake was the final resting place of many bodies, but none of them had wanted to end up there. It was the favorite dumping ground for Red City's cops and crooks alike.

No. Their destination was farther into the hills.

THREE

An hour later, they arrived at a beautiful mountain lake surrounded by pine trees, weeping willows, and white-barked beech trees. This high above Red City, more leaves had begun their yearly transformation from verdant green to their autumnal pageantry.

Ragnar snorted quietly to himself. Apparently, he was still feeling philosophical and a bit poetic after the work and artistry he'd poured into the funerary longship. He looked over at the ship secured safely on its cradle. The runes carved into the wood of the cradle ensured the boat remained safe and upright—it had been a nice piece of rune work by his dad.

A sad smile gently pushed up the corners of Ragnar's lips. His work celebrating his father's life rested in a piece his father had made to commemorate the lives of those in their community.

When the car crunched to a stop in the state park's gravel parking lot near the lake, he quickly got out and opened the door for his mother, helping her out.

"Thank you, Ragnar," his mother said, reaching up to bring his head closer so she could kiss his cheek.

"I got the ship, boy," Uncle Roy said quietly.

Ragnar let Roy take the ship. He wondered when his uncle would stop calling him "boy." He was nearly thirty-two. But in all fairness, Uncle Roy had known him for more years as a child than as an adult. Ragnar had just come back into Roy's life a few weeks ago. Ragnar still didn't know what had caused the rift between his father and the man who'd been his best friend. He'd asked his mom, but she said it was a story for Roy to tell.

The parking lot was unusually full. The mountain air was cool as it approached dusk. A lot of people had shown up to pay their respects to his father. He saw his friends—Melinda, Mississippi Pete, and José standing near the path down by the lake. Melinda wore a black pantsuit and a dark-red shirt. José wore a black suit and a white shirt with a thin black tie. Mississippi Pete, who went by Sippi, was dressed much like Uncle Roy but with the addition of a tall, black-felt cowboy hat that looked a few gallons short of the full ten.

Ragnar turned to look behind him as the gravel crunched, announcing another car entering the lot. A big, shiny black classic Lincoln Continental rolled to a stop. The man behind the wheel sent a shiver up Ragnar's back.

Dax owned a dive bar and had become the target of the Black Suns. On multiple occasions, if rumor held true, they'd used rune-magicked bullets to try to kill but had failed. Those bullets were what had brought the man into his father's acquaintance. Dax had sought out expertise on the runes, and his friend Manman Delphine had called in Ragnar's father.

The tall, skinny white man with black hair walked around the car and opened the passenger door for Delphine. He had a bit of stoop to his neck and shoulders and a beak of nose, which gave the man an almost vulture-like appearance. The tall, Black trans woman had been a close friend of his father's, as well as an acquaintance of Dax's. Though the manbo and Gunnar represented vastly different schools of magic, they'd grown close, mostly over whiskey and cards. His dad hadn't been much of a drinker, but he made an exception when they got together.

Dax, along with Delphine who rested her hand on his forearm, walked toward Ragnar and his family. Delphine stepped forward and kissed Ragnar's mom on each cheek. "Erin, I'm so sorry for your loss. Gunnar was a dear man and wonderful friend."

Erin nodded, a cordial but sad smile coming to her face. "Thank you, Delphine. I'm glad you could join us."

"I wouldn't miss it for the world. And please know, if you ever need anything, don't hesitate to call, even if it's just to hear a friendly voice."

"Of course. Thank you."

Delphine gestured to Dax. "This is my friend Dax. He was acquainted with your husband. Gunnar did some rune consultations for him."

Dax offered his hand to shake. "My condolences, ma'am. Gunnar was a good man and cared very deeply for his community." He stepped over to Ragnar and shook his hand and gave him a nod. "Ragnar."

"Dax. Thank you for coming." Ragnar hadn't expected to see the man, but he appreciated the appearance nonetheless, even if he was kind of a spooky bastard. They'd become allies of a sort after they'd worked together to retake Tallulah's bar and defeat the bikers.

Speaking of the devil, Tallulah rolled up in an old pickup truck and came over to pay her respects.

"I didn't figure to see you with all the work at the bar," Ragnar said to her.

"Ragnar, honey, that's why I have staff." She gave a closed-lipped smile to him. "I'm so sorry. More than you can know."

Since they were all clustered together, he gestured to Uncle Roy, who had been standing awkwardly and quietly out of the way. "Everyone, this is my father's friend Roy." Roy nodded a greeting since his hands were full with the longboat.

Roy looked toward the sun after the last hand was let go. "I think it's time to move down to the lake."

FOUR

Ragnar extended his arm to his mother, and together they led the procession down to the lake, gathering people as they walked. Off to the side of the path, he noticed Constance standing with her parents. They'd been blocked from his view by some other mourners. His eyes, drifting away from Constance, noticed a white woman in a black leather jacket and sunglasses standing a bit away from the other small groups. She had a slight olive cast to her skin. He didn't recognize her. She must've been a friend or relative of one of his dad's many acquaintances. Movement in front of him drew his attention back to Constance.

His gut twisted as she approached and stopped in front of him.

She kissed his cheek and hugged him. "I'm so sorry, Ragnar. You dad was a kind, generous man."

"Thank you," he replied quietly.

Connie turned and spoke with his mother. He didn't hear what they said. He hadn't expected to see her today. He hadn't seen her since she'd stormed out of the parking garage outside the Denver airport a month ago. Although he should have made the effort. His parents had really liked Constance and had welcomed her into the family.

He mumbled responses to Connie's parents before they moved on to talk to his mom. Once Constance and her parents finished, they joined the back of the crowd as they resumed the walk down to the shore of the lake.

His mom leaned over and pitched her whisper so only he could hear her. "Connie is looking lovely today."

It wasn't the first time his mother had mentioned her appreciation for Connie. He thought his mother was holding out hope they'd get back together. With each passing day where they didn't speak, that idea moved further from reality.

When they reached the lake, they joined everyone who'd showed up to honor his father. Bob walked up and hugged his mom, kissing her cheeks, then turned and shook Ragnar's hand, all the while side-eyeing Roy. Bob was his dad's best friend and had been for years. He had grayish-brown hair and a beard and wore a gray suit and white shirt. Ragnar had no idea what his relationship had been with Roy or even if they'd crossed paths. Ragnar didn't remember them ever being in the same space together, but memories of Uncle Roy were still fuzzy and few between, clouded by years and youth.

Bob led the service, but Ragnar didn't hear a word of it. He just stared out over the pristine mountain lake. The cool breeze danced over the water and brought the freshness of the mountains to him, encouraging him to breathe deeply and fill his lungs with it. The fading rays of summer filled the air, though hints of autumn added a bit of spice to combination.

"Ragnar," Uncle Roy said quietly. "It's time."

He nodded and took the longship from his uncle's hands and moved along the corridor the crowd had opened to the water. The sun had reached the point where it lit the sky on fire with oranges, reds, and deeper, darker colors at the highest realms as it slipped behind the western mountains. It was a spectacular sunset.

The breeze picked up, and a few leaves floated on its embrace to land in the water. The steady beat of a shaman drum joined rustle of the wind through the leaves. He wasn't sure who'd brought it, probably one of his bandmates.

Squatting, he set the steel longship in the water. It sank to the perfect level, riding like a real longship. He gave it a push. As soon as it left the shadow of his body, the wind filled the small sail and carried the ship out into the lake.

As it sailed away from the shore, the metal began to glow, first along the lines of the runes. Then the glow intensified and spread to include every inch of the steel longship. As it spread over the mast and sail, a flash of brilliant light illuminated the boat, forcing him and likely everyone else to squint against the brightness. When his eyes readjusted to the growing darkness, the boat no longer appeared small but steadily grew until it was as big as a true longship. Behind him, the mourners gasped once they realized what they were looking at. The murmurs of excitement brought him a feeling of satisfaction. His father would've been proud.

The longship still glowed, but now it groaned and creaked as if it were made of wood and riding up and down the brutal waves of the North Sea.

As the murmuring died down, the sound of singing grew louder, accompanying the drum that had started earlier. He watched his ship sail farther into the lake—a glowing ship of magic as the familiar voices of Mississippi Pete, Melinda, and José sang, "Helvegen."

Chuckling quietly to himself, he shook his head. It was a great song by Wardruna but not a revived ancient death song, as it was often rumored to be, or at least presented. But thematically, it was perfect. That was what his friends had been working on since their return to Red City. Melinda's husky contralto led the melody while Sippi and José dug into the harmonies.

Now that the boat was safely in the middle of the lake, flames began licking across it, rising up the lines and sails until the whole thing appeared to burst into flames like a proper old-school Viking funeral.

Ragnar swallowed around the lump in his throat. "Goodbye, Dad."

FIVE

Ragnar stood at the shore by himself until the last ember winked out, consumed by the lake. When he felt a presence by his side, he looked over and saw the top of his mother's head.

"It was absolutely lovely, Ragnar. Your father would have been so proud of your work."

"Thank you, Mom." He sighed. "I miss him so much."

"Me too. More than you can understand."

He didn't take offense at her words. She'd known his father longer, for one thing. Sure, he'd had breakups with girlfriends, but he'd never known the true loss of one he'd loved for so many years, through good times and bad. Not like his mother. He wrapped an arm around her shoulder, pulling her in close.

"I love you, Mom."

"I love you too." She placed an arm around his waist. "It's time to go. Your friends are waiting for you."

"Let me take you home."

"No. Bob offered. You need to go be with your friends and howl at the moon."

He chuckled. "OK, Mom." He leaned down and kissed the top of her head.

She laughed and gave him a last squeeze. "You've been taller than me since you were twelve. I'm proud of the man you've grown into."

He cast one last glance out over the lake. It was good and truly dark. Not a single piece of his ship was left afloat or aglow. Letting go of his mom's shoulder, he turned around and offered her his arm. Their wolf-enhanced eyes would let them safely walk up to the lot, but he wanted to offer her the courtesy so they'd both have an excuse to share the touch of a loved one. Both of their lives were emptier than they'd been a few months ago, and he needed this closeness.

They walked in silence, the murmur of conversation growing as they neared the sidewalk in front of the lot. The crowd had diminished significantly while he'd stared out over the lake. The only people who remained were his bandmates, Manman Delphine, Dax, Uncle Roy, and Bob. A glint caught his eye, drawing it deeper into the parking lot. The woman with the pixie cut sat astride a sport bike. He wondered —

"Take Roy with you. I think he needs some people around him. He's been too isolated in that cabin in Colorado," his mom said, interrupting his thought process.

Ragnar knew what she meant. After he, Melinda, José, Roy, and Sippi escaped from the Black Suns in the Rocky Mountains and made it home to Red City, he'd noticed Roy's awkwardness over the last few weeks. When action had been needed in the Rockies, Roy was calm, cool, and collected. But ask him to talk to people for more than a few sentences, and he'd find an excuse to fade into the background.

"Have fun, dear." She stopped and pulled him around so they faced each other. Once again, she grabbed his cheeks and brought him down so she could place a kiss on his forehead. "And be safe."

"I will, Mom."

Bob noticed them and drifted over. "Ready to go home, Erin?"

"Yes. Thank you."

"No problem. Glad to do something. Take care, Ragnar." Bob escorted Ragnar's mom toward the cars.

"Fuck," Melinda said.

Ragnar heard it a moment later—the sound of motorcycles. And it wasn't the higher-pitched tone of sport bikes, either. He jogged forward. "Bob, get Mom in the car get her out of here. Now!"

Bob didn't answer, but he guided her into the car, jumped behind the wheel, and sped away just as a group of headlights cleared the entrance of the parking lot. Ragnar watched the car's rear lights fade away. He hoped the bikers hadn't blocked the road farther down the line.

The sounds of boots crunching on gravel grew louder as the bikes shut off one by one. Everyone now faced the bikers, who were approaching on foot.

"Did we break up the little gathering?" one of the bikers asked. He stopped at the edge of the parking lot, leaving plenty of space between himself and the small group of remaining mourners.

"What do you want?" Ragnar barked out, his anger growing. The bikers couldn't even allow him and his friends a single day of grief.

"We came to pay our respects to the man who kept things quiet so we could mind our business." He sauntered a bit closer.

Ragnar clenched his jaw, hate burning in his veins. He took a step forward, but a hand on his shoulder stopped him from taking a second one. He hadn't noticed when his friends had moved up next to him.

Melinda stepped forward, partially blocking him with a shoulder. "Get the fuck out of here. Is nothing sacred to you?"

"It was a nice display; I'll give you that. Too bad it was wasted on this lot." The biker sneered at Ragnar's friends.

Dax stepped between Ragnar and the bikers. "I thought I told you the Black Suns weren't welcome in Red City anymore, and that I'd kill anyone riding with a Black Suns logo."

Ragnar shivered. Dax had done something with his voice, adding weird harmonics and disharmonies into it. Ragnar wasn't sure if it was a trick of the moonlight, but Dax's skin and hair seemed thinner, as if his skull were showing through his outer layers.

The biker's smug expression slipped off his face for a second, and he took a half step backward. "We're not in Red City." The words tumbled from the biker's lips. "This area isn't part of the deal." The biker turned back to Ragnar. "We came here to warn you, Ragnar Gunnarsson. Toe the line or reap the consequences."

"What consequences?" Ragnar bit out and took another step.

"Toe the line. Or join your father."

Ragnar lost it and surged forward, but he was yanked back by multiple pairs of hands and arms. He roared incoherently and tried to break loose, but his friends smothered his movement.

Dax extended his arm. A massive scythe appeared in his hand. "You can't threaten a man on the day of his father's funeral."

The biker managed to pale even further in the moonlight as his jaw dropped open, and he took a few steps back.

"Get the fuck out of here!" Melinda stalked forward. "Slim, put it away. I won't allow killing on the day of a good man's funeral."

That calmed Ragnar a little, and he regained a modicum of composure. Melinda was right. His father wouldn't want there to be violence on a day like this and certainly not because of him.

"Too many good people die every day," Dax said, his voice getting every spookier. "Too few bad ones join them."

"That may be true. But these scumbags won't be joining them today," Melinda said sternly.

"She's right," Ragnar said. "Dad wouldn't want this, no matter what."

Giving one curt nod, Dax seemed to solidify. "You get to live today, biker scum. Now get out of here before I follow you until the clock strikes tomorrow."

The bikers backed away slowly, trying to maintain their sense of superiority, but once they neared their bikes, they turned and ran. Soon the roar of custom motorcycles filled the night.

It had started out a peaceful, quiet night. But the bikers had ruined that too. Everything they touched turned to ashes.

Ragnar and the group watched after the bikers for a while until the engines were no longer audible.

"Come on," Sippi said, breaking the silence. "Let's get over to Tallulah's. We have some drinking and singing to do."

SIX

Ragnar stared out the car window and stewed the entire ride to the Honky Tonk Woman. Why couldn't the bikers have left them one day to mourn without exerting their poisonous presence on him and his friends? He concluded they'd never know peace until the bikers were no more. On that point, he certainly could agree with Dax.

When they finally parked the car, Ragnar took a minute in the backseat after his friends stepped out and waited for him nearby to clear his mind. This was supposed to be a celebration of his father. He also knew it was a show of support and love from his friends in a dark, difficult time. He couldn't drag his anger and desire for vengeance into the event.

He took a deep breath and exhaled it noisily. "OK. Let's do this." He climbed out of the car and joined his friends.

"Ready, Ragnar?" Melinda asked.

He nodded and followed everyone into the bar. A sign on the door read, *Closed for a private event.* Tallulah stood behind the bar and as soon as she saw him, she leaned over and whispered something to the bartender, then cut across the room and gave him a giant hug. "The ceremony was lovely."

"Thank you. I'm glad you were there."

The bartender joined them a moment later with two glasses in her hands. She handed them to Tallulah, who handed one to Ragnar. Tallulah had changed out of her subdued funeral clothes into a red western-cut shirt, jeans, and a pair of boots. Her wavy light-brown hair flowed over her shoulders.

"A dram of the best whiskey in the house." She raised her glass.

Ragnar touched his glass to hers and took a drink. It was indeed some fine whiskey. "Thanks, Lue."

"It's the least I can do. Your table is over there." She pointed at a table with a handwritten sign on it that declared it reserved. A place like the Honky Tonk Woman didn't do reservations, therefore they didn't have premade signs.

"I'll send over the usual drinks for everyone," Tallulah said, heading back to the bar.

Ragnar joined his friends around the table and took another drink of his whiskey.

"It's a full crowd tonight," José observed.

He was right. The place was packed. A moment later, a server with a tray full of drinks distributed them around the table.

Tallulah climbed the two steps up to the stage and stopped behind a mic. "Hello, everyone! Thanks for coming out the Honky Tonk Woman tonight to celebrate the life of Gunnar Magnusson, who unexpectedly passed recently. For you longtime friends of the bar who don't know him, he's the father of the front man of one of our favorite local acts—Ragnar and the Desert Rattlers." Tallulah stopped and looked around the room. "Everyone got a drink?" When no one called out a "no," she hoisted her glass of whiskey into the air. "To Gunnar."

"For Gunnar," the crowd replied.

Tallulah took a drink along with everyone else. "Tonight is a fundraiser for Ragnar and his mother to help them out during these trying times. All proceeds go to them. And that includes tonight's food, which is graciously being provided by Mama Adele's Soul Food. Thank you, Adele, Tomi, and Dax!"

Ragnar looked around the crowd until he found Dax sitting at his table with Manman Delphine, Tomi, an Asian woman he hadn't met, and a short Black woman with an afro. If Ragnar remembered correctly, she was Tomi's cousin.

Catching Dax's eye, Ragnar raised his glass to Dax and mouthed, "Thank you."

"Now we got some bands for you tonight who've also donated their time. And if he's feeling up to it, maybe we can talk Ragnar into coming up and singing some songs with his band. So please be generous! We've got a donation box going up here for folding money and an account set up if you'd like to do it electronically. Now let's have a good time and celebrate the hell out of the good man who gave us Ragnar!"

The crowd clapped.

Ragnar felt touched and a bit embarrassed to be the center of attention in this manner. He liked being on stage and singing, but this was different. He knew some of the people here might pity him, but that didn't matter. The people he cared about had showed up for him.

He'd had no idea this had all been put together. His friends had just told him they'd thrown out an invite to some people to get together and celebrate the life of his father.

Even though Red City was a dark, corrupt place that seemed to draw the worst scum of society at all echelons, it was also filled with really good people who looked out for each other. And he guessed he had a pretty good community. Dax's presence and the donated food was a surprise.

Dax had only had a passing acquaintance with Ragnar's dad, and then with Ragnar as they helped Tallulah get her bar back. Ragnar wondered if Manman Delphine had orchestrated the food, since she was the one intermediary who had strong relationships with his dad and Dax and his circle of friends.

While he was contemplating everything, Tallulah plunked down the bottle of the whiskey she'd poured Ragnar's drink from. "This is for Ragnar. Ragnar, share it as you like."

"Thanks, Tallulah. This means so much to me," Ragnar said, standing.

Tallulah hugged him. "I'm sorry for the reason we're here, but you know we look out for our own. You were here for me when those bikers tried to steal my bar. This is the least I could do for you, honey."

"All the same, I'll never forget it. If you ever need anything, all you have to do is call," he replied.

"Same goes for the rest of us," Melinda said, raising her pint of beer at Tallulah.

"Thanks. Now I have to go help at the bar and check with Adele on the food. The smells coming from the kitchen are mighty enticing."

Ragnar grabbed the bottle.

"Hey, where you going with that?" Sippi asked, looking outraged.

"I'm going to go thank Dax and Tomi." He wandered off before anyone else could protest.

SEVEN

Ragnar stopped a few steps away from Dax's table. "Mind if I pull up a chair for a moment?"

"Not at all," Dax said, hooking a chair with his foot and pushing it away from the table.

Sinking into the chair, Ragnar set down the bottle. "Thought I'd say thanks in person and share a little good spirits."

Tomi eyed the bottle. "Those are some good spirits indeed, but I don't wanna take your goodies."

"Nonsense. It was given to me to share. It's the least I can do for the food." He opened the bottle and poured some into the glasses that were slid his way.

"Thanks," Tomi's cousin said. "This is a choice drop. I'm Little Suzie, by the way. Tomi's cousin. And this is Minh, Tomi's girlfriend."

"And what Suzie fails to mention" — Delphine said, a well-manicured eyebrow rising — "is that she's my new apprentice."

"Congratulations," Ragnar said, but Suzie rolled her eyes. "I guess?"

Delphine smirked. "Suzie has been having trouble accepting the path offered to her. But the well of power contained within her demands attention and an outlet."

Ragnar could understand that. His father had told him much the same thing about his own power. No doubt, Uncle Roy had helped guide the observation. Ragnar's dad, while knowledgeable, hadn't possessed a lot of power. His runes worked well because he was fastidious with their creation and pushed himself to the limit. Ragnar soon figured out his work could outstrip his father's once he hit his teens. Unfortunately, he'd been a bit of an undisciplined student during those formative years. He had tried to make up for it over the last few years, finding his need to connect more deeply with his father and his own talents.

"I'm coming around. I guess voodoo priestess is a pretty punk title to add to the résumé." Suzie winked at the manbo.

Ragnar looked around the table. He didn't know Minh. His wolf sense indicated some variety of supernatural, but not one he was familiar with. That left Tomi as the only mundane human at the table. Most of the people in the room were supernatural, though he did spot a few people he knew to be normies. A few of them he was pretty sure knew about the supernatural. There were a few humans who had either been born into the magical world, like Tomi, or who'd found their way in somehow. But there were also a few people he didn't rightly know about. Tallulah had probably invited a few of her closest friends to the private affair. Those people could also likely be trusted with knowledge of the other world that existed in the same world they called home.

Something sent a shiver down his spine. It felt like he was being watched and his heightened wolf sense tingled. There. Leaning against the back wall was the woman he'd seen at his father's service. She held a drink in her hand and looked around the room noncha-lantly. No one stood near her.

The conversation buzzed on around him, but he didn't pay atten-tion to it. He kept his eyes down and let his head shift to whoever was speaking so it looked like he was involved in the conversation. But he remained aware of the woman. She watched the room with a predatory gleam in her eye, assessing everyone and everything she saw. He had no idea what computations her brain was making. There were a lot of dangerous people in the room. Supernaturals always posed a bigger potential threat to normies.

Especially the people who sat around the table with him. Dax scared the shit out of Ragnar, especially after the little show earlier that evening. He had no idea what the man was, but from what Ragnar had seen, he was not to be messed with. The bikers had found that out the hard way. Manman Delphine was no slouch either. All his interactions with her revealed a kind and generous woman, but no one in Red City messed with her. Every supernatural he'd seen speak with her afforded her nothing but the highest level of respect.

But he didn't know if the mysterious woman was a supernatural of some sort. The two times he'd seen her, they'd been surrounded by supernaturals. It would have been impossible to pick out what she was with all the sensory noise.

He couldn't be sure because was trying not to stare at her, but he thought her eyes kept sweeping toward him—or at least the table he sat at—more than any other place in the room.

Leaning over the table, he caught the attention of a few people and waited until everyone focused their eyes on him. "There's a woman leaning against the wall watching the room, but mostly us. Do any of you know her? Don't be obvious checking."

One by one, they performed quick looks. Those with their backs to the wall and the woman brought out their phones and surreptitiously used their selfie cameras to grab a glance over their shoulders.

"Anyone?" he whispered just loud enough for the table to hear.

"Nope," Tomi said.

Dax shook his head, as did Delphine.

"No idea, but I'd like to get to know her," Suzie added, waggling her eyebrows suggestively.

Tomi snorted. "She's clearly trouble."

"I know. She's just my type." Suzie grinned at her cousin.

Ragnar chuckled. He liked Suzie. She seemed like a fun person. Flicking his eyes back to the woman, he found nothing but empty wall. She'd disappeared. Leaning back in his chair, he quickly swept his eyes around the room. There. She was heading for the front door.

"Well, I'll let you get back to your conversation. I just wanted to thank you and share a bit of whiskey. It was nice to meet you, Minh and Suzie." He grabbed his bottle and dropped it off at the table with his friends before heading toward the front door.

He slipped out into the cool, quiet night. Brow furrowed, he surveyed the parking lot until he saw a shadow in dark leather reflecting some of the lamplight. He took off in her at a jog.

"Hey! Wait," he called out.

She picked up her pace.

"I just want to talk to you."

She turned around at the edge of a pool of light under a light pole, and a gleam passed through her eyes. "Who said I want to talk to you? Go back inside with your little friends."

Now that he had her attention, he stopped and held his hands out to show they were empty. "Why are you here?"

"That's none of your business."

"The hell it isn't. This is a party for my father." He took a step forward.

"Go back inside like a dutiful son before you bite off more than you can chew." She walked away, her stride long and confident.

He jogged after her. When she reached a car at the end of the lot, she walked behind it. A moment later, she stopped and pulled on a helmet. The high-pitched power of a sport bike purred to life. She pulled from behind the car and onto the highway but stopped parallel to where he stood. Raising her hand to her helmet, she flattened it out and gave him a salute that ended with flipping the bird at him. Then she roared away from the Honky Tonk Woman, heading away from Red City.

He watched as her taillight disappeared into the distance. When he could no longer see it, he shook his head and returned to his friends inside.

EIGHT

As Ragnar reentered the bar, he nearly ran into Melinda, causing her to jump back. "Sorry about that."

"Where'd you go?" she asked.

"I was just curious about something."

She nodded and narrowed her eyes. "Let's go see about drowning that curiosity in more of Lue's fine whiskey. And you better hurry or Sippi and José will drink it all."

He chuckled and followed her to the table, taking his chair. Sippi grabbed an empty glass and poured some whiskey into it, sliding it across the table to stop inside Ragnar's waiting palm. He took a deep drink and sighed at the burn.

Sippi had a knowing smile on his face. "It's only been a little over a month since Connie dumped you, and you're already chasing ladies?" He raised his glass at Ragnar. "Thatta boy!"

"What?" Melinda turned sharply to him. "Now's not the time to be looking for that kind of trouble."

"No, it's nothing like that." He sighed and took another drink, this time a sip he could savor. "This strange woman has shown up twice tonight…" He trailed off, his eyes narrowing in thought. "Maybe three times. There was a sport motorcycle parked down the street from the house when Uncle Roy, Mom, and I left for the lake. I mean, it could be a coincidence or a stretch, but no one on the block has one of those bikes. At least not that I'm aware of. Then she was at the lake, and now here."

"Interesting." Melinda sat back in her chair.

"Did any of you see her? Know who she is?" he asked.

"I only saw her back as she walked out the door with you in hot pursuit." There was a lot of amusement in Sippi's voice. "Those leather pants were definitely what one would refer to as flattering."

"I wasn't checking out her ass." Ragnar rolled his eyes.

"Why? You should have been, even just as an objective admirer of aesthetic beauty."

"Sippi, there's a reason you're single," Melinda replied.

"I'm a discerning gentleman, that's all."

Ragnar rested his elbows on the table and leaned forward. "Guys. You're missing the point. If it was the woman I keep seeing, then she's been following me all day. Why?"

"To return to my earlier point, you also have what is considered a nice ass," Sippi said, his grin growing broader.

"Oh for fuck's sake, Sippi. Be serious for a moment," Melinda said, annoyance slipping into her voice.

"What? I'm being serious. You can't tell me Ragnar's ass hasn't drawn its fair share of admirers."

Melinda turned to Ragnar. "Can we kick him out of the band? Please."

Ragnar winked at Sippi. "I'd like to, but he's the best pedal slide guitarist I've ever met."

"Ugh. I'm surrounded by clowns," Melinda said.

"I'm not a clown," José said, finally speaking up.

"No, you're the clown's assistant."

Ragnar raised his hand to stop the banter. "So, none of you got enough of a look to tell whether you know her or not. None of Dax's crew knows who she is either."

"Who who is?" Tallulah said, stopping next to the table.

"Did you see a woman wearing a leather motorcycle outfit? She was a little shorter than Melinda. Maybe five-eight? Dark hair in a pixie cut."

"Hmm. I think so, why?"

"Do you know who she is?" Ragnar asked, a bit of frustration coloring his voice.

"Sorry, honey, no. I don't. I can ask around if you'd like."

He wondered about it for a moment. "No, I'll just keep an eye out for her." He wasn't sure he wanted her tipped off that he was getting overly curious about her.

"Do you think she had something to do with your dad's death?" Melinda asked quietly.

The thought had crossed his mind. But how bold could a person be, showing up at their murder victim's funeral services?

"I don't know. But there's nothing we can do about it right now. She rode off into the night." He gave a frustrated grunt and took another drink. Her identity would have to be a problem for some other day.

He slid his empty glass toward Sippi. "Fill it up, please."

NINE

As the evening progressed, the drinks kept flowing. The only thing that kept the gathering from devolving into a total train wreck was the excellent southern food provided by Adele's restaurant. Ragnar even sang a set with the band, sans drummer. When they finished, he went outside to get some of fresh air and quiet. There was a direct correlation between the amount of alcohol imbibed and an increase in decibels.

Walking out back, he stepped away from the lights around the building and parking lot. This far out from Red City, the light pollution was pretty minimal, and the clear sky was spectacular. One of his favorite parts about camping trips with his dad had been staring up into the sky by the dying embers of their fire, his stomach full of grilled meats and smores.

He wondered if wherever his father was, he was staring at the same stars, just from the other side.

Behind him, the shuffle of feet through gravel drew his attention away from his revery.

"Mind if I join you?" Manman Delphine asked.

"No, not at all, Manman."

She stepped up next to him. "Beautiful night. But please, call me Delphine."

He nodded. "Alright, Delphine."

"That was a special bit of rune work you performed this evening."

"Thank you."

"I'm glad you're tapping into your potential."

"Like Little Suzie?"

Delphine chuckled. "Yes, though she may be fighting it more than you."

He snorted quietly. "You should have been there for my teen years."

This time, Delphine laughed. "I was. Your father and I have been friends since not long after I came to Red City. Damn. Almost twenty years. The time flies."

He nodded ruefully. "I was not always the best pupil back then."

"Boys and their fathers often clash in their teens. But he was always proud of you. Even your more lackluster works inspired him to brag. He would have been singularly excited about what you worked earlier today. It was impressive on a raw magical level, but the complexity and how it all worked together... Only a rune scholar of your father's level could truly appreciate the finer points."

"Do you know the runes?"

She nodded, returning her gaze to the stars. "I do. It's how your father and I became friends. I sought him out when I heard about him. Knowing runes is handy in my line of work. In many ways, it's similar to some aspects of voodoo."

"Hmm." He didn't know much about voodoo at all and wondered how much his father had learned during his friendship with the manbo.

"And while I'm certainly enjoying your company and the stars, I did come looking for you for a reason. Would you be OK if we talked about your father's death?" She laid a hand on his forearm before he could answer. "If I didn't think it was important, I wouldn't bring it up."

His father had trusted the manbo, and it had been a month since his father was killed. Now that some of his numbness had worn thin, more questions about the death seemed to be cropping up in his mind. "Dad always trusted you, so I'll follow in his steps in that regard."

"I was speaking with Dax about some aspects of your father's… murder, and he has some legitimate concerns that need to be brought to your attention."

"Dax?"

She nodded. "Without revealing his secrets, let's just say he has a special affinity for death and the dead. You'd be wise to listen to him."

He thought about it for a moment, then chucked his chin toward the bar. "Let's go."

Together they returned to the bar. As soon as his friends saw him, they poured him a glass of whiskey and set it in front of the empty chair he'd been sitting in earlier.

"I see there's an empty table next to yours. Can you combine the two, and I'll bring everyone over?" Delphine asked.

"Sure."

As Ragnar approached the table with his friends, he grabbed the empty table and brought it over. His friends, picking up on what he was doing, cleared one side so he could make the two square tables into one rectangle.

"What's going on, Ragnar?" Melinda asked, a slight furrow forming on her brow.

"Not sure, but Dax has something to say about Dad's death."

"You going to be OK with that? Why he can't he wait until some other time?" she asked.

He shrugged. "Delphine thinks it's important enough to deal with now. And Dad always trusted her, and she trusts Dax."

A moment later, Dax's crew crossed the room and selected chairs. Delphine directed Dax into a chair in the middle near Ragnar. Jamie, the young wolf shifter who'd helped them retake Tallulah's bar, joined Tomi, Suzie and Minh.

"Hello, Jamie," Ragnar said. "I didn't see you earlier."

"Hi. I was helping Mama Adele in the back. I work at the restaurant now."

"Nice." He wasn't sure what else to say. They barely knew anything about each other than through the context of fighting the bikers. She was young, but she'd proved to be pretty damned tough.

"Thanks for speaking with me," Dax said, his voice quiet.

"Delphine says you have something important to say."

Dax nodded. "I have some concerns. This is all based on the assumption that the bikers might be connected to your father's death."

"That's a fair assumption. Especially after their little visit earlier."

"I'd hoped my threat and eliminating Ivar would have bought us more time. I'm not so naive as to believe they'd adhere to my... banning them from Red City—"

Tomi snorted. "Ban? More like death sentence."

Dax tipped his head to the side briefly and gave a half shrug. "Column A, column B. Anyway, my concerns are based around this assumption and colored by my interactions with the bikers. When they first started targeting me, they were using bullets with rune magic. That's how I met your father."

"And me."

A faint, quick smile twitched one of Dax's cheeks. "Indeed. They also used those bullets to kill one of my bartenders. One of the effects of the magic was to tie his soul to his body. They've used a lot of those bullets, or other similarly magicked weapons, to kill a lot of people. There were many in the city morgue who were similarly denied their rightful journey to the next world."

"Next world?" Melinda asked.

"Don't ask me what that might be. It's different for everyone, depending on their belief systems and what powers claim dominion over their souls."

Melinda's eyes opened wide, and she slumped back in her chair, her hand shaking as she reached for her glass. Ragnar had the same reaction, even though he kept his more internalized. Afterlife? Powers? Did he mean deities?

"Anyway, for a soul to be trapped in such a manner—attached to their dead body—is torture and will drive the spirit mad over time."

"And…and you're worried they might have used a weapon like that on my dad?" Ragnar asked as a pit opened in his stomach. If the bikers had used weapons like that on his father… He'd get his vengeance no matter what. He couldn't fathom such cruelty to not only rob someone of their life but to continue the torture into the next one. Fascism was a hateful ideology.

"Yes. That is my concern."

"What can we do about it?" Desperation seeped into Ragnar's voice.

Dax inhaled, then huffed out a breath through his nose. "I need to see the body and do a proper inspection."

"How? Other than when the cops had Mom identify the body, they've denied my requests to see it."

Dax pursed his lips. "I don't doubt it. The bikers and the cops are just two arms of the same corruption."

"Then how can we get in to see him?"

Delphine leaned over the table toward Ragnar. "Have you met Boudreaux?"

"A time or two." Ragnar wasn't sure what the EMT could do to help.

"He's got a friend who is a coroner. She can get us in. But we should keep the party small. Dax, you, and me."

Melinda caught Ragnar's attention. "Are you sure you want to do this? See your father's body, I mean."

He did. He couldn't explain why. Tonight's funerary ceremony had been intended as a way to say goodbye without having access to the body for cremation or a burial—the body was still evidence in an open murder case—but he needed to say goodbye in person. "Yeah. I need to do it. Especially if what Dax says is true and the bikers used such a weapon on my dad." He turned to Dax. "Can you free his soul if it's trapped?"

Dax nodded. "Yes."

He sounded confident. Ragnar hoped it was earned. The thought of his father's soul being tortured like that would torment Ragnar. "Alright, we do it."

Delphine sat up straight. "I'll text Boudreaux now. Be ready to go when I contact you."

"I'll be ready."

TEN

Ragnar waited for what seemed like a month but what was only four days before Delphine called him. Tonight was finally the night.

As he waited for his ride, he sat on the edge of his childhood bed and stared at the wall, his foot nervously tapping on the carpeted floor. He didn't know how long he'd been sitting but a gentle knock on the door drew him out of his stupor.

"Yes?"

"Melinda is here, honey," his mom said.

He sighed, opened the door, and followed her downstairs. Melinda wore a dark plaid shirt and black jeans—basically her normal non-work outfit but in darker shades. Once he cleared the stairs, she pushed herself off the couch and greeted him with a hug.

"Ready to go, Red?"

He nodded. "I'll be out in a minute."

She winked at him, then hugged his mom and left.

"Bye, Mom." He leaned down and kissed the top of her head.

"Have fun with your friends." She smiled softly and squeezed his hand.

He hadn't told her about what Dax had told him. It was information she didn't need, and it wouldn't do her any good. He was still half unsure if he even believed Dax, but the consequences of disbelief could be catastrophic.

On the drive, he ignored Melinda's attempts at casual conversation. His mind was too occupied. But she shifted to more of a friendly monologue to fill the space, which he appreciated. She generally acted like his big sister and just wanted to make sure he was doing OK. He liked the sound of her voice and found her tone soothing at the moment.

They were the first to arrive at their destination—a dark street a block away from the morgue where his father was being stored. After Melinda pulled to the side of the road, they sat in the car and waited.

"Are you really sure you want to do this?" Melinda asked.

"What choice do I have?"

"The same choices we always have—to do it or not to do it."

"If I don't do it, my father's soul could be condemned to endless torture, attached to his dead body." His tone was getting a bit heated.

"Do you believe Dax?" She sounded more inquisitive than accusatory about what Dax had told them.

"All things considered, it's probably best if I act like I do. The consequences of pretending this might not be real could be…well, more terrible than I want to be responsible for."

"Fair enough." Her brow furrowed. "I think that might be them. I think that's his land yacht."

He turned in the passenger seat and spotted the approaching headlights. It was hard to tell in the dark, but it did look like a large black car approaching.

"I wonder where he got that. It's a hell of a ride," Melinda mumbled, obviously talking to herself.

When the car parked behind them, Ragnar and Melinda got out. Dax was the first out of his vehicle and walked around the front of his big old Lincoln to open the door for Manman Delphine. Tonight she was dressed in a more conservative and less colorful outfit—dark jeans and a thin black sweater. Her headscarf appeared to be black as well. Dax wore his usual black leather jacket, black T-shirt, and dark jeans. Ragnar had just gone with one of his usual tight black T-shirts, and his everyday jeans. All together they looked like a reasonably well-dressed crew of burglars.

After they greeted each other, Delphine directed them down the block in the direction of the morgue. Melinda trailed along at the back of the group. Since no one stopped her, he didn't mention anything about her presence. It would be good to have someone he trusted there as emotional support and as backup.

"Boudreaux is already here with Winnie. They'll let us in the back door," Delphine said, turning onto the sidewalk that wrapped around to the back of the building.

The building she led them to was made of brick and sort of rundown looking. Graffiti covered most of easy to reach surfaces. Even a few spots farther out of reach had been claimed by more ambitious artists. As they left the light of the streetlamp behind, they darted into the shadows of the back of the building, stopping at a door. Delphine rapped on the door three times, paused, then another four times. It cracked open with a squeak that sounded obnoxiously loud against the silence of their sneaking around.

Once whoever was inside confirmed Delphine's identity, the door opened all the way, and they followed the manbo into morgue. As soon as Melinda cleared the entrance, a tall, muscular Black man pushed the door closed. After the man cleared the shadow of the door, Ragnar recognized Boudreaux.

Delphine hugged him and kissed his cheeks, and Dax shook his hand.

"Boudreaux, you remember Ragnar," Delphine said, gesturing at Ragnar and Melinda. "And his friend Melinda."

Boudreaux shook both their hands. "Good to see you again."

"Thanks for getting us in," Ragnar replied.

"Don't thank me, thank Winnie." Heels clicking on concrete drifted toward them. "And here she is now."

An attractive white woman with dark hair and wearing a white lab coat appeared in the hall leading deeper into the building. She stopped in front of them.

"Did you bring anything to scramble the cameras?" Dax asked Boudreaux.

Winnie laughed, though it seemed to have a bitter undertone. "This old building doesn't have any security cameras. Don't think they'll add them, either."

"What was this building?" Melinda asked, breaking her silence.

"It used to be an old morgue, but it sat empty and unused after they built new ones to replace it." Her eyes shifted to Dax briefly. "Then when an assassin tried to kill Dax, they blew up the building I worked in, so now they've stuck me down here."

"I'm sorry about that," Dax said.

She shrugged. "It's not really your fault someone tried to kill you."

Ragnar watched the interaction but didn't say anything. He wanted the discussion to end so they could see his dad. But at the same time, he didn't feel ready and wanted them to keep talking so he wouldn't be forced to confront the specter of his father's death and maybe, if Dax was correct, his dad's actual ghost.

He didn't hold out hope this was all some month-long cosmic joke on his behalf, but seeing his dad's body, lifeless in a morgue drawer, would be a definite final note. And he probably needed to see it, if he was being honest with himself. There really was no other reason for him to be here. Dax could do his thing, whatever that was, on his own. And Ragnar trusted Delphine to ensure everything remained above board and honest.

"Well, are you all ready?" Winnie asked.

Everyone turned to face Ragnar, even though this was technically Dax's show.

There was no backing out now, nor would he, even if a part of him wanted to. Ragnar inhaled slowly through his nose, then exhaled and said, "Yeah. I guess so."

ELEVEN

They descended a couple flights of stairs with Winnie in the lead. "Sorry I can't take you down the elevator, but there's no way I'd trust it with a body that wasn't already dead. If there was an office space down here, I'd use it just to avoid climbing up and down the stairs all day, but alas…"

"No worries. I needed a workout today, anyway," Delphine said.

Ragnar brought up the rear, letting the others continue their small talk. The closer they got to the lower levels, the more the chemical smells increased. He guessed it was from whatever they used to preserve the cadavers but didn't care to find out definitively.

"Only one more floor to go," Winnie said. "The bottom floor has the best coolers, so we keep the most important cadavers down there."

He hadn't met Winnie before, but she sounded as if she were almost babbling out of nervousness, which didn't help his own nerves. He didn't know what to expect; he'd never been in a morgue before. He'd been too young when his dad's dad had been murdered, and there would have been no reason for a child to be brought into a morgue. The grandparents who'd passed of natural causes probably wouldn't have even been moved to a morgue.

"OK, we're here." Winnie stopped outside a door and unlocked it, pulling it open. Her eyes repeatedly flicked nervously to Dax, then away again. "I'm going to stay out here."

The stairwell wasn't terribly well lit, but somehow Winnie looked even more pale than she had upstairs. Ragnar began to wonder what he was about to see. Or had she witnessed what Dax could do?

Boudreaux stepped out of the way of the door and backed up against the wall. "This ain't my rodeo. I'll wait with Winnie."

Ragnar set a hand on Melinda's shoulder and leaned closer to her. "You don't have to come in. I'll be fine."

"Shut up. I got this."

Dax and Delphine had already entered the room when Ragnar joined them, Melinda in tow.

"Drawer seven," Winnie said just before she shut the door.

"What does it feel like in this room?" Delphine asked.

Dax's eyes went blank for a moment. "Not great, but not as bad as the old morgue. I mean the newer one." He sighed. "The previous other one."

Delphine walked to the wall of drawers and inspected them, stopping at one that must've been the one they wanted. "Ready?"

Dax nodded.

Ragnar stood back against the opposite wall. Inside him, a general sense of numbness warred with morbid curiosity and a need for finality. The draw sliding open sounded particularly loud in the cold, silent room.

"I'll remove the sheet," Dax said, stepping forward.

"There is none. Well, a small one covering his waist," Delphine replied.

"Hmm." Dax looked over the body. "Do these look like…?"

"Yeah. They do." Delphine scooted over to make more room for Dax. "Is he…here?"

Dax stood up straight and rigid for a few moments before slouching back to his normal slight stoop. "Unfortunately, yes."

"What?" Ragnar approached the drawer but stopped before coming within view of what was inside.

Dax had an expression of sympathy on his face, which looked out of place on his normally neutral visage. "Your father's spirit is still here, forcibly tethered to his body."

"Can I… Can I speak with him?"

Dax shook his head. "No. That's not something I can do. We'd have to contact a medium or someone who can do a seance."

Delphine's eyes narrowed. "I think in this case, we should leave well enough alone. Let the dead remain dead."

Ragnar nodded. "Yeah. I think that's for the best." He did want to hear his father's voice again, but not like this. If his spirit was in some kind of pain, he didn't want the last interaction with his dad to be an unhappy one. The loving but concerned father he'd spoken with on the phone was the one he'd like to keep with him as a final memory.

Melinda had sidled around to the side of the room but still hadn't gotten any closer to the drawer. Perhaps she was psyching herself up for it.

"Are you sure you want to do this, Ragnar?" Delphine asked. "The killer…" A curious and concerned eyebrow raised as she made eye contact with him. "They did more than just kill him."

"What did they do?" Melinda asked.

Delphine kept her kind eyes on Ragnar. "Are you sure you want to know?"

He didn't want to know, but he had to. Needed to. He drew in a breath and stepped forward. Once he saw his father's face again, a bar of hot lead dropped into his guts, burning and gurgling.

His dad somehow looked younger. The normal worry and laugh lines had been smoothed out by gravity pulling back on his skin and a lack of muscle control to move his skin around into the expressions he normally saw on his father's face. He held his father's face in his vision for a few moments, but then his eyes slid down the nude torso, and he nearly gagged.

The murderer had carved all kind of lines into his skin. He couldn't figure out what they were through his burning eyes. He tried to blink them clear. "What did they do to him?"

"It looks like symbols of some kind. They go all the way down his legs and onto the top of his feet." Delphine sounded distracted as she ran her eyes over her friend's dead body. "They look like runes, but I'm not sure."

Dax grunted in affirmation. "It's hard to tell with the body wiped clean, likely during the autopsy."

Ragnar turned around and stared at the wall for a moment. Something terrible had been done to his dad, more terrible than beyond just murder. His body had been violated.

Detachment. He needed to put his feelings into a little box and leave them there so he could get through this. There was something deeper going on, and he needed his wits to figure out what.

Taking in a deep breath, he held it and turned around, exhaling noisily.

"You OK, Ragnar?" Melinda asked. She still stood at an angle so her view of his father was blocked.

"No. But I'll manage it." He steeled himself, cramming the box lid closed. "OK. Do you think Winnie will let us have copies of the files?"

"I don't know," Delphine said. "We can certainly ask."

He nodded and stared at his father's body. He tried to pretend it was just an inanimate object, that it had no more attachment to his life than a friend's sofa. It almost worked. It would have to do.

Taking his phone out of his pocket, he navigated to his photos and quickly created a folder, then opened the camera app. "We need to get as many pictures as we can if we're going to interpret these symbols."

He held up his phone and took a slow video rolling down the body from head to foot, following the lines of symbols carved into the body. Then he started taking photos, meticulously working from head to foot again. When he was finished, he stared at the cadaver.

"Got everything you need?" Melinda asked, sounding a bit nauseous.

"Only half of it." He looked up from the body at Delphine and Dax. "I hate to ask, but can you help me turn it over?"

Dax nodded. Stashing his phone back in his pocket, Dax helped him flip the cadaver. His fath—the body—was cold and clammy to the touch. Once the cadaver was settled, he stepped back.

Delphine gasped, holding her hand up to her mouth. "Oh my."

TWELVE

"I guess we know what killed him," Dax said in a low voice.

Spread out over the back of the body were ten clear stab wounds. Around each one, more symbols had been carved, breaking the near-linear pattern that had been used on the front. In addition to the symbols forming circles around the stab wounds, more symbols had been carved all the way down the body, the linear pattern repeating except where they'd been forced to curve around one of the stab wounds.

"Hmm." Delphine's hand had dropped to her chin as she leaned forward to inspect the stab wounds. "I wonder. Were these wounds from one weapon applied ten times, or from ten weapons applied once?"

Ragnar couldn't figure out why that would matter; ten was ten.

"What are you thinking?" Dax asked the manbo.

"Well, with the all the symbols, it kind of has a ritualistic feel. Ten stab wounds in the back from ten bladed weapons…" She whistled. "It could be killing method, like the symbols, are also in the realm of the occult or the supernatural."

"Does the number of weapons make a difference?" Dax leaned

closer to the body, imitating Delphine in her inspection of the wounds.

"Many non-supernaturals believe in the occult and practice their own versions of it, be it Wiccan witchcraft or using tarot cards."

"Wait." Ragnar looked up from the cadaver, his brow furrowed. "Wiccan isn't real witchcraft?"

Delphine held up a hand and wobbled it side to side. "It was only invented in the 1940s. Some real witches may use it in their practices, but a lot of neopagan mundanes use it as well."

"Hmm," Dax said.

"Anyway, ten stabs to the back are a symbolic death and hearkens to one of the more potentially sinister tarot cards. None are inherently sinister, especially in multi-card readings, but alone..."

"The ten of swords?"

"Exactly."

Ragnar returned his gaze to the wounds and counted ten, though he'd already done it several times, then looked up at Delphine. "Are you saying a tarot card inspired his murder?"

"Yeah." A muscle in Delphine's jaw flexed. "And if that's the case, then I think it confirms there may be a lot more going on than a random murder of one man. Something very bad and, well, to return to a word I used earlier, sinister."

Ragnar felt just as confused as Dax looked.

Delphine sighed. "I've followed the cases over the years, but none have popped up in this part of the country. They've mostly occurred around the east coast and the south."

"What? What have you been following?" Ragnar asked.

"The Tarot Slayer. The serial killer is now operating in Red City."

THIRTEEN

Ragnar stared at Dax and Delphine, trying to rack his brain for whether he'd heard of the Tarot Slayer or not. True crime and serial killers were not a hobby for him.

"The Tarot Slayer? No way..." Melinda broke her silence.

Apparently, true crime was a hobby for her.

"Why would a serial killer target my father? Don't they usually kill blonde coeds?"

"Some do, but serial killers can have all kinds of preferred targets. Jeffrey Dahmer targeted queer men," Delphine added.

"Well, who does the Tarot Slayer target?" Ragnar asked.

Delphine's frowned and pursed her lips. "That's always been the problem with the Tarot Slayer—no discernible victim pattern."

"There are all kinds of theories, but nothing confirmed by the cops or 'experts.' And even most experts don't agree." Melinda, looking contemplative, folded her arms over her chest.

"That doesn't help much," Ragnar mumbled. To distract himself, he pulled his phone out and resumed documenting the markings.

They all looked up when the door opened and Boudreaux slipped in and quietly returned the door to the closed position. He raised a finger to his lips, forestalling any questions.

"You can't go in there!" It was Winnie's voice. "Stop. You're not authorized."

"This order from the judge gives us the authority, now move aside," replied a male voice.

"Let me see that."

"It's in order," he said, annoyance plain in his voice.

"I don't care. It's my duty to protect the integrity of the bodies here. Anyone can wave a paper at me. You can't take custody of any of the bodies in here without my approval. And I won't give that until after I read your court order and ensure its validity. Now quit flopping it in the air and let me have it."

Ragnar, desperate to complete his task, worked his way down his father's body as fast as he could, then stepped to the other side. Dax and Delphine moved out of the way for him.

Boudreaux joined them. "Get that body flipped back over. And we gotta hide. If we're caught in here, we're cooked and so is Winnie."

"Where are we gonna hide?" Melinda hissed.

Boudreaux hitched a thumb over his shoulder at the body. "Same place as him. Find an empty drawer and get in."

Everyone stared at him.

"Now!" he whispered loudly.

That sent the four of them scrambling, opening drawers while Ragnar tried to get the last of his photos.

"Ew, body," Melinda said, shutting the door with a thump.

"What was that?" the male voice asked.

Something thudded into the door.

"Sorry, kicked the door," Winnie said.

Boudreaux stared at Melinda.

"Sorry," she whispered.

Ragnar finally got the last picture. "Dax. Help me."

Dax let go of the door he'd opened and slipped over next to Ragnar. Together they flipped the body and rearranged the limbs so it appeared as it had when they'd open the drawer. Still, something didn't seem right.

Looking around, Ragnar saw a cloth on the ground, snatched it up, and used it to cover the body's waist and genitals. He slid the drawer in and carefully shut the door.

"Here," Dax whispered, pointing to an open door.

Ragnar jogged over and laid down, letting Dax shut him in. Ragnar twitched when the door clicked shut, and he was plunged into darkness. He didn't like confined spaces with no light. And inside a morgue drawer was about as sightless as one could be confined. He quietly felt around, touching the slab he was lying on, the walls, and the ceiling.

His breathing grew shallower. He felt his eyelids twitching as if he was trying to banish the darkness by blinking. It didn't help. The darkness remained—heavy and oppressive.

The sweat breaking out on his forehead quickly cooled in the electrically generated low temperature required to preserve bodies. Soon, shivers broke out all over his body.

He clenched his jaw, grinding his teeth to keep the scream from escaping. Being buried alive was one of his greatest fears, and now he was trapped inside a morgue drawer only inches away from the dead and a few feet from the body of his dad.

Once his teeth started clacking thanks to the sweat drenching his body, he was forced to clamp them tightly together. Whoever was collecting a body likely wasn't a wolf shifter, or they'd have heard Ragnar and the others in the room trying to hide and burst in. But there was no sense trusting to that guess. Plus it gave him something to focus on.

Even so, every time his hands or feet or a knee or elbow bumped against the metal surrounding him, a wave of panic spread through his body. His jaw was clamped so tightly, and he was panting so hard, the air whistled between his teeth. In response, he pressed his legs together and his arms against his sides. If he was forced to be in this hellish drawer, he'd have to act like a motionless body. Maybe if he avoided bumping into the walls and ceiling of the drawer, he'd be able to control his growing panic.

Since he couldn't see in the total darkness, he closed his eyes. He was just lying on a metal shelf. Nothing more. Not trapped in an inescapable stainless-steel coffin. Slow the panting. In. Out. Slowly. Steady. In. Out.

Once he got his breathing under control, he was able to release a little of the tension on his jaw and reduce some of the pressure running through his head. Now the waves of panic were merely gentle waves lapping at the edge of his awareness. Even the thudding of his heart shifted from the banging of a bass drum to thumps on a medium-sized tom and slowed to a fast but less extreme pace.

Now that he'd managed to slightly compartmentalize his panic, he could hear mumbled voices. He focused in on the sounds, trying to distinguish any words or phrases, but couldn't. Even with his enhanced wolf-shifter hearing, the words were rendered into incoherent mumbles thanks to the thick stainless-steel door blocking the morgue drawer. And no doubt, the speakers were keeping their voices low, something people did in the presence of death.

Then they quieted and disappeared. Any minute now… Any minute someone would let him out and he'd be able to suck in the sweet air of not being trapped in a freezing-cold steel drawer. But no one came.

Soon the waves of his panic grew, lapping farther and farther up the shore of his resistance and growing higher and higher until he feared an inescapable tsunami would come his way and overwhelm him. He could see it coming in the near distance as he ground hard on his teeth and panted quicker.

Something clicked near his head. Then he began so shake and shimmy in a different way than his body had already been shivering. Light flooded through his closed eyelids, which shot open. The moderately dim lights of the morgue hurt his eyes, but the pain felt like sweet relief. As soon as his feet cleared the end, he swung them over and sat on the edge of the drawer, heaving in deep, cleansing lungfuls of air.

"You OK there, Ragnar?" Melinda asked.

He couldn't look at her, he was too busy trying to gather himself. "No. Don't like confined spaces."

"Shit, I didn't realize you were claustrophobic," Melinda said.

"I'm sorry," Dax said.

Ragnar shook his head with a twitch. "Not your fault. What happened?"

Winnie huffed angrily. "They've moved your father's body."

"What?" That pushed his receding panic farther away. "Moved? Where?"

"I don't know. I'll see if I can find him."

"Fuck." Dax folded his arms across his chest. "There wasn't time to help his soul."

Melinda gasped. "Fuck."

FOURTEEN

Ragnar sat quietly in the passenger seat of Melinda's car, staring out the window but seeing nothing. Why had they moved his dad's body? And who were they? Winnie had only described them as a pair of nondescript white men in suits. Ragnar didn't know the Winnie, but she'd seemed angry at the violation of the sanctity of her domain.

"You going to be OK?" Melinda asked when she parked near Delphine's shop.

"Yeah." He paused, thinking about the question. "No. No, I'm not. And I won't be until we can ensure my father's soul is free and whoever did this to him is dealt with."

She reached over and patted his knee. "I know. I hope you know we're all here for you. We'll do whatever it takes to help. We all loved and respected your father. Gunnar was a truly good man."

"Thank you. I appreciate you, Melinda. You've always been there for me."

"Hey, we're family. As long as we can keep Sippi from blowing up anything we don't want him to, the four of us will get this sorted out."

He nodded and chuckled. "Yeah. Not sure bombs are what we really need at the moment. Well…I guess let's go inside and figure out what comes next."

They headed into Madam Thibodeaux's, the official name of Delphine's shop. As soon as he crossed the threshold, he was assaulted by a riot of colors and aromas from all the magical supplies and paraphernalia.

He'd always liked going to the store with his father as a child. It felt a bit transgressive, like he was getting to see something he wasn't. But instead of being an unwelcoming warning, it felt more conspiratorial, as if Madam Thibodeaux herself was letting him in on secrets and welcoming him to share her forbidden knowledge. It had been about twenty years since the first time he'd entered of the shop, and he still felt much the same now as he did then. But now he was a veteran of the hidden world of magic and the supernatural. Well, maybe an open-minded journeyman.

"Ragnar, cher, lock the door behind you," Delphine said as she slipped into the back room through the beaded curtain that separated the front of the shop from the stockroom and office.

He turned the lock and followed Melinda into the back room. Dax had started the water kettle and was getting ready to make what looked like tea. Ragnar wasn't much of a fan of the stuff, but he'd seen Dax's vast collection the few times he'd invited Ragnar into the tearoom.

While Dax played with his tea, Delphine brought out several folding chairs and arranged them into a circle. Once that was done, she pulled out a folding card table and set it up in the middle. It would be cramped if everyone tried to scooch in around it, but it would allow them to set their tea on it.

Delphine sat down and caught his attention with a sympathetic smile. "How are you doing, Ragnar?"

He gave half a shrug, unsure of how to respond. He'd just handled his father's body to catalog all the things that had been done to it, only managing it by going to a deeply numb place. Not that he'd emerged from the deep numbness that had descended on him since his father's death.

Melinda patted his knee. "We don't have to talk about this now."

Her words shook him out of his funk slightly. "No. We do. Who would want my dad's body moved? Where did they move it?"

Dax brought a large teapot over to the table. "I'd like to know as well. And why would someone with official power want a victim of the Tarot Slayer moved?"

"Just who is the Tarot Slayer?" Ragnar asked.

"He's an obscure serial killer." Delphine took a full cup of tea from Dax. "Each of his victims was staged to look like a tarot card. In this case"—she fished a box out of her pocket, opened it, and pulled out the cards, flipping through them—"the ten of swords." She set it down on the table and slid it toward Ragnar.

He picked up the card and examined it. On it, a man lay prone, his face turned away, with ten swords sticking out of his back. A red cloak or blanket reminiscent of flowing blood was draped across his lower body.

"What does this mean? Is it just style or is it a message?" he asked.

"The staging is usually a message," Delphine said. "In this case, one of betrayal or deceit. When the ten of swords comes up in a reading, it tends to lead to a less-than-happy event."

"Betrayal? Deceit? My dad was one of the most honest and honorable men I've ever known."

Delphine nodded. "Agreed. He truly was. Which makes this even more mysterious."

"Upright or reversed?" Dax asked quietly.

Delphine shifted in her seat, looking up at the ceiling for a moment. "That's a good question. Neither reading is good. Reversed might indicate an unpreparedness for inevitable change, or an old event or situation now ending badly."

"Hmm." Dax paused to take a sip of tea. "I wish we'd had more time."

Delphine pursed her lips. "Me too."

"Is there any way to get a look at the police report?" Melinda asked.

"Boudreaux is working on that."

Ragnar had to hope the man could get a copy of the report, or they'd truly be operating with no clue and no clues. "And you're sure my dad's soul is trapped?"

Dax nodded once. "That's the one thing I was able to tell right away."

"Is it painful?" Ragnar asked.

"Yes. But not at first. Though if he's left too much longer, his spirit will begin to suffer. We need to find out where the body is. Then I can cut it free so it can go on to the afterlife."

"Damn."

"Who would have wanted him dead?" Melinda asked, her voice a bit too loud and bright.

Ragnar redirected his mind away from the thought of his dad's spirit suffering to the slightly less morose topic. "The Black Suns are the only people I can think of. They've been hounding my family for generations. They killed my grandfather because he refused to join their racist pack, and because he tried to form a wolf shifter pack against their orders. They threatened my dad with the same fate to keep him in line. Instead of outright revolt, Dad chose a more peaceful option by creating a community of mutual aid.

"He still got periodic visits from the bikers to remind him to keep his head down. My parents tried to shield me from those visits, but my bedroom was on the front side of the house and all I had to do was open the window to hear what the dirtbags were saying on the front steps."

"Your dad would have been an excellent leader of a wolf-shifter pack," Delphine said. "Is there any chance he might have changed his mind?"

"No I really don't think so. We'd been butting heads about his stance for a while, and it only seemed to cause him to solidify his decision." He chucked his chin toward Dax. "You saw several rounds of our arguments. I don't think I've ever quite seen him that angry as when he burst into your bar's backroom." He chuckled humorlessly, then sighed. "It's probably my fault."

"You knock that off, Red." Melinda slapped her hand down on

the table. "You don't control the bikers. You can't control what bad men do."

"Yeah, but he helps us escape the bikers, then winds up dead basically a day later." He shrugged. "It's too big of a coincidence."

"Look, Ragnar," Delphine said, her face full of sympathy. "That's highly unlikely. If the Tarot Slayer is working with the Black Suns, the wheels had to have been set in motion long before you called your dad looking for help. I doubt they just happened to have him on speed dial, and he caught the first flight to Red City. This was probably in the works for a while."

"But," Melinda said, "would the Tarot Slayer work for hire? Would he have killed Gunnar for his own reasons? Does he have reasons? Patterns?"

Delphine huffed and sat back in her chair. "There are theories… But in the case of such a unique serial killer, the police in the various cities where the victims have been attributed to the Tarot Slayer aren't in agreement on a lot of the details, other than the tarot theme. I've listened to some of the podcasts but haven't paid too much attention to the details. I guess I'll be going into research mode."

"If we can get a look at the police report for Ragnar's dad," Melinda said, "it would be great if we could compare it to one of the reports from one of the other killings."

"So I guess I'll start researching the Tarot Slayer in-depth. Once I get a basic narrative assembled, I'll send it out to everyone," Delphine said. "We'll need all hands on deck to access contacts in the targeted cities to see if we can get more on-the-ground information. Sound like a plan?"

Everyone around the table agreed, and Delphine suggested they all get VPNs and new emails for added security. Nobody was surprised Dax didn't have an email, but he said he'd get Tomi to help him set one up.

Their plans all made sense, even if it sounded like getting the reports was an impossible task. But Ragnar couldn't believe he was sitting around talking about tracking down a serial killer and that his father was a victim of that serial killer. But despite the reassurances of the manbo, he still couldn't help feeling responsible for pushing the Black Suns into acting on their years of threats. The timing just felt too close to be coincidence.

The thought that his actions had directly contributed to his father's death brought the sour taste of bile to the back of his throat.

FIFTEEN

Ragnar lay in his bed, staring at the ceiling. The meeting at Delphine's two nights earlier hadn't yielded much useful information. The only bright point had been the call from Boudreaux saying Winnie had a contact who she thought could track down a copy of police report. This was why they'd all agreed to set up new emails and VPNs to cover their tracks in case somebody came looking. Now all he did was wait and check his phone for updates that weren't coming.

With all the free time, self-recriminations over his father's death dominated his idle mind. If Ragnar'd just listened to his dad, the man would probably be alive right now. Ragnar grabbed his phone to check the date. He and his band would've been done with their tour by now and heading home, where he'd sit down for a family dinner with his mom and dad and tell them all the highlights of their trip.

When the phone buzzed in his hands, he startled and dropped it on his face. Groaning, he picked it up and rubbed the bridge of the nose where the edge had landed. It was Manman Delphine.

He answered. "Hey, Delphine."

"Ragnar. I've got good news."

"We've got the police report?"

"Indeed. It's in my email box right now. What's the new address you set up?"

He gave her the email address.

"I'll send it as soon as we get off the phone."

"Right. Talk to you later." He hung up.

A moment later, an email pinged his phone. He found the zipped file in his inbox. It was too big to look at on the phone conveniently. He rolled out of his bed and walked over to the desk and opened the lid on his laptop.

After he opened the file, he stared at the list of files and folders. He wasn't sure he was ready to dig into them. No doubt there were lots of photographs of the scene, including of his dad's freshly killed body. He decided to open the written report first, figuring the lack of photos would make it a little easier, but he found himself staring at the letters of the words as they blurred together into meaningless clumps.

He grew angry at himself. A serial killer had brutalized his father and stolen him from his family. The least Ragnar could do was find the guts to open the images and try to track down his dad's murderer. But in the couple days since he'd sat in Delphine's back room, he'd barely left his childhood room. All he could focus on was the idea he'd somehow directly contributed to his father's death. If he'd just quit antagonizing the bikers, they wouldn't have needed to make an example out of his father like they had of his grandfather. At least if they killed Ragnar too, there'd be no next generation to intimidate.

But if the bikers killed him, then his mother would have to deal with losing her husband, father-in-law, and son to the bastards. Ragnar wouldn't bend the knee to them. He couldn't. He'd already gone too far and made himself a direct enemy of the bikers. After the retaking of Tallulah's bar, he was probably seen as a close ally of Dax, who had been waging an increasingly brutal war against the gang, thinning their numbers drastically.

Finally, Ragnar moved the cursor to the images and closed his eyes, double clicking aggressively to open whatever happened to be under the cursor.

When he forced his eyes open, he stared at a photograph of ten knives sticking out of a bloody back. He swallowed a sudden flood of bile, but he couldn't take his eyes off the image. It started to blur in his vision. Shaking his head, he tried to find the detachment he'd used to examine his father in the morgue. Once he found it, or least he hoped he had, he focused in on the details.

He couldn't see much of the area around the body. The body must have been discovered at night. It was dark. He wasn't even sure if the body rested on pavement or some other surface. The blood looked dark and mostly dried, though some rivulets still had that glossy, wet appearance. He let his eyes move to the thing they'd been most drawn to—the knives. He was a blacksmith after all.

The handles looked fairly basic, like the ones on basic kitchen knives. Some looked like they were made of wood, while others had plastic handles. None of them looked new. Knives like those could be found in any kitchen or thrift store in the city.

He sighed. He'd hoped they'd lead to some revelation. Blinking hard, he tried to get his eyes to focus more closely on the small details, but the laptop was too small. Clicking it shut, he sat back in the desk chair and rubbed his eyes. He needed a bigger screen so he could get more details without having to zoom all the way in. A bigger monitor. Like the one in his dad's office.

SIXTEEN

He stood in the kitchen and stared at the door to his dad's office. His mom was talking to someone in the living room. It sounded like Bob. Ragnar briefly wondered why his dad's friend was here, talking to his mom.

No one had been in the office since his father had passed. At least Ragnar was pretty sure no one had. He hadn't. And his mom very pointedly avoided looking at the door when she was in the kitchen.

Well, he needed that larger monitor. He was sure his father would forgive his son the trespass in the name of finding his executioner. Ragnar stepped across the hallway and opened the door quietly, slipping in and closing it silently.

He inhaled deeply. The room smelled a bit stuffy and musty from being closed for a month, but underlying the stale air was the distinct scent that belonged to his father.

Ragnar swallowed back a thick lump forming in his throat. He hadn't thought his father's scent would linger for so long. All he wanted to do was stand there and inhale the aroma so he could preserve it in his mind for as long as possible.

Hot tears rolled down his cheeks, jogging him from his revery, and he dashed them away and turned around. The room looked exactly like it had the last time Ragnar had been in it. The office had been his father's sanctuary.

Crossing the room, he pulled out the desk chair and sat down. Normally, he would have adjusted the seat down since he was taller than his father, but he chose to leave it as it was. He set his computer down and unplugged the video cable from his father's laptop, plugging it into his own. Then he turned on the monitor and opened the lid of his laptop.

The image exploded across the big thirty-four-inch screen. Choosing to repeat his previous sweep of the photo, he started with the edges. It looked like pavement underneath the body.

The blood looked to be mostly at the nearly dry stage except for a few streams that looked a little more liquid. Leaning in closer, he zoomed in on a couple spots on the ground and along the body that looked odd. He realized it was an area where the blood had been smudged or rubbed away—something to catalog away in his brain for later.

He followed the lines of the slightly fresher looking blood to where they emerged from a knife wound. Narrowing his eyes, he stared at the blade. It had a central edge. Kitchen knives didn't have a central edge. Sure enough, the knife was double edged—a dagger.

Why had a dagger been used in that spot and why was the blood fresher looking? He looked closer at the flesh where the knife was plunged into the skin, then he pulled back in his chair until he could see the entire torso. Reaching up from the keyboard, he touched himself over his heart, imagining the line going all the way through his chest to his back. The dagger had been plunged into the heart.

And it had most likely been the last blow delivered, judging by the rivulets of fresher blood. He'd have to see if he could talk to Winnie directly, assuming she'd been the coroner who'd examined and autopsied the body.

He returned his focus to the one non-kitchen knife and let his eyes roll up the edge of the dagger to the cross-guard and the hilt. The muscles of his cheeks flexed. The dagger looked familiar. Very familiar.

The dagger had been made in the forge behind the house, in his father's smithy. It was his father's dagger. His dad had made it. He'd forged the weapon that had delivered the final blow. The killing blow.

SEVENTEEN

The room began to spin around him, so Ragnar pushed back in his dad's office chair and looked at the ceiling, trying to get control of himself. The chair squeaked as he moved back and forth. As he shifted around, he noticed an empty spot on the shelf and the empty mount where the dagger had been displayed.

The killer had been in this room. They'd taken his dad's own dagger and used it to deliver the coup de grace. The person who'd murdered his father had stood not far from where he now sat. They'd laid their hands on one of his father's prized creations and turned it against him.

His breath came in short gasps and the edges of his vision darkened. Leaning forward, he gripped the edge of the desk until his fingers hurt and lengthened his breaths until the darkness faded from his vision. It took him another minute or two to finally get his spiraling brain under control.

When he felt like he could stand without his knees buckling, he stood up and walked to the shelf. He reached out but drew his hand back. If there was evidence there, he didn't want to disturb it. Pulling out his cell phone, he opened the flashlight app and shined it around on the shelf but didn't notice much other than a thin layer of dust that had accumulated in the time the office had been left undisturbed.

He sniffed carefully but only noticed familiar scents that could have easily just been always present in the room. He sniffed deeper but drew back immediately and turned his head. A sneeze came up on him, and he covered his mouth and nose with the crook of his elbow to catch the three quick, hard sneezes. He'd gotten a big snoot full of dust.

Who was he kidding—he wasn't a tracking hound. No wolf shifter was. He opened his phone's search engine and asked it how old of a scent a tracking dog could detect. The answer wasn't encouraging. Maybe up to two weeks for light traces, but that was at the extreme limit for a well-trained animal with a professional handler.

Out in the other room, his mom laughed. Perhaps Bob had made a good joke. The sound brought a bit of bittersweet happiness to him. He was glad his mom could have a brief moment of laughter to interrupt her grief, but he wasn't sure he'd ever find joy in humor again.

He needed to talk to Bob and find out what his father had been up to in the days and weeks before his death. His dad had trusted Bob and confided in him like a brother. And since he was here, it seemed like the perfect time to ask for a private meeting.

He grabbed the doorknob and looked around the room to absorb some of the lingering presence of his dad but stopped when his eyes drifted over the computer monitor. The grisly picture of his dad's desecrated body was splashed across the massive screen. He went over and shut the laptop and unplugged it, tucking it under his arm.

When he emerged from the office, he found his mother in the kitchen making a pot of tea. Ragnar walked over and kissed her on the cheek.

"What were you doing in your father's office?" she asked with no accusation in her voice.

"Just want to be in there for a bit."

She nodded knowingly. "Would you like to join me and Bob for a cup of tea?"

"Sure. I just need to run up to my room for a moment." He

darted upstairs, then headed to the living room a minute later. His mom was still in the kitchen.

"Hey Ragnar, how are you doing?" Bob asked.

"I'm doing alright, I guess."

Bob nodded and gave him a kind smile. "Yeah. About the same here, honestly."

"I actually wanted to ask you something."

"Go ahead."

"Um, I think it would be better in private."

"Sure. How about you stop by my office? I'm pretty light on meetings next Monday and Tuesday. Come on in and tell my assistant I'm expecting you."

Ragnar nodded but closed his mouth without saying anything else when his mom hustled in carrying a tray with a teapot and three cups. When his mom had entered the room, Bob's attention shifted to Ragnar's mom. Something in his eyes lit up. Bob and his mom had been friends for years.

As they talked, Ragnar drank his tea and mulled over all the details he'd seen in the file. The file didn't seem as big as he thought it might be, especially considering the manner in which his father had been killed. He'd have to check in with Delphine to see if she'd sent him everything or if he was missing a part of the file. But at least he had a place to start.

After he finished his cup, he stood to head back to his room to look over the other documents and photos he hadn't looked at yet.

While Bob regaled Ragnar's mom with another story from their shared past, she smiled at him as he left. Ragnar was glad she had someone to keep her company.

EIGHTEEN

Ragnar stepped into the lobby of Bob's office just after the lunch hour on Monday.

"Can I help you?" a white woman sitting behind a desk asked.

"I'm here to see Bob, please," Ragnar replied.

The woman eyed him over warily. "Do you have an appointment?"

"He's expecting me. Tell him it's Ragnar."

She blinked at him slowly, probably wondering why she should believe him. He certainly didn't look like a corporate type who needed the services of an accountant like Bob. She picked up the phone and hit a button. "Mr. Sever, there's a Ragnar here to see you."

He could almost hear what was being said on the other end, but not quite. She must've had the volume down pretty low for the conversation to evade his wolf-shifter ears. After a moment, she hung up.

"He'll be out in a moment," she said, returning her attention to her computer.

He stood for a moment, then shrugged and sat down in the

nearest chair. Five minutes later, Bob poked his head out of the door with his name on the outside of it. "Hello, Ragnar, why don't you come on in. Can I get you a cup of coffee or water?"

"Coffee, please." Ragnar stood up and headed to Bob's office.

"Clara, can you please bring a cup of coffee for Mr. Gunnarsson."

"Of course, Mr. Sever." She sounded a lot more polite now that Ragnar was a "Mr. Gunnarsson."

He shook Bob's hand and took the seat Bob gestured toward.

"It's good to see you, Ragnar."

"Thanks for seeing me on such short notice."

The administrative assistant entered the room holding a mug of coffee with the accounting firm's name on it. She set it down on a coaster in front of Ragnar. Without a word, she left, pulling the door closed behind her.

"It's not a problem. I'm glad you approached me; we needed to talk anyway. Though I'd anticipated giving you more time after the funeral before having this discussion."

Ragnar raised an eyebrow. He'd been the one to ask for the meeting with his father's friend. He wondered what conversation Bob needed to have with him.

"What discussion would that be?" Ragnar asked.

Bob still hadn't sat behind his desk. Instead, he walked over to the window and looked out it for a moment. He sighed and turned around, his hands clasped behind his back. "I guess it all depends on how much you know about your father's business."

Ragnar felt confused. "His business?"

"I guess I should be more specific. Not his vocational occupation, but his role watching over the unaffiliated shifter population of Redemption City." He quirked a knowing eyebrow.

"I don't know much, really. We didn't agree on his stance of remaining unaffiliated and bowing to the Black Suns."

Bob chuckled. "He and I discussed that on occasion. But did he bring you in on how he kept the peace?"

Ragnar shook his head, confusion writ large on his face. "He never gave me much in the way of details. Just told me it was important that I not antagonize the bikers."

Bob nodded and took his seat in the big, fancy executive leather office chair. Leaning forward, he steepled his fingers in front of his face. "Well, the peace was bought with more than just a lack of resistance. And 'bought' is the correct phrasing."

"Bought? What do you mean?"

"That's an old, long story, but to make short work of it…the Black Suns have demanded tribute to keep the peace. A wergeld, to use the old term."

"A wergeld?" Ragnar's mind had ground to a halt. He had no idea the peace had literally been bought.

"A wergeld is basically translated as the price of a man."

"I know what it means." The words came out with a bit more bite than he'd intended.

"Well, they applied it in two ways. If you met their racial standards, you could join the gang. If someone did, it usually exempted their family from the price of peace. Those who didn't want to join or wouldn't be allowed to join—"

"Non-white people."

"Exactly. Those people had to pay money to secure their peace."

Ragnar sneered. "So a basic mafia protection racket?"

"Yes."

"Corrupt cops. Fucking Nazi bikers. Everyone's trying to shake down the innocent." He hadn't realized that might include his father.

Seeing where Ragnar's mind had gone, Bob held up a hand. "Don't get me wrong, your dad was involved, but he didn't take any kind of cut himself. He just stood between the bikers and the community. He hated that he had to, as you put it, 'shake down' the people he was looking after."

Ragnar wasn't sure that made him feel any better. Red City was rotten to the core. Sometimes people had to do what they could to survive, including stuff that would be morally questionable or illegal in another city. He'd always held his father on a pedestal as someone who'd managed to walk the line between corruption and an upright life. But Red City had even sullied his father.

"I can see the gears working in your head, Ragnar. Your father was a good man. The best I've ever met. But sometimes a man has to put aside the purity of his honor to make sure those he protects stay safe. And he protected more than just you and your mother. He had dozens of families standing behind him, and he made sure the bikers left them alone. Well, as best as he could."

Ragnar grabbed the cup of coffee and held it in both hands as he slumped back into the chair. His mind was both running a million miles an hour and grinding down. He'd admired his father as an upright and honorable man. But he'd also been someone who made sacrifices for those he cared for. Ragnar had seen his father do it many times. But to move money from the scared and weak to the bullies? He was having trouble reconciling it.

He hadn't seen any evidence of his father's activities, and he wasn't some fresh-faced kid. But then again, they hadn't been quite as close in the last few years as Ragnar worked on his band. They'd argued more about the bikers over that time as well, driving a wedge between them.

He sighed. It could have been something his dad would have done — hiding the unsavory business from his family. Ragnar always felt his dad had been overly protective and struggled with letting Ragnar go out into the world on his own and make mistakes.

"Ragnar," Bob said, interrupting Ragnar's train of thought, "Gunnar always tried to shield you and your mother from the ugliness of this city. He did what he had to do to make sure everyone survived, even if it meant sacrificing some of his own dignity in the process."

It made sense in its own way. Sacrifice had been something his dad had always stressed. You sacrificed for your community. And whether Ragnar liked it or not, until he had evidence to the contrary, he'd have to accept that his father had facilitated paying off the bikers.

"What changed?"

"What do you mean?" Bob asked, narrowing his eyes.

"If he was useful to the bikers, why kill him now?"

Bob exhaled noisily and sat back in his chair, which squeaked. "Well, Ragnar, I think you got to him. He came to me a couple of months ago and said he was thinking about stopping the payments.

He said he wanted to actually protect his community. Even mentioned wanting to take things further and form a pack for the shifters who wanted to join." He returned his elbows to the desk and peered through his steepled fingers.

"Gunnar raised you to be an independent and upright person, which I guess backfired on him. I think he realized you were right."

"But why now?"

"I mean, the Black Suns are at the weakest they've ever been, at least in Redemption City. Their underground war isn't going in their favor. They bit off too much by taking on that shit bar owner." He shrugged. "Now seemed the best time possible."

Ragnar sat in silence, his jaw hanging open. His dad had defied the bikers and was planning to form a pack? That didn't seem like his dad at all. But after the revelation of the bribe money, did he really know his dad as well as he thought he had?

"How far had it gone?" Ragnar asked after shaking off his momentary shock.

Bob furrowed his brow and looked confused.

"Forming a pack. How far had it gone?"

Bob shrugged. "I don't know. He only mentioned it one time to me. But not long after that, well, you know."

"The bikers killed him," Ragnar mumbled to himself.

"Exactly."

Another question came to the forefront in his mind, one that had been percolating for a while. "But why the Tarot Slayer?"

Bob's face flashed a glimmer of shock for the briefest of moments. If Ragnar hadn't been paying attention, he'd likely have missed it.

Bob asked. "Where did you get this information? The police aren't saying they have any suspects. They've been pretty tight lipped in fact."

Ragnar, not having meant to reveal the tarot slayer information, scrambled to find an answer that wouldn't reveal his activities in the morgue. He bought himself some time by taking a drink of his coffee. "Um, I can't reveal too much. But I've got a friend who overheard some cops talking in a bar."

"I hope you're keeping your nose out of this. Red City cops aren't known for their friendliness or their forgiveness. And if the Black Suns catch wind of you poking around, they will come after you."

"I know." He sighed. "I just feel so helpless, Bob. It's my dad. I didn't think even the Black Suns would stoop to bringing in a serial killer. Usually they just do their own dirty work, and from what I hear, they relish the opportunity."

Bob nodded thoughtfully, looking mollified. "Well, and this is just a guess, but I think they're pretty focused on their little turf war right now. From the rumors I've heard, there aren't many members of the local chapter left. Most of the ones running the streets these days are from out of town. They probably don't care about a local issue like this, perhaps. Also, your father was a well-respected member of the community, even beyond the world of the supernatural community. The bikers are raising enough noise as is. Being directly linked to your father's death might have been a bridge too far. The media and the public would have demanded a proper investigation."

"How so? Doesn't seem like anyone cares about gangs like the Black Suns."

"The Black Suns have always had to walk a line. They pretty much get free rein as long as they don't make too much noise, go after the respectable elements in the city, or cause too much trouble for those in charge. They're creating a lot of noise now, which is causing issues for the police and elected officials. Being linked to the death of a prominent and well-liked member of the community could have pushed the ruling class into turning against the bikers—at least for a while. But bring in a newsworthy figure like the Tarot Slayer, and they get the job they need done while deflecting from their other activities. Frankly, I'm surprised the media isn't all over this, if it is the work of the Tarot Slayer. It would be a field day for them."

"Me too. They'd normally love something like this."

"And that speaks to the city and the cops working to keep it suppressed." He fixed a stern but friendly expression on his face. "And that means you should stay out of it. If the wrong person finds you snooping around, you could get in serious trouble. You don't want to be on the radar of the Redemption City Police Department."

"That's the truth." Ragnar pursed his lips and a thought came to him. "What's happening with the money if my dad isn't facilitating payments anymore?" Ragnar didn't care about the cash, but if it was a protection payment...

"Oh, don't worry about that. The bikers made sure it was taken care of. They showed up in my offices the Monday after your father's service to ensure the money keeps flowing. I'm handling the collection and handover now."

"Ah. I guess that's good." He wasn't sure if it was actually good or not, but at least the people who relied on not being harassed by the bikers could still buy their sense of peace for now.

Bob looked at his fancy gold watch. "I'm about to head into an important meeting. If you have any last questions, let's make it quick."

"No, I don't think I have any more questions at the moment." Ragnar had plenty of questions but had left off the "for you" from his statement. He might've even had more questions than he'd arrived with. He stood up and extended his hand across the desk. "Thanks, Bob. I appreciate your time."

Bob stood and shook his hand. "Anytime, Ragnar. And remember what I said about not digging into the police's business."

"I don't intend to interfere in the investigation." It was true. He just wanted to conduct his own investigation.

"Good man. Say hi to your mother for me."

Ragnar nodded and left, his mind whirling with a maelstrom of thoughts and questions.

NINETEEN

Ragnar, Melinda, and Mississippi Pete had driven through the area a few times to make sure there wasn't any undue police presence around, but like most sketchy neighborhoods in Red City, the cops seemed more interested in patrolling donut shops and keeping the poors out of the wealthier parts of town.

"Are you sure you want to do this?" Melinda asked.

"What do you mean?" Ragnar asked.

"Well, you know…"

He sighed. He loved Melinda like a big sister, but sometimes she took the role a bit too seriously. "I've seen his body. I've dug through the police report and seen a lot of the photos. Some pavement isn't going to disturb me more than I already am." He hadn't meant to add so much annoyance into his voice.

After he'd left Bob's office, he'd called his friends to explain the next part of his investigation and made arrangements to meet them the following evening to check out the murder site. Although Melinda had objected, she'd demanded to go and to bring Sippi too. "In case of trouble," she'd said.

"I'm sorry, Ragnar. I'm just trying to look out for you."

"I know. I'm sorry for sounding peeved. But this whole thing is fucked up, and I'm so far into it that not much is going to bother me at this point. When I decided to pursue this course, I knew it would be hard and lead me down paths I couldn't expect. Now we're going to check out the spot where he his body was found." He shrugged. "I do appreciate you, Melinda, especially your support. But sometimes I think you forget I'm an adult now. I'm not the annoying little snot-nosed kid who used to tag along behind you when our parents hung out."

She chuckled. "You know, I'm beginning to realize that. I guess I'm having trouble adjusting to this new side of you."

New side? He thought about her words for a moment. He'd been nominally the leader of the band, but they'd run it as a group with everyone having equal say. In band arguments, Melinda usually took his side or tried to anticipate what she thought his side might be. But since they'd gotten involved in investigating his father's murder, he'd been taking charge more and making tough decisions.

"Where do you want to park?" Sippi asked from behind the steering wheel of Melinda's car.

"Find us a dark, out-of-the-way spot," Ragnar replied. Without checking in with each other about what to wear, they'd all dressed in dark, nondescript clothes.

Sippi turned down a street with only a few functioning street-lights and parked under a tree. They all looked around, checking if there were any pedestrians or eyes watching. Ragnar needn't have worried. This wasn't the safest part of town even in daylight. There wouldn't be anyone wandering around now.

When it seemed clear, Ragnar popped out and shut the door quietly. Sippi and Melinda followed a moment later, taking his lead with the silent approach. Melinda slung a backpack over her shoulder. Pulling out his phone, Ragnar checked the location he'd programmed into his phone's map app before leaving.

He inhaled deeply, then coughed. He'd been trying to rely more on his other senses beyond just sight and sound. He was a wolf shifter; he might as well use all the enhanced options he had. But the cool night air was saturated with petrochemical fumes mixed with what must've been raw sewage. Not a pleasant cocktail. He took a more cautious sniff, trying to determine if there were any people around besides himself and his friends. Nothing. At least not in the direction the breeze was blowing.

He picked up his pace as he headed to the pin on the map. The only noise was the sparse traffic on a nearby overpass cutting over and through this little section of Red City. The path took them under the overpass, around a block, and back under the overpass on a different street.

Ragnar stopped and looked around. This was the spot where his father's body had been found. "Melinda, can I get your iPad, please?"

She handed it to him. He'd need to get one of his own. The bigger screen was handy, plus he wouldn't have to rely on her to carry it, especially if she wasn't available to let him borrow hers. He opened the tablet and found the picture he'd queued up before they'd climbed into the car.

His dad's dead and violated body practically jumped out at him and caused him to flinch. Despite his earlier protestations, each time he saw the images of his dead dad, it felt like another stab to his guts. He reached into the place where he'd been storing his numbness and grasped hold of some of it.

"OK." He pointed to a nearby wall. "His body was found over there."

They crossed the distance to the dirty, graffiti-covered wall. There was almost no brick visible through the thick layers of painted tags. Using two fingers, he expanded the image—this one had a much wider angle—on the iPad and tried to find some matching graffiti so he could further orient himself. In the intervening weeks, more tags had been layered over the wall, but he found a section that was recognizable and moved closer to it, then adjusted his position based on the placement of the body in relation to the wall.

He moved closer to the spot where he figured the body had been without stepping on the spot. He didn't know why, but it didn't feel right to step there.

"What direction is the wall running?" Ragnar asked.

Sippi pulled out a compass and opened it up. "Um, looks like the wall runs north-south."

"So the body was oriented with the head to the south." He didn't know why it mattered, but Manman Delphine had asked for the information.

"Here." Melinda extended her hand and gave him the portable black light they'd brought. It was meant to be more of a novelty item for parties or for putting in your van or car. He turned it on and nearly gagged.

The wall and the ground were awash in splatters and streams at about waist height. The wall must've been a regular spot for people who wanted something to piss on. He felt disgusted that some of the streams had run over the spot where his dad had been found. He should have died in bed at a nice ripe age, not on a piss-covered patch of pavement in a shitty part of Red City.

Shaking his head, he ignored the wide swaths of urine stains and widened his inspection area. He looked around on the ground for about fifteen feet on each side of where the body had been found, discovering nothing that sparked further interest. So he moved to the wall, sweeping the beam of black light left to right starting where the wall intersected the ground and working his way up.

"There!" Melinda said, pointing.

Ragnar stopped.

"No, go back about two feet to your left."

He swept the light back to the left.

"Stop! There."

"Indeed," Sippi mumbled.

Ragnar rotated the light bar so it was horizontal. A crude arrow had been smeared on the brick wall about head height. It pointed to the south.

"Can one of you take a photo on your phone?" Ragnar asked.

"I got it," Melinda said.

"Sippi, can you hold the light for me? I want to pull up some photos from the report."

Sippi took the light and kept it trained on the arrow. Ragnar opened the iPad cover and flipped through the images until he found a few that included the wall.

"Interesting. Very interesting," he mumbled to himself. Sippi and Melinda crowded in around him, so he extended the iPad out so they could both more easily see the screen. "Not one of the images has anything marking the wall in that spot. I'll have to check all the written reports when I get back home, but I don't think they noticed this arrow."

"How can we be sure it's related to the murder?" Melinda asked, staring hard at the screen then shifting her gaze back to the wall.

"I guess we technically can't, but it feels out of place compared to everything else here." He examined at the graffiti and how the arrow intersected it. "Look, it doesn't fit in with the graffiti here. Sippi, can you sweep the light around up higher?"

Sippi complied.

"See, nothing up there other than a few splatters that might be bird shit or something else. We've got piss on the ground and from the waist down, nothing real up top, and this one arrow that aligns perfectly with where the body was found."

"It does seem unlikely that it's not related," Melinda said, though her voice indicated she wasn't fully convinced.

"I'm inclined to agree with Ragnar," Sippi said.

"We might have found a clue the cops missed."

She snorted. "Not that that's hard with those incompetent goons."

"And if this kill was affiliated with the bikers, they probably let the cops know so they could bungle the investigation."

"That's true. I'm surprised the police report didn't mysteriously get lost in a tech failure," she said.

"Incompetence and malfeasance make their files a lot harder to trust. If it was one or the other, we might be able to reason our way around the information we've been given, but both issues make it a lot murkier." Ragnar stared at the wall and reached up to scratch his bearded jaw.

Something broke in at the edge of his awareness. Sniffing the air, he moved his head so he could catch the new shift in the breeze, which brought a scent from a new direction.

He smelled someone nearby.

TWENTY

Ragnar had trouble distinguishing the smell because the shift of the breeze carrying it to his nose was blowing over Sippi first. Focusing on the smell, he handed the iPad to Melinda and stepped around Sippi so he could get the scent uninterrupted. Sippi adjusted his position and took up a protective stance to Ragnar's front left.

Clenching his jaw, he put his hand on Sippi's shoulder, then took a step so he was once again in front of him. "Stay there."

Sippi grunted in acknowledgment.

Ragnar concentrated on the breeze, drawing in a slow, careful breath. He did his best to ignore the scent of piss and pollution, homing in on the scent of an unwashed body. There was also a faint whiff of stale beer. He made a snap decision and waved his friends after him as he stalked forward on quiet feet.

His friends picked up on his body language and followed along silently. The scent-laden breeze drew him toward one of the pillars holding up the overpass. There was a small patch of dirt surrounding the base of the pillar. Most of the grass was worn away, but a scraggly bush created a partially private space between it in the concrete rising out of the dirt.

A lump behind the bush shifted and started snoring. Ragnar gestured for Melinda and Sippi to fan out to each side. They moved quickly around to the head and foot of the lump under the ratty blanket, blocking it in. Ragnar waited until they were in position to move around the bush. He squatted next to the sleeping person. The snoring stopped, and the body grew unnaturally still. They were awake.

"I can see you're awake. No one is going to hurt you or take anything from you," Ragnar said softly.

"Go away," said a sleep-stained, masculine voice.

"I just have a few questions to ask, then we'll leave you alone."

"I don't know nothing. Go away."

"We'll make it worth your while," Sippi said.

Ragnar shot a hard look at his friend. Twenty dollars, all the money Ragnar had in his wallet, was hardly enough to make anything worthwhile.

"How worth my while?" the person asked from under their blanket.

"I've got twenty bucks you can have," Ragnar said.

The top of the blanket flipped down to reveal a dirty white face covered in a long, thick dingy-blond beard. "Nope. Not worth it. Go away."

His "go away" didn't hold the same vehemence it had a moment earlier. Ragnar cast a hard glance at Sippi, who got the picture and pulled out his wallet.

"I can add thirty-seven more," he said, staring into his wallet.

"Go away." This time the tone held a note of curiosity.

When Ragnar looked over to Melinda, she rolled her eyes and took out her own wallet. "I can add one hundred to the total."

A grin split the dingy beard. "She gets it. What do you want?"

Some of the building tension fell from Ragnar's shoulders. "Do you usually sleep around here?"

"Money first."

Ragnar sighed and pulled the twenty-dollar bill from his wallet before putting the billfold away. He stood up, took the stack of bills from Sippi, and added Melinda's hundred-dollar bill to the pile.

Squatting back down, he put the money in the homeless person's waiting hand. He flipped through the bills, his smile growing as he neared the bottom bill. Then the money disappeared.

"Yeah. I sleep here."

"How about six weeks ago? The night the body was found over by that wall."

The homeless man tensed up, his eyes flicking toward Melinda and Sippi. And with Ragnar basically squatting over him, he had nowhere to escape to. "Don't know nothing about that. Didn't see nothing. Nothing."

"That's a bingo," Sippi mumbled.

"We're not cops. We not here to roust you or drag you off. I'm just looking for a few answers," Ragnar pleaded.

"Not worth it."

Melinda sighed. "You fuckers owe me." She pulled out two more bills. "Would another two hundred take care of it?"

The man nodded eagerly. She reached down but drew her hand away before he could take the money. "This is all you're getting. We get answers until you legitimately don't know anything more. If you try to hold back and shake us down for more, I'll just kick the answers out of you."

Ragnar held up his hand to Melinda but made sure he caught the homeless man's attention before speaking. "That won't be necessary, will it? It'll just be some quick questions and answers, then we'll go away, and you can go back to sleep and dream of all the things you'll do with your easily obtained money. Right?"

The homeless man nodded. "Right."

Melinda handed the money to the man, and he carefully took it from her, probably trying to avoid irritating the woman who'd just threatened him. Ragnar knew she wouldn't assault the poor guy, but when she was annoyed, she liked to bark, even if there was rarely any bite to back it up.

"What do you want to know?"

"Were you here on the night the man was killed over there by the wall? The guy with all the knives in the back."

He nodded.

Ragnar exhaled in relief. Answers. "Did you see what happened?"

"I saw some of it." He paused, then his eyes flicked to Melinda, whose face was still hard. "He wasn't killed here."

"What?"

The man gave Melinda one last glance and took a moment and closed his eyes. He exhaled and opened them again. "This is all I know. I was sleeping here when a car screeching to a stop woke me. I rolled over and hid under the bush there, but I saw everything. It was a white van. Someone came around back and opened up the back doors—"

"What did they look like?"

"I don't know. They wore all black and had their face covered. Maybe average build." He eyed Ragnar up and down. "Shorter than you. Maybe about her height. I don't know. It was hard to tell from here."

Ragnar nodded, cataloging the information.

"Anyway, they reached into the back of the van and dragged out something wrapped in black plastic. They laid out the bundle, then cut the plastic apart the long way. That's when I saw the white flesh. Then the knives. It was a lot of knives." He shivered. "I retreated back farther and grabbed some dirt to rub into my skin so they wouldn't see me.

"I figured they'd take off after that, but they pulled the plastic out from under the body and threw it into the van. After that, they draped a red blanket over the lower half of the body and posed the… corpse."

"Did they do anything to the wall?" Melinda asked.

"Yeah, but I couldn't see what because they blocked the view, but they rubbed something on the wall. After they moved, I couldn't see what they'd done though. Then they stared at the body for a few minutes before turning and getting in the van and driving off."

"Did you call nine-one-one after the van left?" Ragnar asked.

The man shook his head. "No. I got the hell out of here. I don't want nothing to do with killings and cops. This right now is more than I want to have to do with it, but it's not like I got a choice, and you paid me."

"Honestly, it was probably a good thing he did run away. The cops would have likely dragged him in and pinned it on him. Kill two birds with one stone. Clean up the streets, solve a murder," Sippi said.

The man nodded vigorously. "I ain't got much out here, but at least I ain't getting shanked in prison to make me go away forever."

Sippi and the man were probably right. It was exactly what the Red City cops would do. They'd declare it a victory against crime and say something callous about the accused killer being murdered behind bars, saving the taxpayers' money to house and execute him. It would have saved the cops a much more elaborate coverup, such as taking the murder victim's body out of the morgue. Ragnar couldn't blame the homeless man for not wanting to get involved.

"Anything else you can think of?" Ragnar asked. "Smells, sounds? Anything?"

The man thought for a moment, before shaking his head. "No. Can't smell much but piss around here. And it's noisy with the road overhead. I can't think of nothing else."

The man was likely a normie. Ragnar couldn't detect anything magical about him, not that he could detect everything in the supernatural world.

"Thanks. I do appreciate it."

"We made a deal. You paid, I gave you all the information I had."

Melinda snorted. "Might be the one honest person in Red City."

Ragnar couldn't disagree, though he considered most of the people he knew to be pretty honest, at least not less so than the average person. Then again, most citizens keeping their heads down and trying to get by in Red City were pretty honest, except when they might need to lie out of necessity to protect themselves. It was a murky city that did bad things to good people, but Melinda's statement still held. This city made liars of everyone eventually.

"Well, we'll—"

He heard the scuff of a foot on pavement nearby—boot sole, gravel, and asphalt grinding together. He stood up rapidly and held up a hand to quiet everyone. Edging over the side of the pillar, he peeked around it. He saw the distinct shape of a human body in the distance. The shadow in the darkness stood still, but a glimmer of light glinted off whatever they were wearing. It looked like leather in the dim light under the overpass.

They stared at each other, at least Ragnar assumed the figure was staring his way—it looked like he was seeing their front more than their back. The shapes and shadows didn't look quite right for the back. Then the person spun and dashed away.

TWENTY-ONE

"Backpack!" Ragnar barked out.

Melinda shucked it off in a split second and held it out so he could snag it as he took off at a sprint. He was glad he'd put on his running shoes in the interest of having a quieter option than his normal cowboy boots.

As he ran, he unzipped the back pocket of the backpack and pulled out a little plastic disk. Behind him, he heard the car fire up. He yanked the zip closed and slung the pack over one shoulder. He tried to get his other arm through the second strap but missed the first few times. Once he managed it and got the backpack situated, he poured on the speed.

While he'd fiddled with the backpack, he'd somehow kept pace with the person he was chasing. Now that he could focus entirely on them, he gained on them slowly. Digging deeper, he pulled out some of his power and speed from his wolf side. Now he moved faster and was truly gaining.

The person disappeared behind another of the overpass's pillar.

He darted to the right and found them climbing onto a motorcycle. "Stop! I just want to talk."

They turned their head. It was the woman who always seemed to be popping up wherever he was.

"You! Stop, please!"

She crammed her helmet down over her head and turned away from him. Just as she fired the motorcycle to life, he lunged forward and grasped for the bike. At first, his fingers dragged across plastic. But when they hit metal, he unfolded his thumb, letting the plastic disk he'd pulled from backpack go. It stuck to the metal as she tore away, her back tire spitting bits of gravel in his face as he fell to the ground.

As he pushed himself off the pavement, Melinda's car screeched to a stop next to him. "Get in," shouted Sippi.

Ragnar dove into the waiting open back passenger door. Melinda smashed the gas pedal down, and they took off. Sitting up, he contorted to get the backpack off in the tight confines of the back seat and pulled out the iPad. He opened the tablet and brought up the tracking app tied to the little GPS tag he'd planted on the bike.

It was an idea he'd gotten from Jamie when she'd helped them retake Tallulah's bar. Apparently, Dax's crew used the tags quite a bit in their war with the bikers. Ragnar and his friends had missed most of that while they were on tour, trying to take the next step in their band's evolution. He hoped it worked for them now.

"I think I can still see the taillight in the distance," Melinda said.

"See if you can make up some distance while I get this app working." He closed it and reopened it. That did it. A flashing light popped up on the map. "OK. We're working."

"Still want me to catch up?" she asked.

"Yeah, let's get a little closer at least," he replied as he watched the map, zooming in on the dot marking the fleeing motorcycle.

He fed Melinda directions as needed, his foot nervously tapping on the floorboard of the back seat.

"Ragnar, knock it off. You're making me nervous." Melinda shot him a half-hearted scowl.

"What?"

"The foot. Stop tapping."

He stilled it, then fed her the next turn. "Looks like she's heading toward downtown."

"Good place to lose someone this time of night," Sippi said, twisting in the front passenger seat to look back at Ragnar. "Lots of traffic and activity from clubs, restaurants, and such."

"Yeah."

"Sippi, sit straight and buckle up. I don't want to get pulled over," Melinda said, casting a glance at him.

"I am buckled up." He caught the edge of the belt with this thumb to demonstrate.

Melinda huffed, annoyed by Sippi's proximity.

In all honesty, Sippi got on everyone's nerves from time to time, as Ragnar was sure his bandmates felt the same way about him too. It happened when you spent a lot of time with each other, often in confined spaces—the hazards of being a touring band. But to be fair, it wasn't like Melinda was an experienced car chaser, tailer, or whatever someone would call it. They were all doing the best they could in unfamiliar circumstances. He just wished he had a hammer with him. Without one, he always felt a little defenseless, even though he was wolf strong and could handle himself in a fight.

He had no idea what kind of trouble the mysterious woman could be leading them into. They still had no idea who she was or why she kept popping up wherever he was. If she was the killer, it seemed strange that she'd be so interested in the family of her victim. He really needed Delphine to come up with a contact who could provide more information on the enigmatic Tarot Slayer.

TWENTY-TWO

Sippi had been right. The woman on the motorcycle had led them straight into the district of downtown known for clubbing, though it contained a world well beyond dance clubs and drinking establishments. Nearly whatever vice a person wanted to indulge had real estate here and was easy to find. Although drugs and sex work weren't legal in Red City, it didn't matter as long as you had the money to pay the "fines" or bribes. These activities were only illegal to the poor who got caught in their webs. But the neon lights were pretty.

Melinda had steadily gained ground on the motorcyclist without getting too close. Now they were waiting in traffic to see where she'd go next. Ragnar guessed she hadn't discovered her unwanted tail.

"Doesn't look like she knows we're here," Sippi said.

Just as he spoke, the motorcycle whipped out of its spot in traffic and shot down the double yellow lines between the lane they were in and oncoming traffic.

"Damnit, Sippi. You jinxed us," Melinda said.

"Hey, that's not how this works," he replied.

"Well, you spoke, then they took off." She turned her head toward Ragnar. "What do you want to do?"

Ragnar sighed, trying to clear his head of their bickering. "We've got her on the GPS. Just stick to traffic. No sense creating mayhem. This isn't the kind of car we can do that in, anyway."

"Well, if we hadn't blown up my van…" Sippi left the statement hanging unfinished.

"You blew it up yourself. We could have left it whole and tried to recover it." Melinda sounded smug about it. "It was your choice."

They could have tried to recover it. They had to go back eventually to get their instruments and the cash they'd stashed in the mine on Roy's property in the Rockies. But Ragnar doubted the bikers would have left the van intact. They would have taken out their frustrations on the vehicle they'd been following for days.

"And as much as I loved your van, it would've been even worse for zipping through traffic. About the only thing that can keep up with a sport bike is another sport bike."

"Maybe we can get some fancy schmancy motorcycles. Like Dax has."

Melinda snorted. "He takes them from the bikers. Last time I checked, those dirtbags aren't riding imported racing bikes."

"I'd look pretty good on a Harley." Sippi pantomimed gripping handlebars and revving a bike.

"How you going to keep your cowboy hat on as you're riding?" Melinda asked, making a turn Ragnar had pointed out.

"I'll get a chinstrap for it."

Ragnar laughed. It was the first good laugh he'd had in a long time. "You'd look fucking ridiculous wearing a cowboy hat with a chinstrap. And the metal tip on your bolo ties would hit you in the face in all the wind."

"I could pull it off."

"Sure, whatever." Melinda had a smile on her face as well.

"She's stopped moving." Ragnar zoomed into the spot. "Looks like an alley."

"What do you want to do, Red?" Melinda asked.

"Park as soon as you can. You go check on the bik—" Ragnar stopped speaking as he narrowed his eyes. "Is…is that her?"

A woman in what looked like black riding gear strode around a corner and walked to the head of a line waiting to get into a club. She disappeared inside.

"Not sure, Ragnar," Sippi said. "So now what's the plan?"

"Here's how we'll play it," Ragnar said. "Melinda, you slip around back and check out the bike. Sippi, you wait outside the club. I'm going in to see if I can track her down."

"You sure that's a good idea?" Melinda asked. "She could be dangerous."

Ragnar stared at the club entrance as they found a close spot through some miracle. "So can I."

TWENTY-THREE

As soon as the car stopped rolling and Melinda put it in park, Ragnar stepped out and strode to entrance to the club. He stopped in front of the tall, muscular-looking Black man working the door.

"Did a woman in bike leathers with short dark hair enter a couple minutes ago?" Ragnar asked, folding his arms across his chest.

"Lots of women been entering all night. I just check the IDs and collect the fees." To punctuate his statement, he took the ID from a short blonde woman in a shiny dress, gave it back, took her twenty-dollar bill, and waved her in.

"Would a little some—" Ragnar shut his mouth, his teeth clacking as he remembered he'd given his last twenty to the homeless person. "Any chance I can go in and look?"

"All the chance in the world. Back of the line, pay the door when it's your turn." The bouncer turned away to grab another ID. He took care of a few more people before he looked up again. At first his brow furrowed in annoyance at seeing Ragnar still standing there, then his eyes opened in recognition and a big smile spread across his face.

"Mother fucker! Get over here," the bouncer said, stepping out of line toward Ragnar.

He was confused. He didn't recognize the man and couldn't think of what might account for the sudden shift in demeanor. Then Mississippi Pete stepped up to the big man and pulled him into a hard, back-patting hug.

"It's been a while, Sippi."

"Sure has, Deon. How you doing these days?" Sippi asked.

"Oh, you know. Same ol', same ol'." He chucked his chin at Sippi's head. "Where's that goofy-ass cowboy hat you always got on?"

A mischievous grin spread across Sippi's face. "Left it at your mom's house."

"Shit, cuz, if I ever find your hat at my mamma's house, you won't have anything left to put it on." Though the words made it sound like a serious threat, his tone and the friendly smile spoke toward the humor intended in the statement.

"Then I'll be sure not to forget it next time." Sippi laughed, nodding his head at Ragnar. "This is my friend, Ragnar. Ragnar, this is Deon."

Ragnar shook his hand and gave him a friendly smile. "Good to meet you."

Some young white guy in a shiny shirt with too many buttons undone leaned over the velvet rope cordoning off the line. "Hey, man, we're waiting to get in here."

The smile slipped off Deon's face as he turned to the guy who'd spoken. "If you don't want to go to the back of the line, shut up." Then he turned back to Ragnar and Sippi.

Sippi winked at him. "If you want to really annoy the little douche, mind letting my friend in? We're looking for someone."

Deon chuckled. "As long as you don't cause any trouble in my club. I don't want to have to throw your ass out." He looked Ragnar up and down. "Might actually make me work for it too, if I had to."

"I'll mind my manners. Just want to have a word with someone," Ragnar replied.

"Alright, go in. And Sippi, if he causes any trouble, I'll kick your ass too. I'll go easy on you though, since we're friends. Now get out of my way so I can go back to work."

Sippi laughed. "Much appreciated. But I'll hang out here and keep you company while you admire driver's licenses." He placed a hand on the small of Ragnar's back and pushed him forward.

"Thanks, Deon." Ragnar passed the large man and stepped through the door. To his left was a coat check with a bored-looking hostess behind the counter. It had been a warm day, and there were few coats coming in to keep her busy.

The next stop was a fireplug of a bald, white man holding a metal detecting wand. "Arms out to the side, spread your legs," he said with a disinterested tone.

Ragnar complied and waited as the man ran the wand around his body. He was glad he didn't have any weapons on him. Hopefully, the mysterious woman had been similarly checked out. If she pulled a knife or a gun on him, he'd have to act to protect himself. Perhaps he'd have to spend some time in the forge and see if he could create a series of runes he could place on a weapon to fool mundane detection devices like the metal detector.

"You're good. Go on in." The bald man had already moved on to the next person. "Arms out, spread your legs."

TWENTY-FOUR

As soon as Ragnar stepped through the door and into the club proper, he was assaulted by the steady thump of electronic bass and a whirlwind of lights.

He wasn't familiar with club music, but he didn't dislike it. Bobbing his head, he tried to ignore the assault on his senses and blend in. With his dark jeans and tight black T-shirt, he didn't look out of place as long as no one noticed his basic black running shoes. Most of the men in the club had tended toward flashy button-down shirts, some with elaborate patterns and others made from shiny materials.

After his senses acclimatized, he pushed his way into the dense crowd. He was glad he stood a few inches taller than most of the people as he swept his eyes around, looking for the woman in motorcycle leathers with the pixie cut. She'd stick out—most of the women in the club wore skimpy dresses.

As he eyed the people, he collected his fair share of glances. Though where his was clinical, trying to identify his target, the glances the women cast his way might've best been described as appreciative. He was tall and muscular. His Norse heritage gave him height, his wolf shifter duality helped with strength, and his years spent blacksmithing had built a good base of muscle.

And if he was being honest with himself, he knew he was a good-looking man. He kept himself well-groomed and wore shirts and jeans that flattered his physique. He tried not to be vain about it, but he wasn't going to hide it either.

But he wasn't there to look for a date, not that he had any interest after the breakup with Constance and his dad's death. He was there to find someone who might be the one responsible for that death or at least know something.

There. He thought he caught a glance of flashing light reflecting off leather. Using his size, he cut his way through the dense crowd of dancers, parting them like the prow of a ship cut through waves. Once he was close enough to get a better look, he shook his head in disappointment. It was just a woman in a leather or vinyl dress.

Since he was now near the center of dance floor, he took a moment to look around the entire room. While he searched, a white woman in a blue dress slipped in front of him and started dancing at him. It took him a second to respond, but he moved into the rhythm of the music and the woman's dancing, half-heartedly trying to blend in a bit better.

He continued his surveillance as he danced with the woman, using the movement to adjust his body to see more of the room. His eyes met up with eyes staring at him. Then they flashed away as soon as she saw him notice her. She had the same dark hair and pixie cut he'd seen several times now.

Gently placing his hand on the woman in the blue dress's shoulder, he moved past her and pushed his way through the crowd. The woman with the pixie cut tried to ignore him, distractedly dancing with no one and shifting just enough to put a tall guy between them.

Ragnar couched slightly and tried to blend in as he changed directions from directly at her to a more round about path. The next time she looked back to where he'd been a moment before, her brows furrowed, and she rotated her head, trying to find him. He kept low and danced his away around a couple small groups dancing in their own circles. As he came up on her back, he stood to his full height and resumed the rhythm of the dance just as she turned around.

Ragnar leaned in just close enough to pitch his voice to her ear. "Fancy meeting you here." If she was a human, she might not hear it. He kept a respectful distance, not wanting to find out the hard way if she had managed to sneak a weapon into the club.

"You know, just fancied a little techno." She resumed dancing, the momentary shock of finding him so close dismissed.

"Why have you been following me?" he asked, deciding not to go directly to the hard questions in case they sparked that trouble Deon was trying to avoid.

"Coincidence?"

"Ha. Not buying it. Just happened to be waiting on my street before my dad's funeral. Just happened to go to the same lake as me, over an hour away. Then just happened to show up at the same bar I was in, all the way across the Red City basin? Then at a random underpass in a sketchy part of town? Not buying it at all."

She snorted. "Well, I'm not selling anything." She didn't say anything else, eyeing him warily. "Can't a woman go about her life in this city?"

"Certainly." He wasn't sure how to respond to that. He'd never really tried to interrogate anyone before. And he'd definitely never tried to do it casually on a dance floor. "But what does your life have to do with my father's death? Are you some distant friend or family member I've never heard of?"

"Yes, you've never heard of me before. Now why don't you mind your own business and leave me to mine." A touch of annoyance had seeped into her voice.

"Not if your business has to do with my dad's death." He narrowed his eyes and leaned in closer. "Was my dad's death your business? Did you kill him?"

She looked genuinely shocked for a split second. If he hadn't been watching every detail of her heart-shaped face, he might have missed it. But quick as lightning, her expression returned to same mild neutral one she'd had for most of their interaction.

"That's fairly rude. You stalk me halfway across the city, then accuse me of murder?" She shook her head, tsking at him. "Not a good first impression on a lady."

"Stalking *you?* Why are you stalking me? You've shown up at a handful of places I've been, including the funeral service for my murdered father."

"Just visiting this fine city and seeing the sights. I can't help it if you don't believe in coincidence."

He snorted. "Fine city? Now I know you're lying. If you didn't have anything to do with my father's murder, there shouldn't be any issue talking to me."

"What are you, a cop? 'Cause that's the kind of shit a cop says." She smirked, appearing to be enjoying messing with him.

Ragnar found himself somewhere between amused and annoyed, and he wasn't sure where to take the conversation next. He didn't think he could trick her into saying anything, and she clearly wasn't interested in volunteering anything. They shifted their rhythm slightly as the song changed.

"At least tell me your name," he said.

"Why?" She tilted her head in curiosity.

"Please?"

"Since you asked so nicely. It's Judy a…" The second part disappeared into a mumble. She reached out and touched his stomach. "Oh, such nice abs."

"Judy what?" he asked, distracted. When she squeezed, he flexed his stomach muscles.

"Judy and…" She slammed a lightning-fast fist into his gut. "Punch!"

The air wheezed out of his lungs as he curled over, his knees shaking. Hunched over, he could only see her boots stalking away toward the back of the club. He dropped down to one knee and held himself up with a hand on the dance floor.

No one seemed to notice or care that he was there with a string of drool hanging from his lip. She'd struck faster than a snake. And the power… He struggled for air, trying to get his diaphragm to work and open his lungs.

As he knelt there, he saw a foot coming at him. He yanked his hand away, but not quite quick enough. He dragged his fingers free before the person could put their complete pressure on his digits. The movement forced him upright, and he clasped his hand to his chest. His stomach and chest finally seemed to be loosening up a little. He forced himself to his feet, swiping the spittle from his lip. He lurched in the direction he'd seen her boots stalk off.

Not even bothering to avoid being seen, he pushed his way through a door into a hallway filled with kegs and cases of beer. Ahead, he saw a door that likely led outside. He shouldered it open and burst out into the cool evening as the sound of a motorcycle disappeared into the distance.

He leaned up against the brick wall, trying to draw in a full breath. On the other side of the alley lay Melinda, splayed out against the ground. Groaning, he pushed off the wall and went over to her. She matched his groan as she rolled over and pushed herself into a sitting position against the brick of the opposite building.

Ignoring the stink of the alley, he slid down the wall to sit next to her. He still panted to catch his breath. "What happened?"

She coughed, shaking her head. "I don't know. The door opened, I saw a fist coming at my face" — she rubbed her cheek on the opposite side of where he sat — "and then a roundhouse kick that sent me tumbling. What about you?"

"She punched me in the stomach." He cradled the spot, feeling the tenderness. "After she fondled my abs."

Melinda laughed then groaned. "She flirted with you to get the drop on you? Come on, Red. You gotta stop thinking with your crotch."

He frowned. "You know me better than that. I was trying to get answers from her. She distracted me by touching me, then hit me."

"Did you get anything useful?"

"Not much." He sighed. "I don't think she killed Dad."

"Are you sure?"

"Not really. But when I accused her of being involved, it was the only time she lost her cool. She seemed genuinely shocked at the accusation."

"She could just be shocked that you fingered her."

He snorted a laugh, then winced in pain from the muscle contractions.

"Ugh. What are you, twelve? I mean when you accused her of murder." He could practically hear the eye roll in her voice.

Ragnar collected himself, pushing his urge to continue laughing away. "Ignore my momentary decent into juvenile humor, you could be right. But it didn't feel quite like that kind of shock. I also think I got her name."

"Oh?"

"She said Judy and…" He trailed off.

"And what?"

"She said Judy and Punch, but she said it as she punched me."

Melinda started chuckling, then it built into a full-on laugh. Ragnar felt a little offended at the laughter, but he couldn't pinpoint why she was laughing so hard at the name Judy. Finally, her laughing ended in a wheeze as she wiped the tears from her face.

She hissed as she wiped her injured cheek. "Fuck that hurts still. She got me hard."

"What's so funny?" Ragnar asked.

"Punch and Judy. It's a super old-school English puppet show, usually very violent." She chuckled again. "She gave you a thematic fake name so she could punch you. I got to give it to her; she hits like a Mack truck and has a sense of humor."

"Hmm."

"Was she English?"

"I don't know. Hard to tell with the club music and trying not to talk about murder too loudly." He shook his head. The mysterious woman—Judy, it was the only name he had at the moment—had gotten him good. At least they still had her bike GPS tagged. They'd be able to track her down.

TWENTY-FIVE

Grunting in pain as he engaged his core to stand, Ragnar got up and offered a helping hand to Melinda. She took it, and he pulled her upright. He looked around the alley one last time, then followed her out of the alley to the street at the front of the club.

When they rounded the corner, they went looking for Sippi. They found him standing near the front of the line, which seemed longer than when they'd arrived, talking to his friend Deon.

"What the fuck you doin' coming out the alley?" Deon asked, holding up a hand to stop the line. "You didn't cause any trouble up in my club, did ya?"

Ragnar shook his head. The floor had been so packed and the lights so distracting that no one had even noticed he'd been punched right in the guts.

"Don't worry. I didn't cause any trouble in the club," Ragnar said.

"What about the alley? Why you snooping around back?"

"Don't worry, big guy, we didn't steal any of the garbage or the stank. Nor did we break anything." Melinda sounded annoyed by the interrogation, but more than likely, she was just doing her best to hide her anger at getting dropped so fast. Melinda prided herself on her toughness and her ability to thump some skulls in a bar fight.

"No worries, lady. No need to be terse." Deon snorted a laugh and turned to Sippie. "Your lady friend here is a fierce one."

Sippi laughed. "You don't even know the half of it. Best stay on her good side."

"I'll keep that in mind."

Ragnar hoped the banter would take a bit of the wind from Melinda's angry sails. "Hey, Sippi, did you see the motorcycle come out this way?"

"Nope."

"Alright, I'll be right back." Ragnar jogged down the block to the car and grabbed the tablet from the backpack. When he opened the app for the GPS tracker, he didn't understand what he saw. So he closed the app and reopened it. The dot wasn't moving. And when he expanded the map, he found that it was only about a one hundred yards away in the alley.

Locking the car, he tucked the tablet under his arm and returned to the alley. He looked around where he'd found Melinda but didn't see anything. Then he walked down the alley in the direction the bike had disappeared. Still nothing.

He was about to give up when he walked by a dumpster and saw a bump stuck to the side that looked a little too symmetrical to be a dent or some bit of garbage. It was their tracker. He peeled it off the dumpster carefully, using his T-shirt to shield his fingers as he pinched the sides. He hoped they'd be able to get a fingerprint off it. Not that it would do him any good. It wasn't like he had an actual contact with the police who could run the print for him. But maybe he could at least check it against any other evidence they gathered. Besides, gathering fingerprints seemed like the kind of thing a detective would do.

He wished he had something to put the tracker in and keep it safe. He made a mental note to pick up some plastic sandwich baggies to carry around with him. Then he rejoined his friends as they chatted while Deon checked IDs and waved people inside.

"What's up, Ragnar?" Melinda asked.

Ragnar's eyes flicked to Deon. "Just had a thought, but it's not important right now."

"Ah. I guess we should get out of here," she said picking up on what he was getting at. "Deon, it was nice to meet you. See you later."

"Likewise. And Sippi, we'll catch ya later." The big bouncer paused the line to give Sippi a goodbye hug.

Ragnar shook the man's hand, then followed his friends back to the car. He waited until they were situated and rolling away with Melinda in the driver seat.

"You going to tell us what's up?" Melinda asked.

"Yeah. I, uh, found the GPS tracker."

"Those sound like good words, but the tone says something else," Sippi said, leaning forward from the back seat.

"It was stuck to a dumpster in the alley. She found it on her bike."

"Well shit." Melinda gripped the steering wheel. "Where does that leave us?"

"I'm not sure. We can't track her down and interrogate her, and she's gotten the drop on us anytime we've gotten close to her," Ragnar said.

"She's a slippery one, that's for sure."

"Wait, how'd she get the jump on ya, Melinda?" Sippi asked.

"I don't want to talk about it," Melinda said quickly.

Ragnar chuckled but stopped when his still aching stomach muscles reminded him why that was a bad idea. His wolf healing was doing a good job of repairing the damage her punch had caused, but it still hurt. "She sucker punched me in the gut, then dropped Melinda like a sack of potatoes in the alley."

"It'll be the last time she gets the jump on me," Melinda ground out through clenched teeth. "I owe her, and I intend to pay her back with interest."

Melinda usually made good on her threats, and Judy—for lack of a better name option—had gotten Melinda hard. But Judy was fast and strong, and he wasn't sure even Melinda would be able to make it even steven. Of course, in the mood she was in, Ragnar chose to keep that thought to himself. He didn't feel like getting sucker punched twice in one night. He'd never been accused of being a genius, but he wasn't an idiot either.

TWENTY-SIX

It had been nearly a week since they'd surveyed the site where his dad's body was found, and they'd gotten virtually nowhere in the meantime. His eyes burned from staring at the large monitor. He'd resorted to moving it to his room. His mom knocked on his bedroom door but not on the office one. Apparently the potential of mutual embarrassment from walking in on Ragnar potentially naked was enough of a threat to warrant the extra privacy.

He didn't feel burdened by his mother's attention. After all, he was grateful that she'd let him stay with her until he could get back on his feet after the tour had ended abruptly early.

He didn't even have the money from the tour. When they'd fled through the old mines near Uncle Roy's house to get away from the Black Suns thugs hunting them, they'd had to leave most of the cash they'd been paid by all the bars and events they'd performed at. Once things were settled with his father's murder, they had to go back and recover their property and money so he could pay out his friends, including Constance.

Melinda, who was still pissed at Connie, said she shouldn't get anything since she quit the band. But Ragnar couldn't do that to Constance after everything that had happened, including losing some of her drum kit. Constance had performed in every show they'd done; she'd earned her equal share just like the rest of them.

Rubbing his eyes, he leaned back in his chair and grabbed the bottle of eyedrops he'd picked up to deal with the dryness his fixation on his father's file was causing. It was barely even noon. It was too early for his eyes to already be this tired. But he couldn't pull himself away from his monitor. If there was something he'd missed in the partial police files Delphine had sent, he needed to find it. He had to find his dad's killer before they struck again. He wouldn't let the Tarot Slayer get away with this and add yet another victim to their already long list of murders.

When a knock on the door came, he quickly tabbed out to the backup window he kept open for just this purpose. Just like a teen hiding his porn window.

"Come in," he said.

His mom stepped inside. She gave him the sad smile she always seemed to present to him. "Still looking at guitars?"

"Yeah. I miss playing." It was true. "And I have no idea when we'll be able to recover our instruments." Also true. But he wasn't sure why he felt like he was lying to his mom. Maybe because he was using the truth to hide the dark secret of his obsession with solving his father's murder.

"You need to get out of this room. Go see your friends. Have a beer. You're looking positively dyspeptic after spending so much time hidden away in this room."

He had been spending time with his friends, but it certainly wasn't fun time. Anytime he left the house, he had to come up with legitimate excuses to hide his actual activities. But that had been a week ago. "I will. I'll give them a call later."

"Tell you what. I'm going to intervene. Why don't you take your mother out to brunch?"

He opened his mouth to object.

"I won't take no for an answer. Come on, we both needs this."

"Alright, mom. I'll meet you downstairs in a couple minutes."

She nodded and pulled the door closed as she left. A few minutes later, he was behind the wheel, heading to a brunch spot his mom liked in the neighborhood.

She was right. They both needed a little time to reconnect. In his effort not to lie to her, he'd avoided her, and she'd noticed it. He couldn't tell her why he'd been doing it yet, but he promised to make more time for her.

They were just about to ask for the bill after too much coffee and plates full of brunch classics like French toast and bacon and eggs Benedict when the sound of motorcycles rumbling into the parking lot weighed his already-full belly down with a feeling of nausea.

The bikers didn't scare him not really, but they'd picked the worst time—or the best in their perspective—to roll up on him. If he'd had his crew with him, he'd have been able to even the odds if it came down to a fight. But by himself with his mom? He had to do whatever it took to get her out of there safely.

He flagged down the server and requested the check. Pulling out his wallet, he was disappointed to see so little money staring back at him. He needed to figure out some way to earn some bucks and fast. He peered out the window, hoping that the visitors were from some other group of bikers. But the Black Suns logo—a white sun with spidery thin rays coming out of it—on black leather vests dashed that hope instantly.

Scanning the lot, he thought about doing a dine and dash and rectify it later, but the bikers already had his car surrounded. He straightened his back and waited for the inevitable as a handful of bikers dismounted their bikes and headed toward the front door and a few to the side door, leaving another dozen sitting outside on their bikes, engines still rumbling.

The tension in the restaurant grew palpably thicker as the scent of fear filled the room, spiking his own senses and causing a surge of adrenaline.

"Well, well, well. Out to brunch with mommy."

"Sigur, I see you're back from Colorado," Ragnar bit out.

Sigur's face darkened briefly. Ragnar and his friends had caused a lot of pain to the bikers, shooting several of them, probably multiple times. And it was possible they'd blown up several of the bikers in the various explosions Ragnar's friends and Roy had set up. That brought some satisfaction along with a cruel smirk to his face.

"I'm surprised you have the guts to show up within city limits after Dax's pronouncement."

Sigur scowled. "This is our city. We're the ones who have the say."

Ragnar had gotten under Sigur's skin. He'd seen the briefest flash of fear dance across the biker's eyes at the mention of Dax.

"I'll be sure to convey your greetings to Dax."

Sigur's jaw clenched briefly before he leaned over, bracing himself against the tabletop with both arms. "Look, you little pissant, I'm only going to give you this warning once. Stay out of business that doesn't concern you."

"Or what?" Ragnar asked, moving his face closer to Sigur's.

"Ragnar," his mom said, a tone of warning and pleading threaded through the two syllables.

"Or your mom might get to witness a second family funeral in as many months. Or maybe you will." Sigar grinned wickedly and leered at Ragnar's mom.

He was about to launch himself at Sigur when his mom's hand on his forearm stopped him. She gave a gentle squeeze and looked to the biker with a stern face. "You have delivered your warning. Now go and leave these people alone to enjoy their brunches."

Sigur stared at Ragnar's mom for a second and pushed off the table, rattling the dishes still sitting on it. He chuckled. "Your mom's got some stones, Ragnar." He reached out and patted Ragnar on the cheek a couple times. "Best heed my warning."

It was one of the most condescending things anyone had ever done to him. A firmer squeeze on his arm from his mother kept his butt in the chair as he clenched his jaw. Sigur chuckled again and walked away.

Ragnar's mother left her hand on his arm until well after the sound of the bikes had disappeared into silence. Slowly, the restaurant returned to life as tables were cleared, and people paid and left. He sat in silence, steam practically pouring off his head. Pulling out her wallet, his mom paid the check and left a generous tip.

"Let's go, honey." She stood up and kissed him on the forehead.

Without a word, he followed her out. Since she'd walked to the driver side, he slumped into the passenger seat. Off in the distance, he heard the sound of a motorcycle but relaxed once he realized it wasn't a custom road bike or a Harley. The sound grew quickly louder, then zipped by, leaving only its doppler effect. He caught a brief glimpse of a bike he thought looked familiar. At least Judy hadn't flipped him off as she went…that he could see.

He was getting damned tired of these supposed coincidences. They were making his teeth itch. How did she always end up being nearby when he was up to some kind of trouble? If he ever got his hands on her, he'd have to ask her most pointedly.

And more importantly, how had the bikers known when to come harass him? He knew correlation didn't equal causation, but both Judy and Sigur being at the same place at the same time where he'd made an unannounced-to-the-world stop to have brunch with his mother was just a bridge too far to call coincidence.

TWENTY-SEVEN

Ragnar couldn't tell if he was hearing the sounds in his dreams or if they were coming from the world of the awake. He hadn't been sleeping well, especially over the last three evenings since the bikers threatened him and his mother at brunch. Grumbling, he rolled over. And promptly fell out of the small bed and onto the floor with a thump and a whoosh of air from his lungs. His phone continued ringing. Calls this late at night were never a good thing.

As he reached for it, it stopped. He scowled at it and grabbed it off the nightstand to see who'd been calling at…shit, three a.m. As he opened it to check the call log, it started ringing again. He almost dropped it. He couldn't quite make out the name through his sleep-blurry eyes.

He answered it. "What do you want?"

"My, aren't we grumpy," Sippi said.

"Sippi, you better have a reason for waking me up at three in the morning, or I'm going to… I don't know, I'm too tired to think of what I'll do to you."

"Give me the damn phone," Melinda said in the background.

There was a tussle, then her voice sounded directly in the phone. "We need you to come pick us up."

"Are y'all drunk? Call a fucking taxi."

"No. Well, I mean yes, kinda. Sorta. But that's not it. Sippi got a call from that weird friend of his."

"The Rat," Sippi said in the background.

Ragnar had met The Rat a few times. He was definitely one of the weirder characters in Red City but overall seemed pretty harmless. As long as you stayed on his good side. Ragnar had no wish to insult a man who controlled the city's rat population.

"What?"

"The Rat called. Said we had to meet him over in the industrial section on the west side of town."

Ragnar sighed, rubbing his eyes. "Can't it wait until tomorrow?"

"I don't know. I mean, I don't think so. He seemed insistent that it was very time sensitive," Melinda said.

"He was really agitated and anxious," Sippi called from the background. "Well, more anxious than normal. Trust me, we need to go see what he wants. He wouldn't call me if it wasn't important."

Mississippi Pete had the oddest, most eclectic network of people. All Ragnar had gotten out of Sippi was that he'd helped The Rat once. It was Sippi's kidnapping that had persuaded The Rat to help when they wanted to kick the bikers out of Tallullah's bar. Along with whatever allegiance The Rat had with Dax and the young woman Jamie.

"Alright. Where are you at?" Ragnar asked, defeat coloring his voice.

"At Tallulah's," Melinda replied.

"Fuck. That's way out of town." He held the phone away from his ear to check the time, needing to see the numbers to goad his sleepy brain into mathing. "I'll be there in an hour. Start sobering up some." He didn't bother waiting for an answer and simply hung up.

He got up off the floor and pulled some jeans, a T-shirt, a hoodie, and socks and underwear from his dresser. Dropping his pajama pants, he quickly dressed and went downstairs to find a thermos mug. While the coffee pot brewed, he left a note for his mom so she wouldn't worry about him when she didn't see him in the morning.

With a full mug, he climbed into his mom's car—she'd been letting him use it since she was using his dad's car—and headed out to the Honky Tonk Woman to pick up his drunk and wayward friends.

TWENTY-EIGHT

Ragnar arrived at Tallulah's bar almost an hour to the minute from when he'd hung up on his friends. Parking out back, he walked in the back entrance since he knew it would be unlocked in anticipation of his arrival. The front lot was virtually empty since the bar was closed for the night.

He set his now-empty mug on a counter in the kitchen and hit the bathroom before heading out to the bar, where he heard voices. He picked up his mug and found the rest of the band, minus Constance, sitting around a table with Tallulah. Pausing, he ran a hand down his face. He really had to stop thinking of Constance as part of the band. It had been nearly two months since she'd dumped him and quit.

Feeling composed enough, he dropped into an empty chair at the table, which had an open bottle of whiskey on it along with four partially filled tumblers. Everyone had pint glasses of water in front of them. A pitcher of water stood next to the bottle of whiskey.

He sighed and shook his head. "I said to start sobering up."

"We are!" Sippi held up the glass of whiskey. "See, we're drinking water." He looked at the whiskey in his hand, giggled, and set it down to pick up the water. "See. Water. And"—he used the pint to point at the whiskey bottle, sloshing water over the rim and onto the table—"we switched to eighty-proof whiskey instead of the cask-strength stuff we were drinking."

Next to him, Tallulah was trying to contain her smile and chuckles. "Good to see you, Ragnar. It's been too long. Try not to be such a stranger."

He hadn't been out to the Honky Tonk Lady since the party they'd held in honor of his father. "Sorry, Lue. I'll try to get out soon."

"Come play a show. I can fit y'all into the schedule."

"We don't have a drummer."

She snorted. "Since when was a drummer a requirement for a country band? Besides, if you're desperate for one, we can find one to sit in with you."

"I'll think about it." He fixed a firm expression on his face and eyed his bandmates. "Go use the bathrooms. I'm not stopping until we get to wherever The Rat wants us."

"Yes, father," Sippi said, doing his best impression of a petulant teen. He stood up and shuffled off with his head hanging, though the laugh he let out as he entered the bathroom belied his faux seriousness.

José and Melinda laughed and got up as well.

As soon as they were alone, Tallulah leaned in closer. "Don't be too hard on them, hon. They came out to blow off some steam."

He exhaled heavily, trying to let go of his frustration. "I know. I just wish they'd be a little more serious right now."

She laid a hand on his forearm. "They are. But they're good-natured people who just wanted a little fun. You need to balance the two, especially in hard times. You don't want to grow hard from being too serious for too long."

It sounded like a pointed, but well-meaning and friendly criticism of his demeanor as of late. He tried to take it in the manner it was intended.

"I know, Lue, I know. It's just… I'm not meant to be investigating a murder, let alone the murder of my dad. I should've been here tonight with them. Playing music and drinking and passing out in the bunkhouse." They'd called and asked him to hang out, but he'd said no. "But here I am, sober, my hands haven't touched a guitar since the night of my father's service, and I'm sleeping in my childhood bed in my mom's house."

"I understand, Ragnar. It's hard. You loved your father, and he was good man. Too many good people die by violent hands in Red City. And most of them will never get justice, and their families will have to live not knowing who did it. Unless someone steps up to investigate. Sometimes you don't get to choose what you're called to."

He snorted. "I'm certainly not being called to be some sort of investigative vigilante. I'll leave that to Dax."

Tallulah shivered. "Yeah. You'd think the bikers would be smart enough to heed his warning and stay the fuck out of town. I don't know why they aren't scared shitless of him. I know I am."

Ragnar wasn't exactly scared of him, but he also gave Dax plenty of respect. He didn't know what Dax was, but Ragnar could tell both by the man's presence and by others' reactions to him that he was potentially a very scary and powerful man.

Tallulah stood up and patted his shoulder. "I'm going to go get you some more coffee. I'll also fill up some to go cups for your friends."

"Thanks, Lue."

"And think about what I said. I'd hate to see this whole thing dim your fire."

He sat quietly while the crew got ready to depart and thought about what Tallulah had said. He couldn't help feeling a bit grim after losing his dad, but he couldn't force everyone around him to be in deep mourning like he was. Everyone handled their grief in different ways. And after the stress of helping him investigate his father's death, they needed to cut loose for an evening so they could recharge and keep up the fight. He couldn't begrudge them that. It wasn't their fault that something had cropped up at this particular moment.

"Ready to go, Red?" Melinda said. "Tallulah has your coffee."

"Yeah. Let's do it." He stood up and headed toward the kitchen, taking his full mug from Tallaluh. He gave Tallulah a big hug. "Thanks for the talk, Lue. I'll take your words under advisement."

TWENTY-NINE

Two giant mugs of coffee coursed through his veins, the caffeine making him twitchy and anxious. He wondered what the hell Lue was using for beans. It must've been some serious trucker-level go juice, because it hit him like a sledgehammer.

His eyes flicked to every movement or reflection of moonlight or streetlamp as they worked their way into the western industrial district of Red City. Too many manufacturing jobs had been shipped overseas by companies looking to exploit cheaper workers while blaming local workers for not letting themselves be as exploitable, leaving a lot of derelict buildings.

Because of all the abandoned buildings, a lot of homeless people congregated in this area. And unless the cops needed to meet some quotas or some city council member wanted to seem tough on crime, the cops largely didn't bother patrolling around here, preferring to keep their protection racket in neighborhoods that had something worth shaking down.

He glanced at his phone on the dash mount, checking how far they still had to go. The address The Rat had sent them was only a couple blocks away. Making a turn, he found a parking place in a pool of light from a streetlamp.

"José, you stay with the car. Sippi and I will go with Ragnar," Melinda said. The Rat hadn't told Sippi to come alone. The odd little man tended to only communicate directly with a people he felt comfortable with, so they were all going to see what he wanted.

"Gotcha." José got out of the back seat and walked around to lean against the hood.

For the second time in the last few days, Ragnar wished he'd taken the time to rune spell a new sledgehammer. Hell, he should at least buy one. Even a mundane weapon in a wolf shifter's hands could still do serious damage. Well, if they got in trouble, they could resort to fists and their enhanced healing. And if it was supernatural trouble, they could go full wolf on the situation.

He grabbed his phone from the cradle and stepped out of the car, joining Melinda and Sippi. Together, they followed the map the rest of the way until they came to one of the entrances into the underworld of Red City. He'd never ventured into this world, but it looked like he was about to whether he wanted to or not.

They stopped outside the entrance. It looked a service entrance, but it was open aired except for the vertical bars and the barred door, which kind of lent it the look of a jail cell. A moment later, a shadow appeared behind the bars and resolved into the small figure of The Rat once he stepped into the light spilling in from a nearby streetlamp.

"Hello, hello," The Rat said waving both hands twitchily. "You came and fast. Much thanks to friend Sippi."

His voice was on the higher-pitched side. He couldn't stand more than five-four. He wore baggy clothes that looked well worn, but were, surprisingly, reasonably clean. His brown hair was shaggy and poorly cut, as was his beard. Reaching up, he grabbed the bars with knit-glove-covered hands and peered through, a lopsided grin splitting his shaggy beard

"Anytime," Sippi replied.

"Ready?" The Rat asked.

"Ready for what?" Ragnar asked.

"To see the mystery upon my doorstep." The Rat waggled his eyebrows and gave him a toothy grin.

"I guess so."

"Good, good. But be careful. Walk where I walk. Touch nothing. Don't want to leave evidence. No. No evidence for Red City cops." He scowled momentarily before returning to his normal slightly jovial expression.

"We'll be careful."

"Come, come." He pulled the door in, opening it for them. "Time to join friends, living and not so living." He gave a high-pitched chuckle and walked into the tunnel.

"How far do we have to go?" Melinda asked, standing outside the gate.

"Not far, not deep."

Melinda joined Sippi and The Rat, while Ragnar stared after them. After being trapped in the morgue drawer, his claustrophobia had become more acute. The tunnels system under Red City was impressively vast, but the walls and ceiling still looked so tight and confining. But it was all concrete, bricks, rebar, and stone. What could go wrong? The system was only built by the lowest bidder in a city famous for contractors cutting corners and outrageous skimming.

His friends stopped, waiting for him. Finally, he just closed his eyes and plunged past the line demarking inside the tunnel versus outside. If he focused on his senses, his immediate surroundings, and why they were there, he could get through this.

Ragnar raised his nose and sniffed lightly. He was doing a better job remembering to tap into more of his wolfish senses. A general dirty mustiness dominated the aromas. He cataloged the now-familiar scents of Melinda and Sippi and added The Rat's uniqueness. Nearby, he thought he picked up the aroma of small rodents — the rats that almost always accompanied The Rat.

After they took their first turn to the right — Melinda groaning quietly as the light grew fainter — he picked up a new smell. One that seemed a little familiar. The scent of an unwashed body. A dead unwashed body.

The Rat turned his head and slowed down briefly. "OK. Close now. One more tunnel." He stooped and reached into one of the pockets of his oversized coat. "But first, booties! Must be fashionable." He chuckled.

Ragnar took the pair handed to him and leaned against the wall to slip them over his shoes. Taking their cue from him, Sippi and Melinda did the same. The Rat already had a set on his feet. It made sense—they were about to tromp around a murder scene and leaving evidence would be a serious mistake. They were probably pushing it even being there. But there was one thing they could always count on—the sure indifference and incompetence of Red City cops.

"OK. Now sexy in your booties!" The Rat cackled in his high-pitched tone. "We go now. Walk where I walk. Friends waiting. Yes. Yes."

Ragnar listened hard but didn't hear anything but the footsteps of his friends and The Rat—maybe there was a faint squeak in the background, but he couldn't be sure. The Rat stopped when they reached a side tunnel.

Looking around The Rat's shoulder, Ragnar saw his waiting friends. Manman Delphine, dressed in black athletic gear, stood next to a medium-sized silvery wolf—Jamie. He wondered why she was here and in her wolf form. On the other side of Jamie stood Tomi's cousin Little Suzie, wearing ripped black jeans, Docs, and a black band shirt with the collar and hem cut out. Behind them stood a tall shadow of a figure he couldn't quite identify since Delphine blocked the light. He nodded at them in greeting.

The Rat tucked up against the wall, clearing Ragnar's view his body had been blocking. Ragnar now saw the reason for the late-night emergency—a body. It appeared to have been posed. Stepping sideways to get a better angle without entering the tunnel, he stared at the homeless man who'd witnessed the murder of his father.

THIRTY

The man's dingy, beard-covered face was turned toward him.
A ratty blanket had been fashioned into a rough poncho
that appeared to have a few stitches worked into the side to
form a crude tunic of sorts. It came down to about his mid-thigh.
Even in the thin light, he looked far paler than he should've.

"Has anyone touched the body?" Ragnar asked. As soon as he
said it, he saw what looked like spots on the body that had been
savaged by animals.

"Yes. Little rat friends think they find delicious food. I called
them off as fast as I could. But us here? No. No humans…" He
trailed off and looked around, then giggled. "No humans indeed."

"Manbos and manbos' apprentices are human," Delphine said
with a bit of sass in her tone.

"Yes. Yes. Human, but supernatural. No unmagicals here." He
looked down at the body. "Well, one unmagical. But not alive."

Ragnar squatted to get a different angle. One of the dead man's
hands was draped across his lap. Two knives were wired to it so he
looked like he was holding them by the handle. The other hand lay
beside him, and another knife handle was wired to it. Two more
knives lay on the ground nearby.

"Five knives," he said, looking to see if the two on the ground might have fallen from somewhere else on the man.

"Not knives. Swords," Delphine said.

"Swords?" He looked at the five knives which were clearly knives, but symbolically… "More Tarot shit?"

"Yup," Delphine replied. "Five of swords."

Ragnar rubbed the bridge of his nose. "The Tarot Slayer?"

"It looks like it," she said.

"All I know is that it's fucked up." Suzie folded her arms across her chest. "Being a bartender never required me to go crawl around dirty tunnels to find dead bodies."

He snorted. He couldn't disagree with her. Being Manman Delphine's apprentice would lead the young woman down some interesting paths, some of them dark, like this one.

"What else do you notice?" Delphine asked Ragnar, a teacher's tone slipping in.

He looked at the rough garment and the ground. Other than a few rosy spots on the homeless man's skin that might've been smears of wiped-off blood, he couldn't find so much as a drop on the ground. And as pale as he was, he couldn't have too much left inside him. Ragnar tilted his head, noticing a ragged line coming out along the man's neck below the jaw. The head draped forward nearly obscured it.

"No blood. Looks like someone cut his throat and bled him out. But not here." He looked up at Delphine. "Body dump?"

"Yeah. That's no shaving nick on his neck. If someone had cut his weasand here, there'd be blood everywhere. Jamie did a preliminary inspection while we were waiting on you. She smelled hardly any blood, other than a drop or what little bit wasn't cleaned off his body."

The wolf next to Delphine nodded a couple times, which looked like a strangely human gesture for a wolf to make.

"That also means they went to a lot of effort to clean up the body before bringing it here to be posed."

"Which I guess fits the M.O. of the Tarot Slayer." Delphine swept her eyes over the scene, a furrow in her brow. "The only things that are missing are the two figures standing in the background you usually see on the five of swords card."

"Hmm." He pulled off the backpack and took out the black light bar, flicking it on. He swept it around the scene, landing on the wall near the torso and head. "There."

Two stick figures had been drawn on the wall with something that provided some texture and reflection. The arrow drawn on the brick wall where his father had been found had been much fainter and flat, but it had been over a month since it was initially drawn. This was fresh.

He looked up when he heard something snap. Delphine was pulling on a black nitrile glove. She placed a bootie-covered foot gingerly next to the dead man, leaned over the body and carefully touched one of the glowing figures on the wall with her index finger. The figure didn't look much different than it had looked before she'd touched it; all she'd done was shift the swirls and thickness of the lines around a bit.

Stepping back, she brought the glove up to her face and rubbed her finger against her thumb. She took a quick sniff. "Huh. I think it's petroleum jelly."

"I didn't know petroleum jelly glowed under blacklight," Melinda said quietly behind him.

"Me either," Ragnar said. "But I can see why it's a good option. It's thick, it sticks, and it's hard to wash away."

Delphine nodded. "And it's a good way to leave clues so the average person won't see them."

The shadow behind Delphine snorted and spoke in a low voice. "The Slayer may be asking too much of Red City's donut chasers."

Delphine chuckled. "Yeah, Dax. They're not what you'd call competent. At least when there's no one to shake down for a bribe."

So she'd brought Dax with her. It made sense, if he had an affinity for death and the dead.

"Hey, Dax." Ragnar stood up and gave him a quick wave of greeting.

"Ragnar."

"So what's your opinion on this whole thing?"

"Not much. There's very little along his life thread. A brief intersection with yours. A few days before his death."

"Can you tell who the killer was?" Ragnar asked eagerly.

The shadow shook his head. "No. I don't know the presence, and as best as I can feel, neither did the victim. I can't even tell if he was aware of being taken. There's vagueness around the period of his death. But one difference I noticed between your father's body and this one—his soul is gone."

"Gone? As in…"

"Moved on. When he died, his soul moved on to its next phase."

"So it's not tied to his corpse?" Delphine asked.

"Correct."

"What's that mean?" Melinda asked. "Why do that to the first victim and not the second?"

Everybody looked around at each other, waiting for someone to speak up or give a theory. Ragnar rummaged through all the facts of the case in his head, trying to find answers or links between clues.

"Maybe…" He paced back and forth across the entrance of the tunnel where the body lay a couple feet away. "There are a lot of assumptions here, but let's look at the information we have. We're assuming the bikers are the facilitators of my father's death. And I have a bit of information I haven't shared with y'all." He held up a hand to stop any comments. "I've needed to think about it and mull it over. I wasn't intentionally withholding it."

He sighed. "I spoke with my dad's friend, Bob. Dad was paying the bikers to leave everyone alone. He collected money from the community to keep the bikers off everyone's backs."

Behind him, Melinda gasped.

"Hmm," Delphine said, "that sounds like something he'd do. Sacrifice his own feelings to protect others."

"It sounds like he was useful to the bikers," Dax said. "Why would they want to get rid of him?"

"He was talking about stopping the payments and forming a shifter pack. I guess maybe something I said got through to him or he just got tired of being used by racist scumbags. He must have figured the time was right, with Dax weakening the local biker chapter."

"I still have work to do on that front," Dax said quietly.

Ragnar nodded. "Good. But anyway, if word got back to the bikers or if he declared the gravy train was done, they'd have to make an example of him."

"But why not just kill him themselves? Why go to someone like the Tarot Slayer?" Melinda asked.

"I don't know. Dad was respected by people beyond just the supernatural community. Maybe the bikers didn't want so much public scrutiny. Maybe they're scared of Dax and don't want to be that closely linked to the murder. Hell, the Tarot Slayer could be their tool. A serial killer would be an interesting choice to use as an assassin. It certainly would create a distraction and point away from the bikers to a far more sensational killer."

"That all makes sense," Delphine said. "I'm honestly surprised the press isn't having a field day with this. There's nothing they love more than the red meat of a salacious story. A serial killer definitely fits that profile."

"Yeah. I've been thinking about that too. I've been looking up the news articles about the Tarot Slayer's other killings. The press went nuts over them. Why hasn't the press in Red City been running stories about it twenty-four-seven?"

"They don't know." Delphine looked around, realization dawning on her face. "The cops are keeping the details silent. I know that often happens in serial killer cases. The cops don't release some very specific trademark both to avoid copycats and to be able to tell if a death is the real deal. Damn it all. We need to get some real information on the other killings."

Ragnar wasn't sure he'd ever heard her this frustrated. She usually was the picture of calm confidence. He wasn't sure why — he didn't know her well personally, she'd been friends with his dad — but her frustration shook his already wavering confidence in the way things should be.

To cover his concern, he turned his eyes back to the body and was drawn to the marks carved into the skin. Stepping carefully, he moved closer and squatted again, using the black light to see if there were more details they'd missed. The body—what wasn't covered by the rough poncho—was covered in figures and symbols similar to the ones carved into his dad's skin. The blood-stained edges of the marks didn't glow, but the black light served to create a greater contrast.

"What are you seeing?" Melinda asked.

"The marks. They're not as neat. And there aren't as many."

"What do you mean?" Delphine asked, bending down to look.

"On dad's…body, they were neat and precise. I still haven't figured out what they might mean, but each individual mark was carefully cut. And they were a lot more of them in much closer proximity to each other. Here, they look a bit… I don't know. I want to say rushed? And there's maybe only half as many. Huh."

"I see what you mean," Delphine said. "What about the knives? Anything unique about them?"

He swept his eyes over them, even though he didn't need to. As a blacksmith who'd made plenty of knives, there wasn't a store-purchased knife in his collection or in his mother's house thanks to him and his dad. He'd instantly cataloged these weapons when he'd arrived. "No. There's no rune carved dagger. Just another mix of used kitchen knives."

"So what separates this kill from your father's? The runes aren't as precise, and there's no personal connection with the knives," Delphine said, answering her own question.

"Couldn't one of the knives here have belonged to the man here?" Dax asked.

"I guess it's possible, but I doubt it. I'm not sure any of these would be convenient to carry for personal protection or use."

"Also, we didn't see a knife when we talked to him," Sippi said, finally speaking. "If he'd had a knife, he'd likely have waved it at us when we woke him up. I know I would have."

Ragnar nodded, thinking back to their encounter with the homeless man. The man had never even made so much as the smallest movement to reach for a hidden weapon. "You might be right."

Delphine pulled out her phone. "Can you shine the light over him so I can try to get some good pictures of the symbols?"

He adjusted the angle of the light and held it steady, letting his brain wander around the clues he'd assembled, both old and fresh, while Delphine cataloged the symbols.

"Um, what about under the tunic?" Melinda asked. "Didn't Gunnar have the marks all over?"

"Do we disturb the body?" Delphine asked. "It risks leaving evidence, and we don't want to give the cops any excuses to put us on their radar. At least not more than we already are."

A low, deep growl emerged from Jamie's throat. It was so low that likely only one of the other wolf shifters could have heard it.

"What is it, girl? Did Timmy fall down the well?" Melinda asked, sarcastically.

If it was possible for a wolf shifter to shoot daggers from her eyes, Jamie was stabbing Melinda repeatedly. He didn't understand Melinda's antagonism toward the girl. She'd been nothing but friendly and helpful in their interactions.

"Shush," Ragnar said. "I think I hear it now."

Everyone stopped moving and seemed to be controlling their breathing. Not so much as a twitch rustled the fabric of their clothes. It sounded like the general rumbling of a lot of approaching feet. A squeak broke the silence. A moment later, three rats zipped down the tunnel they'd come from and scrambled up The Rat's leg and up his coat to sit on his shoulder. The biggest jostled for position next to The Rat's head so it could squeak into its master's ear.

The Rat nodded, looking like he was listening intently. When the messenger stopped squeaking, The Rat looked to Delphine. "We must go. People come. Lots. Shiny people."

"Shiny people?" Melinda whispered.

"Badges and guns, I think he means," The Rat replied. "Cops."

THIRTY-ONE

"Fuck. Any last evidence we can gather?" Ragnar looked frantically at the people assembled around the dead body of the poor homeless man who'd fallen victim to the same murderer who'd killed his father.

"No time, must away. Scurry away like little rats in the darkness." The Rat pantomimed legs scurrying by waggling his fingers. "Follow me. But still, all carefulness."

He stepped gingerly around the dead man in the narrow tunnel and moved through a gap between Delphine and Dax.

"Come, come," The Rat said.

Sippi didn't wait for another invitation and slipped by the corpse to join the group on the other side. Melinda, her eyes looking a bit wild, breathed shallowly as she stared into the even-smaller tunnel. Ragnar wasn't sure if was the claustrophobia, a fear of being underground, or the consuming dark—or a little of each—but his friend was terrified. He knew he didn't like the increasingly confined spaces, but she hadn't mentioned anything about her experience in the morgue, not that he was in a position to pick up much as focused on his dad as he had been. Perhaps that explained her rudeness to Jamie a moment ago.

He grasped her hand. "Come on. I'm right here. I'm not going anywhere."

She nodded and swallowed. He moved into the tunnel and only felt a slight tug when he reached the end of his arm's length before he knew Melinda was following him in. As soon as they joined the group, The Rat led them deeper into the darkness.

In this section of the tunnels, there was almost no light from the sparsely placed lights meant to illuminate the way for city workers. They were entering some of the least-used tunnels, at least by those who didn't dwell down here like The Rat did. Fortunately, the nearly forgotten black light in Ragnar's hand provided a bit of light to guide his steps.

"OK, stop," The Rat whispered. "Now away, my little pretties."

A pair of rats zipped by Ragnar's feet and through the path of the black light on their way back to the corpse.

"Now silence and darkness," The Rat said.

Ragnar had to pull his hand free of Melinda's tight grasp. As soon as cool air brushed against his sweaty palm, she grasped at his hoodie. He turned off the light and went to remove his backpack.

"Fuck. The backpack." Ragnar reached forward and grabbed the nearest person and pulled them back, then transferred Melinda's hand to theirs.

Turning the light back on, he dashed back down the tunnel as quietly as he could on his bootie-covered feet. If anyone whispered for him to stop, he didn't hear them.

Once he got closer to the body and there was enough ambient light, he switched off the black light, hopped over the body, and snatched the bag from the entrance of the tunnel. As his head barely poked past the corner of the tunnel, he saw a cluster of people about twenty feet down the tunnel they'd come through to find the body. In the brief glance, he saw several backs belonging to uniformed cops and what were probably detectives in suits. Snapping his head back, he stood up and carefully backed up.

"Are you sure this is the right place?" one of them asked.

"The tip said there should be a tunnel up here on the left and that's where the body is," a man with a deep voice replied.

"We sure this ain't a prank, sir?" a woman asked.

"Who knows," said the man with the deep voice. "Doesn't matter. If it's a legit tip, we need to take care of it before the press finds anything out."

Ragnar exhaled a silent sigh of relief. It didn't seem like they'd seen his bag or him. He backed away on silent feet until he felt he was far enough away, then he turned and dashed back to his waiting friends as quickly as he could without making a racket of feet flapping on concrete.

"Damnit, Ragnar, where'd you go?" Melinda hissed.

"Forgot my backpack. We'd be cooked if the cops found it." He stuffed the black light inside it, zipped it, and slung it over his shoulder.

"Quiet," The Rat hissed. "Some cops have supernatural ears."

Supernatural cops? Ragnar had never really thought about that possibility before. He'd assumed the police department was full of normies. But there was nothing stopping a supernatural from becoming a cop. It wasn't like normies even knew such beings existed, so how could they screen them out? Being a cop was a cushy job that paid well and didn't require any real work. It made sense that some supernaturals would join. And with the ongoing national issue of police departments being filled with white supremacists, it would be a logical move for the bikers to place their people inside the department they worked with and around.

Letting his mind work through the concept of supernatural cops kept Ragnar from focusing on their current dilemma—being trapped in a dark tunnel with a body and cops. If they were discovered this close to a murder victim, they'd be spending their foreseeable futures as residents of the city jail.

He shifted on his feet, getting tired of standing still. The only sound was the faint breathing of his friends and the occasional scuff of a foot not placed carefully enough. He wasn't sure why The Rat had haltered their progress here. But these tunnels were his domain, so they had to trust to his knowledge. When the rats skittered by emitting faint squeaks, he tensed up and his heart rate increased slightly as they scrabbled up The Rat to deliver their whisperings to his ear.

The Rat was an interesting character. And trapped deep within his territory, Ragnar was glad the little fellow was on their side. He was incredibly loyal to his friends and to people who treated him well. He called both Sippi and Jaime "friend."

What an odd crew Ragnar had assembled here. Two voodoo priestesses—one in training—four wolf shifters, a "specialist" in the dead, and The Rat.

"Come close," The Rat whispered.

Once everyone gathered into a tight group with their shoulders touching. The Rat laid out their options—wait or go deeper underground so they could get away from the cops and escape the tunnel.

"The cops will be bringing in their crime scene people. It could be hours before they're done. And that's assuming they don't leave people here to watch over the scene," Delphine said. "And they might bring in K-9 units."

"You know my vote," Melinda said, her voice subdued.

Ragnar did. She wanted out of the tunnels, like, yesterday. He did too. It was everything he could do to keep his skin from crawling.

"I can hide us more effectively if we need it," Dax offered.

That raised Ragnar's eyebrow. What else could the mysterious dive bar owner do?

Ragnar needed to get out so he could look for the killer who'd now taken a second life in Red City. "We can't wait around here for who knows how long. I say let The Rat take us around the long way."

That received a general rumble of agreement from the rest of the people who hadn't spoken up. No one wanted to hang out where they were, hoping the cops didn't discover them.

"OK. Into the darkness we go. Friendships and hands. Grasp tightly. Trust to each other. Much darkness before The Rat will lead you into the light." The Rat tittered at something a rat squeaked into his ear. "Yes. Yes. Furry messiah. Bringing them into the light."

THIRTY-TWO

Ragnar thought Melinda was going to break his hand, her grip was so tight as The Rat navigated them through the nearly lightless tunnels of Red City's vast underground warren. After his eyes fully adjusted, he realized it wasn't entirely dark. He could pick up the faint grayness and vague lines of their surroundings.

He had no idea how The Rat navigated in the tunnels, but then again, he had no idea what The Rat was, other than a supernatural with an affinity for rodents. At least he could understand Jamie. If he had wolf shifter's eyes like she did, he could probably cautiously navigate these tunnels. It was probably his shifter eyes that allowed him to pick up what he was seeing. Still, he was glad they'd formed a chain with their hands to make sure they all stayed together and didn't get lost.

Occasionally, Jamie brushed against his leg as she moved up and down the line, no doubt doing her part to shepherd them forward and protect her flock. At first, it caused him jump and nearly yelp. A solid rub against the leg in the darkness was probably a hard trigger wired to the reptilian part of the brain.

They kept silent except for an occasional whimper from Melinda whenever there was a slight change in the tension of the arms holding her hands.

It took him a while to realize it, but the walls around them had started to appear more substantial. They'd found a tunnel with a bit more light finding its way down its embrace. In her haste to get into the light, Melinda bumped into his back as she tried to increase her pace.

"Can all see?" The Rat asked in a whisper.

His voice sounded like he was shouting after the long, dark silence.

"Good, good," he said after getting assents from everyone. "And let there be light!" He giggled at his joke. "Now let us pause, must send scouts ahead. Close. Very close to where we were. But also where we want to go."

Ragnar watched as two rats scurried away from them.

"While they go, we walk a bit closer, but quiet again." The Rat waved them all to follow him.

Melinda finally let go of Ragnar's hand. He wiped it against his leg and wiggled his fingers around to work out the tension of her crushing grip.

Once they reached a junction, they stopped. Ragnar slipped up to the corner and peeked to the right. In the distance, he saw the glow of artificial lighting and shadows passing in front of it frequently. It looked like a swarm of activity as the cops investigated the homeless man's murder. He felt comfortable poking his head out into the tunnel. With all the light blasting the police in the face, they'd not see one shadowy lump in a dark tunnel.

Curious, he turned and looked down the left tunnel. Narrowing his eyes, he focused in on a patch of darkness that absorbed the light in a slightly different way. He drew his eyes up to a pale patch curtained by short, black hair.

"Fuck," he hissed.

It was the woman. How she always managed to be right there whenever they were near one of the Slayer's victims, he didn't know. She'd said she wasn't the killer. Had it been a mistake to believe her?

He ducked back into the tunnel and shifted to the other side, away from the light. If she looked his way, she'd have a partial view into the entrance of the tunnel they hid in. He waved everyone to get along the wall next to him so they couldn't be seen by her. They looked confused but quickly complied without having to be told why.

Looking around, he didn't see any dirt to smear on his face to darken his skin. But why would he this, deep down a maze of concrete tunnels. So he lifted his T-shirt up over his nose and just below his eyes so it covered his face in dark fabric. Flipping up the hood of his hoodie, he pulled it down so it sat as low over his face as he could get it. He slowly peeked around the corner.

She was still there, looking down the tunnel at the cops—no doubt admiring her handiwork. He pulled his head back quickly and turned to the person behind him—Manman Delphine—and whispered into her ear, "Pass it down. Send Jamie up here but have her stay behind me."

Delphine nodded and turned to the person behind her. A moment later, Jamie slunk up the line until she stood next to Delphine. Ragnar squatted and waved the wolf forward. He stopped her when she was close and leaned toward her ear.

He whispered so quietly, he barely engaged his vocal cords, but he knew she'd hear him. "There is a woman in a tunnel to our left. Might be the killer. Can you track?"

Jamie nodded once.

"Good. If I move, I need you on my heel immediately. Understood?"

She nodded again.

"I knew I could trust you."

He stood up and motioned Delphine forward. "We might need to move fast. If I go, everyone follows me. But silently."

She winked and relayed the message down the line.

Taking a deep breath, Ragnar pulled his shirt back over his nose and looked toward the woman—Judy. He found her immediately, but now she stared right back at him. A grin split her lips, and she raised her hand and wiggled her fingers at him in a mocking wave. She rotated her hand around and folded down every finger save for the middle one. Then she turned and dashed down the tunnel she was hiding in.

He jumped into the tunnel moved to the left, running as lightly as he could. He didn't want to turn it into a three-party chase by attracting the cops' attention. As soon as he reached the tunnel the woman had been hiding in, he angled into it and picked up his pace. He looked down to his side, but Jamie had slid to a stop and lowered her head to the ground to snuffle around.

She was a wolf. She could catch up easily. In the distance, he could still see Judy. But if he didn't hurry, she'd soon leave him behind. Damn, she was fast.

He picked his speed, hoping the distance and another set of walls would keep the slapping of his feet from echoing down to a supernatural cop's ears. He'd just have to hope they didn't hear, or there were only normie cops on the job.

Pumping his arms, he swiped the hoodie back and dug deeper. He hated running in jeans, but at least he'd gone with his black sneakers so he could sneak around. She swung wide and went down a tunnel to the left. He heard everyone else running behind him, though some were falling behind. Soon it would likely only be Melinda and Sippi behind him.

And Jamie.

She jogged up, easily loping along beside him. He didn't want to put her in danger, but she could probably catch up to Judy and maybe stop her. Though Judy might be too much against even a wolf shifter in wolf form. The way she'd gotten the drop on him and Melinda left a lingering sense of embarrassment and a phantom pain in his gut where she'd punched him.

"Jamie, go. Left turn up ahead. Careful, she's tough."

Jamie yipped an acknowledgement, then took off, bunching her muscles as she dashed forward. She extended out, using the full power of her wolf body as she tried to catch up to Judy. Only slowing slightly, she arced around the left turn and disappeared from sight. He didn't want to risk a look over his shoulder, but he only heard two sets of feet slapping concrete behind him. He bet Sippi was regretting his choice to wear boots. And although he and

Melinda were now sober thanks to their wolfy nature, they'd still be feeling the effects of their drinking. No doubt they were dehydrated and struggling on this mad sprint through the tunnels.

When it came his time to make the corner, he slowed and threw a quick glance to the side. Melinda and Sippi weren't too far behind. Melinda was ahead of Sippi. Then he saw one more shadow in the distance. He wasn't sure who the last person was, but they were doing a valiant job of trying to keep up.

Ahead, he didn't see anyone. But a patch of light indicated another tunnel, so he aimed for it. He slowed as he approached it and stopped, looking to his right. He saw a distant wolf shape and not far in front of it, a human form. He looked behind himself and yelled, "First right."

He hoped they'd heard him; the light was making it difficult to see down the darker end of the tunnel.

He sprinted toward the light. By now, sweat poured down his forehead. He swiped it away with the sleeve of his hoodie. He wished he didn't have the backpack thumping on his back. It was getting obnoxious, especially with all the loose stuff in it jumbling around. He sounded like a rolling junk shop as his feet slapped on the ground.

He was so close to the outside world. He smelled a bit of fresh air —fresh in the polluted, dirty sort of way that was normal in the industrial part of Red City, but at least it smelled of the outside. He squinted against the growing light. He hoped overcompensating by squeezing his eyes nearly closed would protect them and allow a quicker adjustment as he blasted out into the morning light.

He wasn't sure what time it was. He hadn't pulled out his phone for fear of stray sounds or lights. Right now, he needed to catch Judy, he'd worry about what time it was later.

His stomach grumbled, reminding him he hadn't eaten in a long time—not since he'd had dinner with his mom. He wished he'd thought to grab a snack to bring along. He'd have to add it to his detective backpack along with the rest of his junk—and a method to keep it all quieter and more stable. At this rate, the stuff might all break from all the banging around.

He wanted to whoop in relief at bursting through the tunnel into the outside world of Red City. He adjusted his aim for the shadows that looked like a wolf and a person. A moment later, the pained yelp of a wolf drew an angry growl from his own throat. The silhouette of the woman was growing closer. She'd slowed or stopped to do something.

If she were hurting Jamie, he'd never forgive himself for putting the young woman in danger. Finally, his eyes adjusted to the huge increase in light, and he could see clearly enough to get a better picture.

The wolf stood up on wobbly legs outside the tunnel exit. At least she was ambulatory. Not far away, the woman lifted her leg and hoisted it over the back of a motorcycle. A few seconds later, the bike roared to life. Judy turned her head and winked at him, then tugged her helmet over her head. As she sped off, she raised hand to wave at him. And once again, she ended the gesture with a middle finger.

He couldn't resist. He slid to a stop and raised both hands, giving her the double bird in return. She probably hadn't seen it, but he hoped she'd caught the gesture in her mirrors. He was getting damned tired of being outsmarted by that fucking woman

THIRTY-THREE

As soon as the motorcycle tore off carrying Judy away, Jamie laid down on the ground with her jaw open and her tongue lolling out in a pant. He stopped next to her and squatted, looking her over for any blood or other signs of serious wounds.

"Are you OK, Jamie?"

The wolf nodded a couple of times.

"You sure?"

She nodded again, giving him a small yip. He'd have to trust to her word until she could regain her human form and her ability to speak. If they were pack, he could have simply communicated to her through the pack link, but there were no packs in Red City except the Black Suns.

That fact galled him. Packless wolf shifters were weak without the strength and companionship the link offered them. The world was a lonelier place without it.

He stood up and looked around, checking out the surroundings to make sure there wasn't anything to worry about. He didn't need any new dangers and wasn't equipped to deal with much. Hard breathing and feet running drew his attention back toward the tunnel. Melinda and Sippi emerged from it and slowed to a walk.

They stopped next to him. They both bent over and rested their hands on their knees as they tried to catch their breaths.

After a couple minutes, Delphine exited the tunnel and joined the recovery session. It was another few minutes before Suzie emerged.

She stopped by Delphine. "This is bullshit. You never said this voodoo stuff would require sprinting through underground tunnels to get away from the cops."

"What? Got a problem with tunnels and cops?" Delphine asked, an eyebrow raised.

"Nah, tunnels are cool, and you should always run from cops." She pointed down to her Docs. "These ain't running shoes."

Delphine chuckled, then looked around. "We didn't catch our snoop?"

"Who were we chasing, anyway?" Suzie asked.

Jamie stood up, yipped, and walked over to Suzie with a bit of a limp.

"Oh, I guess we better get you dressed. Um, will the tunnel work? The Rat is there getting his eyes acclimated before exiting." Suzie hitched her thumb over her back to the small backpack she wore.

"No, The Rat is here now. But very bright." He strolled out of the tunnel, shading his eyes with his hand.

Suzie and Jamie walked into the tunnel until they were no longer visible, reemerging a few minutes later with Jamie in her human form, fully clothed. She still had a slight limp.

"Sorry about losing her, everyone. She swept my legs with a low spin kick and knocked the wind out of me."

"Stone cold Cobra Kai move, right there." Suzie tsked and shook her head. "Next time you'll have to pay her back with a crane kick to the face."

Ragnar patted Jamie on the shoulder. "No worries, Jamie. You did a great job keeping up. Do you think you'd recognize her scent again if you came across it?"

"I think so."

"Did you pick up anything interesting in her scent?" Delphine asked.

"Hmm. She's a supernatural of some sort. I'd venture shifter maybe, but not wolf. I'd recognize a wolf shifter instantly."

"That would explain her speed and strength," Melinda said.

"Yeah. That's three times she's gotten the drop on one of us." Ragnar pursed his lips.

"Is the fast lady the killer?" The Rat asked.

Ragnar sighed. "I don't know. So far she's been at the scenes of both murders."

"Murderers sometimes like to see the aftereffects of their handi-work, especially serial killers." Delphine spread her legs wider and bent over, stretching. "Sorry, don't want to neglect myself after a hard run like that. I don't have shifter healing abilities."

"And if she's a shifter, it's more believable that she can lug a body down a long stretch of tunnel without leaving traces of a wagon or wheelbarrow." Sippi shifted on his feet, looking uncomfortable. When Ragnar raised an eyebrow at Sippi, he looked a bit abashed. "Gonna have some blisters. Like Little Suzie, I made a poor footwear choice."

"Ugh. Right?" Suzie joined Delphine in stretching.

"I always thought it was total bullshit that a cat can lounge about all day, then just do all kinds of acrobatics without pulling a muscle. Yet I have to work out all the time just to not hurt myself getting off the couch." Delphine changed positions to stretch some different muscles. "Anyway, so the evidence we have against our mysterious shifter—"

"Judy," Ragnar said.

"What?"

"She said she was Judy. It was an obvious fake name she used as a joke when she punched me. You know, Punch and Judy. But I've been using it to tag her in my brain. Saves having to call her the mysterious shifter or something else."

Delphine chuckled. "Judy is definitely not an intimidating name for a serial killer. So Judy then. She's been at the scenes of two murders. And you said she was at the funeral. And we all saw her at the party at the Honky Tonk. Do we have any other evidence? Jamie, did you pick up her scent on the body?"

Jamie shifted on her feet, folding her arms over her chest as she thought about it. "Maybe around the area. I'm trying to search my memory and sift through the scents that were there. But I'm not sure if her scent was on the body or just around it." She swallowed, looking a little paler. "I'm not a professional sniffer dog. I've just been using my nose a lot to help Dax and fight the bikers. Also, dead bodies are gross, and I was struggling not to vomit on it."

"That's OK, cher. You're doing a great job. No one here probably has as much experience using their nose like you have." Delphine looked around to the other shifters.

"I know I don't," Ragnar said. "I've been trying to tap into my wolf senses more as I investigate this murder, but it's so foreign to me. Since we've been forced into solitude, in wolf terms, and not allowed to form a pack, so many of us aren't very familiar with our dual nature."

Sippi and Melinda nodded along.

Delphine narrowed her eyes and tilted her head in thought. "Why not form a pack?"

"What?" The thought hadn't occurred to him. His father had been the leader, and though they'd argued about it, Ragnar followed his dad's lead on the subject. But if Bob was telling the truth and his father had changed his mind… "But that's maybe what got Dad killed."

"I don't mean to make light of that or the current situation, but you can't really make the bikers much angrier, can you?"

Jamie looked between Ragnar and Delphine. "We're already at war with them."

"The kid's right, Red. If we all surrendered and capitulated to their demands, the best result would be them increasing the money the community has to pay for peace. But more likely, they'll expect a sacrifice in blood."

Jamie scowled at Melinda at the word "kid" but didn't say anything. "I've never been in a pack. The closest I ever came was my friend Cory. And even though we weren't pack, I miss that close connection."

Ragnar thought about it while everyone watched him. Finally, he looked around at his friends. "I'll think about it. But I can't make a unilateral decision without checking in with a few people."

A slight smile spreading across Delphine's face. "Spoken like a true leader. Now back to our potential suspect."

"I don't know," Ragnar said, "something doesn't feel right about this situation. Yeah, she's been near two of the sites, but something is telling me it's unlikely she's the one who killed either victim."

"Is that something your hormones are telling you?" Melinda asked, an eyebrow rising along with a smirk.

Ragnar clenched his jaw. "No, Melinda. It's not my hormones. I'll concede it's possible she might be involved somehow, but I'm just not sure she's a serial killer. Or at least not a brutal one like the Tarot Slayer."

"Hmm. Hmm. Interesting. And what should The Rat do if she comes in my tunnels again?" The Rat asked, lowering his hand from his eyes but still squinting strongly.

That was a scary thought. If Ragnar gave The Rat the green light to attack the woman, he'd swarm her with an army of rats, and she'd die in a terrifying and painful way. But if she was involved with the Tarot Slayer, she might deserve that kind of brutal justice. She might. But he couldn't be the one to sign her death sentence, not based on coincidences and hunches.

"Just follow her and listen in, if you can. We need evidence, not misplaced 'justice.'"

Delphine nodded as if she approved.

"Now what, then?" Melinda asked.

Ragnar sighed. Leading a band was much easier than leading people in serious matters. "I don't know what. We keep digging into the evidence and hope we find something." He looked around at his friends. "And thank you. Let's keep the lines of communication open."

He was about to invite everyone to go get some breakfast together—his stomach was getting quite insistent on being filled and it was making it hard for him to think as clearly as he wanted—when Dax sauntered out of the tunnel, one hand stuffed in his pocket. Ragnar had completely forgotten the man was even with them. He realized he hadn't seen him since they'd fled from the approach of the cops.

"Where the hell have you been, Slim?" Melinda asked.

Dax seemed to ignore her, saying nothing until he joined their circle. His brow furrowed as he inspected Jamie. "Are you OK, Jamie?"

The teen rolled her eyes and made a disgusted noise. "I will be. My pride is hurt than anything else at this point."

Dax quirked up an eyebrow.

"She knocked my legs out from under and me and I hit the ground hard. I'm mostly fine."

"You better be, or Mama Adele will have words with me about not taking care of you."

"Ugh. I'm an adult. I can take care of myself." Jamie didn't sound too vehement about her protest.

"I know. I'm older than all of you. Combined. And then some. But Mama Adele takes care of those she adopts into her family. And that's you and me these days, so we don't have much of a choice. Just don't get me in trouble."

Jamie chuckled. "Understood. I'm fine. Really."

Dax nodded once, then turned to Melinda. "As to your question, I was curious."

"Curious?" A bit of heat slipped into Melinda's voice.

Ragnar decided to head off the argument. "Curious about what?"

"I wanted to listen in on the cops. See what they had to say."

"Don't you think that's a bit reckless? Aren't you worried about getting caught?" Melinda asked.

Jamie snorted. "They won't see him, not if he doesn't want them to."

"And definitely not in a dark tunnel where I can pull in the shadows," Dax added.

The Rat nodded, trying to move a bit farther away from Dax. "Very sneaky, very stealth. Very scary."

Curious. Ragnar wondered what The Rat had seen and what he knew about Dax. The Rat seemed pretty unflappable. Whatever he'd witnessed had left an impression.

"Don't worry. They saw and heard nothing." Dax squinted up at the sun, scowling. "But to assuage your curiosity, I didn't hear much of worth. They don't know much. All they've been told is keep this tightly under wraps. They were just preparing the scene for when some higher-ranking cops showed up."

"Oh well. It was worth a try," Ragnar said, unable to keep the disappointment from his voice. He wondered if mysteries were always like this—each new piece of evidence raising more questions than it answered. His stomach growled, reminding him he was getting increasingly hungry. "Let's get breakfast and talk over what we've got so far."

THIRTY-FOUR

By coincidence, they'd all parked near each other. But it kind of made sense, since they'd basically come from the same side of town. They stood in a circle around Melinda's car as they made plans for where to have breakfast.

Jamie held up her hand. "Quiet." She tiled her head so her ear pointed toward the sky. "Helicopters. Getting closer."

"Multiple?" Delphine asked.

"I think so."

There. He heard them in the distance now too. Jamie had good ears. Soon everyone looked up at the sky in the direction of the approaching helicopters. A few seconds later, the first aircraft came into view.

"Shit. It's a news copter," Suzie said.

They stared as the helicopter flew above the buildings toward the entrance of the tunnels. A moment later, a helicopter from a competing station joined the first one.

"Guys, I'm going to make a suggestion here," Melinda said. "And that is for us to get the fuck out of here. There are probably going to be news vans rolling up soon, and we don't need Ron Burgundy up in our business." She looked around the group, her eyes lingering on Dax and The Rat. "And we're a sketchy looking bunch."

"She's right," Dax said. "Let's get move out. Split up. Try to look for overpasses to drive under. Take your time. Don't draw attention."

"We'll see you at the diner," Delphine said. "Breakfast is on me and Dax."

Dax furrowed his brow at her, then shrugged. "Let's go."

There was a bit of power in Dax's voice, and they all obeyed. Ragnar climbed into the passenger seat while Melinda got behind the wheel and Sippi got in the back. Dax, Delphine, Jamie, and Little Suzie calmly walked over to two small cars. Dax got in Delphine's and Jamie got in Suzie's. Taking a quick look around, Ragnar didn't see The Rat. He needn't have worried. This was his part of town. The Rat had no doubt slipped into the shadows and would soon be safely ensconced deep in his tunnels with his army of rodents.

Melinda, her grip on the steering wheel white knuckled, did her best to drive in a non-suspicious manner.

Sippi, who was looking over his shoulder out the back window, pointed. "Just in time. The vans have arrived."

Ragnar glanced over his shoulder. Sure enough, they had. A fresh flood of adrenaline zipped into his veins. On his empty stomach, it caused his hands to shake. He was going to need a double order of a tall stack of pancakes to deal with the burning hunger. The thought of a steaming-hot stack of pancakes nearly made him drool in anticipation. Although he wanted to hurry so he could get some food, he resisted the urge to ask Melinda to speed up. They didn't have flapjacks in jail.

They all made it to the diner Delphine had suggested without incident, and Ragnar was able to take care of the gnawing pit in his stomach. Even though they spent much of the morning talking over everything, no one came up with anything that might send them in the right direction. Even the mystical Dax had nothing much to contribute other than adding the mysterious woman to his list of people to watch out for.

THIRTY-FIVE

Ragnar stared at the pictures of his dad's corpse on the monitor, trying to interpret the symbols carved all over his body. He just couldn't make sense of them. He recognized a lot of them and knew what they meant individually. The others he'd looked up, recording their meanings in a journal he'd picked up at a bookstore. But no matter how he arranged the symbols in his head, he couldn't make any of it comprehensible.

He nearly jumped out of his skin when his phone rang through his noise cancelling headphones. He'd had the music up loud and the unexpected ring tone came through sounding extra obnoxious. Picking up his phone and answering, he saw it was Melinda.

"Turn on your TV to the news," she said without any preamble.

"What channel?"

"Doesn't matter. Probably could do the cable news ones too."

"Alright…"

"Call me when you're ready." She hung up, and his music resumed.

"What the hell?" he mumbled to himself.

He turned off his headphones and took them off. Expecting the normal quiet of his house, the noise from the street startled him. He heard shouting and cars punctuated by the occasional horn. A helicopter buzzed overhead.

"Oh no..." He stood up and ran downstairs. Snatching the remote from the coffee table, he turned on the TV. After he found a local new station with *Breaking News* running across the bottom of the screen, he sank onto the couch.

He recognized the house on the screen. It was his parents' house, the one he'd grown up in. He stared at the screen blankly for a minute while he tried to gather his brain. Finally, he homed in on the chyron running along the bottom of the screen.

"Local man might be one of the latest victims of the Tarot Slayer."

Someone had leaked the Tarot Slayer information to the press. Again. This time he and his family were the victims of whoever was feeding details to the police. He wouldn't put it past the bikers or some elements of the cops to do this. Standing up, he walked to the front door and peeled back the sheer curtain that covered the tall, narrow window next to the front door.

Reporters lined the sidewalk and news vans were parked down the street. He couldn't quickly count the cameras pointed at the front of the house. There had to be more stations present than just the local ones. He pushed the curtain farther to the side to create more space to see. At the movement, the reporters surged forward in a scrum to see who could be the first to get to the door, their shouting growing louder and closer.

A moment later, multiple fists pounded on the door. Someone repeatedly mashed the doorbell button, adding its ring to the mix. In a daze, he opened the door.

"Mr. Magnusson can you tell us..."

"Mr. Magnusson, how do you feel about..."

"Mr. Magnusson, Mr. Magnusson, NCN News, we can promise an exclusive..."

"When did you first learn the Tarot Slayer might be your father's killer, Mr...."

Each time he picked up on a voice, someone else quickly drowned it out. A forest of microphones had been thrust in his face. Cameras peeked over and through gaps in the maelstrom of reporters. He couldn't concentrate with their intense focus targeting him.

"My… My name…"

The reporters quieted down.

"Mr. Magnusson is my father."

The reporters stared at him, a few of them even opened their mouths in surprise.

"Is that a joke?" one reported asked another.

Ragnar's eyes went wide, and he took a step back. The reporters collectively took a step forward. But before they could cross the threshold, he slammed the door shut, turning the deadbolt and sliding the chain along its channel. Then he backed away from the door, staring in horror.

He hadn't intended to make the classic dad joke. Mr. Magnusson *was* his father. If someone was to affix Mr. to Ragnar's name, it would be Mr. Gunnarsson. His family adhered to the old ways when it came to their surnames. If Ragnar had had a sister, she would have been Miss Gunnarsdoter. He did have an aunt who was a Magnusdoter, but she'd passed away in an auto accident when he was young.

Now the press probably thought he was some callous idiot, making a joke at the expense of his father when they were there to get an interview with someone in the family about the Tarot Slayer and dad's death. He looked around, wondering where his mother was. He hadn't seen her in a while, but then again, he'd been busy in his room looking through the files yet another time. He'd joined her for lunch a few hours earlier but had gone back upstairs.

He went into the kitchen as the pounding resumed on the door. In the center of the island sat a note. He picked it up and read it—it was from his mother. She had gone out to dinner with Bob. He saw Bob more now than he had when his dad was alive. It was good his mom had someone to talk to in addition to her own friends, someone who'd known his dad intimately.

He was about to run upstairs and grab his phone to warn his mom when the pounding on the door stopped and the shouting receded. Running back to the window, he peeked out. He couldn't quite tell what had attracted the reporters' attention, but they swarmed around someone, only parting when two people pushed through. It was Bob and his mom.

Ragnar scrambled and barely had the door unlocked before they reached the threshold. Yanking it open, he backed out of the way, then swung it shut quickly before the reporters could get in. He wasn't sure why he assumed reporters operated under the same rules vampires did regarding thresholds. He didn't even know if the rules were true for vampires.

There was a nest or two of them in the city, but he'd never encountered any. For all he knew, the threshold thing could be pure fiction. Either way, the reporters were once again banging on the door and ringing the doorbell.

He turned around. His mom was sobbing in Bob's arms.

"Ragnar, can you help your mother? I'll go take care of this mess," Bob said.

Ragnar wrapped his arm around his mom's shoulders and guided her onto the couch. Sitting next to his mom, he aimed his ear at the door, hoping his enhanced wolf hearing would let him pick up Bob's words.

"Can you answer any questions about Mr. Magnusson's death and the potential involvement of the Tarot Slayer?" asked one reporter, who either had won some contest or had just gotten lucky to get his question out before being drowned out by their colleagues.

"Not at this time," Bob replied.

"Who are you?"

"I'm Robert Sever. I'm the family's attorney. They will not be taking any questions at this time. Please withdraw from the property immediately before I call the police."

"Mr. Sever. Mr. Sever..."

"There will be no questions." The door opened a moment later and he stepped through, shutting it quickly behind himself.

He leaned against the door for a moment and sighed. "Vultures." He shook his head and stood up straight. "Anyway, that'll keep them off the lawn for now. I can't do anything about them being on the sidewalk or the street since that's public property. But they can't be on your property without permission now that we've withdrawn it."

"You're our attorney?" Ragnar asked. He wasn't sure why it was the first place his brain had gone, but he was curious.

Bob rolled his eyes. "I am a lawyer, but in tax law. So technically it's true, since I've done the family's taxes for years. But more importantly, 'attorney' is a particularly magic word when dealing with the press."

"Ragnar, honey, would you get me a glass of water, please?" his mom asked in a weak voice.

"Sure, Mom." He unwound his arm from her shoulder and fetched a glass of water from the filter pitcher in the fridge.

She took it and drank about half of it before setting it on the coffee table. "Robert, thank you for dealing with the press, but I think I need to be alone tonight."

Something flashed across Bob's eyes, but Ragnar didn't quite catch the full meaning. "Of course, Erin. Just call if you need anything and I'll be right over. Also, I'll assemble a list of attorneys who would be a better fit for this situation. I'm not sure a tax lawyer will be able to help much with all this."

Ragnar's mom nodded. "Thanks, Bob. I appreciate it. Ragnar will see you out. When you're done, come see me, please, honey."

"OK, Mom." Ragnar got up and walked Bob to the door. "Thanks for stepping in and getting Mom through that mess."

"No worries, Ragnar. Glad I could be here for her."

Ragnar shook Bob's hand and locked the door after he left. His mother had disappeared, probably up to her bedroom.

He went upstairs and knocked on the door. "Mom, it's me."

"Come in, honey."

He entered. She sat in a rocking chair in the corner. It had always been one of her favorite pieces of furniture. She gestured to the wingback armchair that had been his dad's. "Please sit. You're too tall for an old lady to stare up at." She smiled warmly but sadly.

He reluctantly dropped into the chair. It felt odd to sit in his father's place. Especially the one he'd sat in when he spent quiet time with his mother in their private sanctuary.

"I need to ask a few questions, and please be honest."

He sighed. He'd known this was coming. "I haven't been dishonest, Mom. I just haven't been as open as I could have been."

"It's a fine distinction to make, but I'll concede the point. I take it you knew about this? The T-t-tarot Slayer?"

He nodded.

"And you and your friends have been looking into it?"

He nodded again.

She grew even paler and raised a shaky hand to pinch the bridge of her nose. They sat in silence for a few moments before she spoke again. "Ragnar, I can't make you stop. But I can't go to your funeral too. It would kill me. I know you're a grown man and a very capable one, but please, for the love of all that's good, please be careful. Please put your safety first. You're all I have left. And all I have left of Gunnar."

He tried to put on a reassuring smile. "I promise I'll be careful."

THIRTY-SIX

Later the next day, Ragnar stepped into his father's forge and turned the lights on. He was tired of running around dangerous neighborhoods and being threatened by scumbag, Nazi bikers and needed something to defend himself. He wasn't a gun person, nor did he wish to become one. But hammers… Those were more his speed.

He'd stopped at a local hardware store and purchased a good old-fashioned, ten-pound sledgehammer with a hickory handle. The salesperson had tried to talk him into one of the fancier ones with a handle made of fiberglass or some other synthetic bullshit, but he'd politely declined. He picked up a couple short-handled, smaller sledges as well—again, wooden handled. He didn't need the added ergonomics or shock absorption of the synthetics. He could rune those features in. What he needed was a natural product that he could cover in magical runes, and wood and good iron and steel made better receptacles than the fake shit.

Looking longingly at the furnace and bellows, he sighed and went looking for his dad's special engraving tools. Someday when he had the time and the desire, he'd construct his own weapon by hand, but for now, retail was good enough.

Once he found his dad's special tools, he set up the sledge in a vice on a work bench. He could muscle the rune marks in with standard tools, but the extra-hard forged and tempered steel of the sledge's head would make it more difficult. Plus, if he forced it, he risked slipping and gouging the steel, breaking the tool, or hurting himself.

His father's tools had been specially tuned to keep the hand steady and compensated for the material being engraved. They were a true marvel of ingenuity. While his father hadn't brought a ton of innate power to the process, he'd more than made up for it through scholarship and cleverness.

At his current education level with the runes, Ragnar couldn't have created a set of tools like this, at least not ones that would have delivered the finesse his dad's tools could. Maybe someday. That thought brought with it a punch to the gut. So much wasted time. His dad would have loved to have shared his knowledge and teach Ragnar his tricks. Now he'd never get a chance.

He brought out the yoga mat his father kept in the forge and laid it out so he could meditate and center his mind before working the runes. To make the magic flow, intention and concentration were needed. His father had always taught him to seek a still mind before lifting the tools. It took Ragnar longer than usual to get to the place he needed. The tumult of the last several weeks seemed to keep his mind in a constant state of motion, turning it into a tornado of overthinking. But being in the forge where his father and he had spent so many good times allowed him to calm his mind and find the place needed.

He started with the head of the hammer, working in his favorite patterns—the ones he'd created himself for his last hammer, which now was buried under the earth in a locked chamber in the mountains of Colorado, along with several of his favorite instruments. He pushed aside that intrusive thought and returned to his work.

By the time he finished with the steel of the head, every inch of it was covered with intricately carved runes and designs that served both a decorative and power-enhancing function. A drip of sweat ran down his nose and fell from its tip when he finished. Instead of shining on the metal, the steel drank in the drop of sweat as if the runes had rendered it desperately thirsty.

Sitting back, he grabbed a rag and wiped the sweat from his head and the back of his neck. The handle was next. He reached for the electric woodburning kit but stopped his hand just before picking it up. This weapon called for the old methods.

It took him a while to find his dad's old wood burning tools. His father stuck mostly with the electric setup for convenience. However, Ragnar wanted to take the extra step. Part of the reason he was in here was to make a new hammer. But the other part was to escape the chaos in the world outside this room, this forge, and focus on his hands and his craft. He needed to feel in touch with something real. The tools. The hammer. And his hands and the sweat from his brow.

So now he had to create the fire and coals he'd need to heat the tips of the burning tools. The fire would be welcome. The night had gone cool and the sweat evaporating off his body only served to chill him further.

The handle took another couple hours all told, but by the time he was nearly done, he'd found his center once again. He just needed to finish one last rune sequence. It was one his father had taught him when he was young.

Gunnar Magnusson had been fundamentally a tinkerer and had created a lot of new ways to use the runes. One of his favorites involved purpose and intent of the user. His dad had made all kinds of variations from the silly to the profound.

At first, Ragnar had thought of making his new hammer only useable by himself. But he thought back to the time he'd lent one of his other hammers to Jamie. So instead, he created a series of runes that checked the intent of the wielder. If someone gripped it with the intent to harm Ragnar, it would cause immense pain and force them to drop it. He also added a neutral identifier that would render it a mundane sledgehammer if someone picked it up off the ground—as long as they didn't have ill intent. The third piece worked in harmony with the first two rune collections, allowing Ragnar to directly hand the hammer to someone. Only then would it remain a powerful magical item. But he put a safety check on that rune too. The handoff required the proper intentionality.

Once the last rune flared and glowed, he admired his work while the runes faded to look like normal wood-burned carvings. He'd taken a plain industrial tool and turned it into a powerful magical weapon and a thing of beauty.

He straightened his back and rotated shoulders. He'd been hunched over his work for too many hours, but now he was done. His back cracked, and he groaned as his tight muscles stretched out. It was good work his father would be proud of. Ragnar wished he could show it to him. Then his mind drifted to Roy. He hadn't seen him in a while. His dad's old best friend would appreciate the work too.

Closing his eyes and lowering his head, he thanked his dad for everything he'd taught him and promised to free his soul. Then his eyes fell on the user intention series of runes. For the first time in weeks, the work had rendered his mind calm and clear. The wheels began turning. The intention runes had been taught to him by his dad, who'd used them on most of the things he created.

Ragnar stood up and picked up the hammer by the shaft just below the head and stalked out of the forge into the darkening evening. The coals and the tools would need to be attended to, but right now his mind was firing, and he needed to check on something.

Moving through the house, he walked into the living room, where Bob was talking with his mom.

"Ragnar, honey, what are you doing with a sledgehammer in the house?" his mom asked.

"Nothing. Just need to check something in one of dad's books." He didn't stick around for any more questions and stalked through the kitchen and threw open the door to his dad's office.

Along one wall was a sliding closet door. He opened it, revealing shelves of journals and photo albums. His dad had been a scholar of the runes. He'd documented every rune he'd carved in both writing and photos. It had been his life's work in many ways.

He'd always complained that so much of the old learning had been lost because it required being passed from person to person, mouth to ear. There were almost none who knew the runes anymore. Not in the way that forged mark and tool and item into magic, anyway.

It seemed like hundreds of books stared back at him from the shelves as he ran his eyes over them. If his father had been this organized about documenting his works, he'd also have some sort of cataloging system. Ragnar's eyes drifted over to his dad's computer. It was password locked, and he hadn't tried to get into it yet. If the cataloging system was there, it would take him some serious time to get in.

He returned his focus to the books in front of him, moving to the left. He grabbed the leftmost journal from the top shelf. Butterflies and hope churned in his stomach as he opened the book to the title page. Yes!

Of course his dad had placed the catalog first. His father might have catalog listings on his computer, which would be easier to cross-reference and search multiple parameters, but a man who was preserving knowledge would also make sure he had a physical copy to go with physical books.

Ragnar shut the office door and sat in the desk chair. It squeaked as it took his weight and as it had taken his father's when he used to sit there. With a smile on his face, Ragnar flipped through the pages, admiring his father's neat and precise handwriting. Ragnar's had always been two steps above raw scribbles. The only thing he could write neatly were the runes.

Of all the things in the house that belonged to his father, these journals might've been the most important and personal thing that hadn't been something given to him by Ragnar's mother. He'd have to ensure his mother didn't let anything happen to them until he got his own place and he could move them there.

He let himself fade into the presence of his father through the writing and words, without actively looking for what he wanted. Those pages weren't going anywhere, and he wanted to absorb the moment of closeness while he could, because he knew another one might not come again. After a while, he was simply flipping the pages slowly and reverentially running his fingers over the paper.

Until he stopped at a page maybe three-quarters of the way through.

The word *dagger* jumped out at him.

"BACKSCRATCHER" — Double-edged dagger
    Owner — Gunnar Magnusson
    Reference — Journal 7 (Page 59, Photo album 10 (Page 31))

"THANKS, DAD." Ragnar laid a hand on the book and smiled before closing it and setting it out of the way on the desk.

He found the two referenced books and pulled them down, opening them to the pages notated in the journal entry. His general sense of peace and connection to his father wavered. The dagger that had been used to perform the killing blow stared at him from color photos arranged on the archival pages of his dad's photo album.

Taking a deep breath, he exhaled slowly and tried to return to clarity before it slipped away fully. Putting the album aside, he picked up the journal and read over the runes and notes describing their creation and the intentions placed behind them.

He found exactly what he'd wanted. His father had engraved user protections into the dagger. Shifting his gaze back to the photos, Ragnar found the one with a naked handle, before it had been wrapped with silver wire. The runes had been laid onto the handle and then covered to hide them from unsuspecting eyes.

Not only would the dagger mark the user if it was used to harm its owner—anyone of Gunnar's blood—but if the dagger was brought back into the presence of the villain, the marks would be renewed, even if they'd healed. Even years later.

Unfortunately, he didn't have the dagger to use as a marker of guilt. It was tagged and bagged in some police lockup, no doubt where almost no one knew where it was. Just like his father's body.

"Fuck." Ragnar needed to consult with the only person who'd know what these runes could do. Uncle Roy.

THIRTY-SEVEN

Ragnar picked up a couple of bookmarks from the stack his father kept on his desk and placed them in the pages of the journal and the photo album. After putting away the catalog book, he grabbed his hammer and the two books and went to his room. He stuffed the books into an empty backpack.

A stray flash of light glared across his window. He walked over and peeled the curtain back a little to look out.

"Damned press. Fucking vultures."

There had been two leaks to the press regarding the Tarot Slayer. The first had revealed the latest victim stashed away in the tunnels. The second had revealed that the murder of Gunnar Magnusson had a much more sinister cause than the information initially released by the cops. Since then, the press had been camped out on the street, hoping to get interviews with Ragnar or his mother. His mother hadn't left the house in the last two days. He'd only gone out long enough to buy the hammers, and they'd hounded him as he left and returned. The only connection they had to the outside world was through their phones and the few visitors who'd braved the harassment of the press, such as Bob.

He had no doubt the press had parabolic microphones and were listening in to whatever they could. He thought about storming out and clearing away all their equipment and vehicles with his hammer. He could do it, too. It would only take a few minutes of rage-induced joy to turn everything into scrap.

He thought he almost felt the hammer thirsting for the destruction through his contact with the handle. Looking down at the hammer, he smiled and let himself indulge in the fantasy for a few moments. But if he couldn't solve the problem of the press with his runed hammer, perhaps he could still find a way to use runes to arrive at a more covert solution.

If his father had been here, Ragnar could've consulted with him, and they'd no doubt come up with a solution. Hell, there might even been a solution in his dad's journals, but he didn't have time to skim through dozens of volumes. Ragnar would need to solve this problem himself.

Slinging the backpack over his shoulder, he took it and the hammer with him and returned to the forge. He was glad he hadn't extinguished the fire and put away the tools. He grabbed a small wooden slat—it was rough and no more than couple inches wide and maybe six long—and warmed up one of the rune-carving tools.

With a grin, he went to work. It didn't take him long. He'd formulated the runes he wanted while he'd waited for the heat to take hold of the wood-burning tool. The mischievous feeling only served to help his intuition as he worked the runes into the slat of wood. The only problem was, he had no one to test the runes on.

Then the sound of the press shouting drew his attention. Bob must be heading home. If Ragnar was going to use his handiwork to fool the press, he might as well make their presence useful. He set down the hammer, not wanting to seem like a threat in case his runes failed, and headed around the house to the front lawn. Across the street, Bob climbed into his car and drove away.

Ragnar wandered out to within fifteen feet of the horde of people on the sidewalk and stood there as they returned their attention to the house. Eyes swept right over him and moved on. He strolled to the walkway leading from the sidewalk to the house and back. Not a single person noticed him.

"Holy shit," he muttered.

A few heads jerked toward the sound.

"Did you hear something?" someone asked.

"Maybe..."

They looked around, squinting into the darkness, but when neither of them spotted anything, they returned to what they were doing. Ragnar would have to be quiet. But he'd effectively rendered himself invisible. At least in the dark, while in the shadows.

He grabbed his hammer on the way by the forge and climbed over the wood fence, dropping into the yard behind their house. Once he was a few blocks away and was sure he'd ditched the press, he pulled out his phone and prepared to summon a ride share but stopped before pushing the final button.

If his rune caused him to be invisible or undetectable, he wasn't sure how good the effect actually was. It had appeared to work. So how would he get into the car? If he dropped the slat with its runes so he was visible, he couldn't pick it up after getting in, otherwise he'd suddenly become invisible in the back of a stranger's car. And he certainly couldn't leave a magical item like that just lying on the sidewalk.

If he was going to visit Uncle Roy, he might as well impose on Roy and see him a few minutes earlier. He sent a message to Uncle Roy, requesting a pickup—Ragnar would "explain later."

Twenty minutes later, an old, beat-up pickup truck pulled to a stop in front of him. Roy leaned out the window. "Going my way?"

"Thanks, Uncle Roy. I'm going to do something, so don't be alarmed. It's a bit of rune work." Ragnar bent over and picked up the slat off the ground.

"What the hell?"

"What do you see?" Ragnar asked.

Roy squinted at the spot where Ragnar had disappeared from. "Not much. Maybe a bit of a shadow or a disturbance in the air."

"Fuck yeah! I'm going to walk around in front of the truck. Watch for me as I pass through the headlight. Then I'll climb in."

Ragnar walked slowly, though his excitement compelled him to run in front of the truck and get in so he could talk over the magic with his uncle. Once he shut the door after climbing in, he set the slat on the dash.

"Sure that's a good idea, boy?" Roy asked. "If people can't see us, that'll be pretty dangerous."

"Good point. I don't know exactly what all this thing does." Ragnar picked up the slat.

"You didn't test it properly?"

"No, but I didn't have much of a choice. I needed to get away from the press." He sighed. "And I need to talk to you."

"You know I'm here whenever you want me to be." Roy pulled away from the curb and took the next turn.

"I know. I want to start by apologizing that I haven't really seen you since the funeral."

"No problem. I haven't been in your life for most of it. I can't expect us to pick up where we left off when I moved away. You were only seven."

"I understand, and I want to get to you know you better. It's just I've been so stuck in my own head about my dad's murder. And investigating it."

Roy raised an eyebrow and cast a side glance at Ragnar. "I wondered if you might be doing something like that. But let's save that topic for after we sit down at the bar."

"OK. And thank you, Uncle Roy."

Roy reached over patted Ragnar's knee. "If you want me to be in your life, then I'm here, and we have plenty of time. Now tell me about that nifty piece of magic."

A bit of warmth seeped into the empty place the absence of his father had created. Roy was right. He and Ragnar did have plenty of time…as long as poking around in the business of an infamous serial killer didn't result in his death.

Ragnar explained everything that had led to the creation of the slat, including the dagger used to kill his father. "So tell me, how did I look in the headlights?"

"Not as great as in the dark. You were still hard to see, but you cast a normal shadow. When we get time, we'll have to experiment with it to see how exactly it works. Be bad to need it in a situation and have it betray you."

Ragnar nodded, his mind churning with ideas for new versions of the runes and ideas to expand their usefulness, including a runed pouch that would nullify the slat's power so he could carry it around without having to be invisible.

"Penny for your thoughts?" Roy said.

Ragnar's mind stopped. Uncle Roy had taught his father and him the runes; he'd be the perfect sounding board for Ragnar's ideas. And for the first time in weeks, the words spilled freely from Ragnar's mouth. It felt good to talk about something that wasn't his father's death with someone who could understand rune work. Roy listened intently, making occasional grunts of acknowledgement or simple comments or suggestions. Ragnar didn't even notice when he parked in front of a shabby-looking bar.

THIRTY-EIGHT

"Isn't this a bit too public?" Ragnar asked, staring at the dingy bar.

"Nah. Nobody here cares what you say. In fact, they aggressively mind their own business. It's why I like it." Roy opened the driver's door on the pickup. "I'm buying. And leave the slat under the pickup, not inside. It ain't much, but I don't want it getting rammed."

Ragnar climbed out and set the slat on the gravel, nudging it behind the front passenger side tire. Taking a step back, he examined the truck. As far as he could tell, it looked perfectly normal and visible. They really would need to find the time to explore the full potential of the magic he'd created and how exactly it worked in practice. He could put all the correct intentions in it during creation, but until the item was properly tested in real world situations, he wouldn't know the results of the magic.

Rune magic wasn't precise. It required focus, experimentation, and testing. Lots of testing.

Once he was satisfied, he followed Roy into the working-class dive bar. Roy bought two beers and nodded toward an empty table in the corner. It was a fair distance from the pool table, jukebox, and the bar, so very few people had taken seats in the area. Perhaps Ragnar could create a circle of silence device.

They sat down, and Ragnar caught up with what Roy'd been doing since the funeral. Then, Ragnar took the bottom of his shirt, wiped the table dry, pulled the journal and the photo album out of his backpack. He explained about his father's dagger and the runes hidden under the wire-wrapped handle.

"That sounds just like Gunnar. He was always impressed with his own cleverness. And those runes are very clever indeed." Roy said it in an affectionate manner. "Even without a lot of innate power, he could make the runes do things far more powerful people couldn't. Just proves hard work and study can make up for natural talent."

He finished his beer and walked to the bar to get another round. "But I can see on your face you've got ideas percolating—beyond the stick you created."

Ragnar nodded. "Yeah. I'm wondering if I can use the rune patterns he engraved on the dagger's handle to match his intention as best I can."

"To what end?"

"To find the killer. If the weapon marks the person who betrayed the owner, Dad in this instance, then it can help me find the one who used it."

Roy sipped from his bottle of beer, thinking about Ragnar's idea. "It's kind of a hard idea to test. But it's not like I have anything better. I say go for it."

Ragnar smiled. "Want to help?"

Roy's mustache twitched in a smile. "Anytime."

"How about tonight? You can crash in the guest room."

"Alright, but I'll need to stop by the motel and pick up a change of clothes. Also, do you think you could create one of those sticks for me? We can't pull in up front of your house and just walk through the press."

"Would it work with simple carvings?"

Roy wobbled his hand side to side. "Probably well enough for one trip in when no one's watching."

"Sounds good, let's go. I've got more beer back at the house."

THIRTY-NINE

After a nice breakfast, Ragnar and Roy went out to the forge to work on creating a simulacrum in hopes of being able to trigger the original runes' magic. Since most of the runes on the dagger had to do with functions such as rust prevention and blade edge maintenance, Ragnar skipped those and focused on imparting characters that would mark betrayers.

Roy turned over the piece of scrap metal Ragnar had used as the base to hold the magic and the runes. "It looks pretty good." He cast a glance at the journal and the photo album. "I can feel the power. I guess we'll know if you get close to the person who committed the murder."

Ragnar nodded. "It's the best idea I've got at the moment."

"It's a good piece of magic, well applied. It's got a better chance of finding the murderer than the cops do."

"That's for sure. Do you want to work on making a few more of my shadow sticks and help me test the limits?"

"Maybe after—"

Someone knocked on the door to the forge. Ragnar opened it and found his mother.

"Hey, Ragnar. Elaine. Nakamatsu is here to see you. She says it's important."

"Can you send them back here?"

"Sure, but they requested to speak with you alone."

"No problem," Roy said. "I was just about to say I need a bite to eat before doing more work."

Roy and his mom left, and a Japanese American woman of medium height appeared in the door.

"Thanks for seeing me, Ragnar."

"No problem, Ms. Nakamatsu."

"Please, call me Betty." Betty, an old friend of his father's, twisted her hands as she stood nervously. "Quite the media frenzy out there." She gestured vaguely toward the front of the house.

"This must be important if you braved walking through that swarm of vultures. Please, come in." He backed away and made room for her to enter. "What can I do for you?"

"I, uh, didn't want to bother you while the family is still in mourning, but several members of the community have come to me."

"OK. Go ahead." He wasn't sure why she was coming to him. No one had selected him to replace his father as the de facto community leader.

"Well, I hate to discuss money, but I promised I'd bring the concerns to you. Everyone trusted your dad. The protection money was a necessary evil, and your dad handled it and made sure it actually went to protecting us."

Ragnar nodded, confused. "But Bob said he was taking care of it for now."

"Well, he is, but apparently the bikers want more. And not just a little bit more. It's almost double what we were paying before."

"Damn, that's a big increase. Did he say why?"

"He just said the bikers are demanding it for our protection. He said he'd ask for a lower fee, but for now to pay it so we didn't anger them. But whenever anyone asks him about specifics, he brushes us off."

"And you want me to talk to him? Why me?" He was perplexed. He'd never put himself out as a leader in the community.

"People respected your father, and we see a lot of him in you. You stick up for your friends and family against the bikers. Most people are too scared to do that."

He hadn't realized people, beyond his dad, had been watching.

"It's a lot of money, and a lot of people are on the edge as is," Betty said.

He nodded. Too many people in Red City had been pushed to the edge of poverty because of the corruption that allowed companies to pay rock-bottom wages, trapping people in a cycle of poverty which wouldn't let them escape to better cities and jobs with better pay.

"I'll talk to Bob and find out what's going on." He added Betty's contact to his phone. "I'll reach out when I know something."

"Thank you, Ragnar. I knew I could count on you." Betty smiled, looking relieved.

After he walked Betty to the door and she left, he sat down and mulled over the issue. He didn't know what he could do if the bikers had raised the amount. It wasn't like he had a contact inside the gang. He wasn't even sure if he reached out that they wouldn't use the opportunity to remove him from the map.

But so far, all they'd done was warn him and make threats. Now that he wasn't alone on the road with only a few friends like he had been on his tour, he might pose a bigger threat as a potential flashpoint to unite the shifters of Red City. And with their war with Dax draining their resources, they might be more interested in letting him live instead of creating a two-front war. Perhaps he could parlay that into a reduction of the fee to the previous amount. He'd be able to help out the community and buy himself some much-needed time.

FORTY

The next day, Ragnar decided to visit Bob and see what he could find out about the payment increases. Plus, it gave him an excuse to get out of the house. In the days after his father's service, he'd rarely left his childhood home, nor had he wanted to. But now that he was practically blockaded in by nosy reporters, he itched to escape.

He and Roy had spent the afternoon after Betty's visit testing the limits of the shadow sticks, as they were calling them. After they'd gotten a solid idea of the uses and limitations of their new toys, Ragnar raided his dad's leather stash—pieces he kept on hand for wrapping handles or making scabbards and bags—so he could make a couple magic-nullifying pouches.

They decided to wait until the neighbors on the backside of the house had gone to work before using their shadow sticks to hop the fence and escape the reporters. In bright light, the sticks didn't completely hide them like they did in darkness and the shadows of deep shade.

Once the street was clear of any people and traffic, they put their sticks away and left the protection of the tree they were hiding behind. Roy had parked his pickup truck a few blocks away in their effort to evade the reporters. When they neared Bob's office, Roy drove around the block so they could check for any reporters staking it out since Bob had proclaimed himself the family's lawyer to the press.

"Looks all clear. I'll drop you off out front and park nearby," Roy said.

"You want to come in with me?"

"Nah. Not sure it would be very productive. Bob and I didn't get along, and I don't think that's improved over the years."

Ragnar narrowed his eyes, a smirk spreading across his face. "Honestly, that might work in my favor right now. Come on."

They got out and headed up to Bob's office. Clara, Bob's assistant, was slightly more polite this time, though she did give Roy a more than cursory inspection. He was a bit scruffier than Ragnar with his unshaved face and thick mustache.

"I need to speak with Bob, please."

"And your name?"

"Ragnar Gunnarsson."

"And your friend?"

"Roy LaGrange."

She picked up the phone and called Bob. She gave him the information and hung up. "He'll be out in a moment. Please have a seat."

"Damn! Ouch!" Bob yelled from inside his office. He emerged a moment later holding his hand.

"Are you OK, sir?" Clara asked.

"I cut my hand. I'll be right back. I'm going to run to the kitchen and get the first aid kit." He turned to Ragnar. "Sorry, give me a minute. You can wait inside my office. Clara, can get you some coffee or something?" He walked down the hall and disappeared.

"Can I get you a coffee?" she asked.

About the time she'd delivered the cups to Ragnar and Roy, Bob returned from the kitchen with a bandage wrapped around his palm.

He sank into his chair, holding up his right hand. "You'll have to forgive me if I don't shake your hands."

"What happened?" Ragnar asked.

Bob rolled his eyes. "I reached into my drawer and the letter opener must have been propped up on something and it stabbed me."

"Do you need stitches?"

"No, it's not that bad. It'll heal quickly. Anyway, what can I do for you today, Ragnar?"

"Well, I got a visit from someone who was... Well, let's just say they're concerned with the increase in the payments going to the bikers."

Bob's face darkened, and his eyes flicked to Roy. "I'm not sure this is a discussion for everyone's ears."

"Roy can hear what you have to say," Ragnar replied.

"But I'm not going to talk about it with him here."

"I'll wait in the lobby." Roy stood up and winked at Ragnar but made sure it was at an angle Bob couldn't see.

As soon as the door shut, Bob relaxed some. "Sorry about that, but old rivalries." He paused and exhaled. "So someone came to you to complain about the payments to the bikers?"

Ragnar nodded. "Yes. They said it's gotten a bit expensive, and some people are struggling to get the funds."

"Hmm, I don't see what the problem is. It's the same amount of money your father collected from them."

Ragnar startled slightly but hoped he got his surprise under control before Bob noticed. Interesting. He and Bob were both being vague about it. Ragnar was glad he hadn't been more specific. He'd already resolved to protect the name of his informant, but now he decided to play it close to the vest and see what he could get.

"Is there any chance I can speak with the bikers? It's possible we can negotiate. They've got to be desperate to settle the issue, with all their other problems."

"I don't think that's a good idea. Especially since you've gotten on their nerves. If anything happened to you, your mother would be crushed. If you're willing to trust my advice, I'd say keep your nose clean and once things settle down, you can plan another tour with your band and let everyone else worry about what's going on in Redemption City."

Ragnar did his best to not to betray his reaction at being told to go play with his friends while the adults handled the important issues. He took a sip from the coffee to buy time to collect himself.

"And another piece of advice from a friend," Bob said to fill the silence, "I'd keep out of the bikers' other business as well. I know you loved your father, but if they brought in the Tarot Slayer to deal with him, then that's probably more than you're capable of handling. I'm just looking out for your mother here, Ragnar." Bob leaned closer and lowered his voice with a quick flick of his eyes toward the door. "And speaking of which, there's a reason your dad asked *him* to leave town."

"I appreciate your care for my mom," Ragnar managed to say without too much heat.

"It's always smart to be selective about who you take advice from." His eyes moved to the door again. "I was your father's closest friend for most of your life. I'm just looking out for you, Ragnar, like your dad would want me to. OK?"

"Thanks, Bob. I appreciate that." He stood up. "I think I've taken enough of your time today."

"You're always welcome here. And if anyone comes to you about things like this again, just direct them my way, OK?"

"I sure will, Bob. And I'll think about what you said." He pulled open the door and headed for the exit, waving Roy after him.

Roy waited until they were back in the pickup before he said, "I take it you heard something you didn't like."

"You could say that. He says the amount the bikers are demanding is unchanged from when Dad was collecting it."

"But that woman said it had nearly doubled?"

"Yup. Then he told me to go play with my friends and leave the tough stuff to the adults."

Roy snorted. "He doesn't know you very well, does he?"

"I guess not." Bob had always been a fixture in their home, and because Ragnar was a well-behaved young man, he'd respected his father's closest friend. "He also said I'd be wise to not place too much trust in you."

And that was the contradiction for Ragnar. In the short time he'd known Roy after his long absence, he'd come to trust the man who he'd known as Uncle Roy. But he also trusted Bob because his dad had trusted him.

"What are you thinking, boy?" Roy asked.

"I'm beginning to think I need to look into what's going on with the money."

Roy grunted an affirmation.

FORTY-ONE

Ragnar was getting tired of being forced to sneak in and out of his own home, but the constant attention of the press camped out on the sidewalk of his mom's house necessitated it. Parking a few blocks away, Roy stopped the truck, and they got out. They activated their shadow sticks once they got close and made sure no one was watching them.

"I'm going to go take a nap," Roy said, after quietly shutting the back door.

"No worries. We'll talk later. I need to sit and think for a bit."

"Is that you, Ragnar?" his mom called from the living room.

"Yeah, Mom."

"There's an envelope on the counter for you. A courier dropped it off for you earlier."

"Thanks, Mom."

Roy raised an eyebrow and made no move to depart for his nap. Shrugging, Ragnar found the large yellow manila envelope. It wasn't thick, but it had some weight to it. Folding back the metal tabs, he peeled the sealed envelope flap open carefully. A few corners of glossy paper slipped out the opening. He caught it before it could fall out and tumble everywhere.

He extracted a thin bundle, which looked like a cover letter on top of a stack of card stock. The top piece of paper was an ordinary piece of printer paper. Thick black letters printed on it, all capital, in a large font read, *BACK OFF OR THERE WILL BE CONSEQUENCES.*

He showed it to Roy. "That's not what you'd call subtle."

Roy snorted. "No, it's not."

Ragnar set down the small stack of papers on the kitchen island, making room for Roy to look as well, and flipped the cover threat over. Ragnar's stomach immediately dropped, and nausea rose. Swallowing hard a few times, he stared at a photograph of his mom standing in front of the house. It looked very recent. Around his mother's face, the sender had drawn the Black Suns logo in permanent marker—almost like it was a target.

Ragnar unclenched his teeth. "Shit."

"Yeah. What else is there?"

Ragnar flipped the photo of his mom to reveal another. And another. And another. All told, there were thirteen. The last one had a tarot card taped to it. The Fool. It was upside down.

"What does that mean?" Roy asked.

Shaking his head, Ragnar sighed. "I don't know. But I do know who will."

"I guess I'm not going to get that nap I wanted," Roy said.

Nodding, Ragnar pulled out his phone and texted Manman Delphine to check if she was in the shop. Then he sent out a message to Melinda, José, and Mississippi Pete.

Even though everyone responded quickly, the wait was excruciating. By the time they all started arriving at his house, he was ready to crawl out of his own skin as he paced in the kitchen like a caged predator. On one of his passes past the island, he stopped and reset the photos, setting the envelope on top of the stack just as the first knock on the door sounded through the house.

Ragnar made to go answer it but was stopped by a hand on his shoulder. "I'll take care of it," Roy said, exiting the kitchen before Ragnar could react.

"Hello, Delphine," his mom said in the living room. "It's good to see you."

"Hello, Erin. How you holding up?" Delphine asked.

"Tired of being cooped up in the house."

"I can understand that. The press doesn't seem to be showing any signs of wanting to leave you alone."

Another knock interrupted them.

"So the gang's all here," Erin said, greeting Melinda, José, and Sippi. A moment later, she appeared in the kitchen with everyone trailing behind her. "I'll go upstairs so you can talk in private." She looked at Ragnar knowingly. "I'm sure I don't want to hear the details of whatever you're up to."

She kissed Ragnar on the cheek and departed. Ragnar gave her a minute to make it to her room while Roy grabbed beers out of the fridge for everyone around the table.

"Thanks for coming. Delphine, I appreciate you closing the store early and braving the press," Ragnar said, turning to his friends. "Same goes for you three. Thanks for coming."

Delphine smiled. "Don't worry, cher. Suzie is handling the register while I'm here."

Ragnar nodded, then took a deep breath, trying to calm the wolf inside him, who still paced angrily and anxiously. "I received this today." He flipped over the envelope, revealing the threat.

Melinda gasped and Delphine leaned closer. José covered his mouth with his hand while Sippi shook his head, a look of disgust on his face.

Ragnar flipped the threat over to show them the first photo. No one made a peep as he looked through the thirteen photos one by one until he got to the last one with the tarot card on it.

"What does it mean, Delphine?" Melinda asked, parroting Roy's earlier question.

"Well, that's The Fool card." She looked up at Ragnar. "Was this the same orientation it was in when you opened the envelope?"

"Yeah. He was very careful to keep everything the same as it came out of the envelope," Roy said.

"The Fool in the reverse. It could mean a few things, but in context with the threat and the object of that threat, I'm going to guess it is reinforcing that the sender thinks this is a mortally reckless path you're on. That you're in over your head and that if you don't stop"—she paused and licked her lips, her eyes flicking up at the second floor—"they'll kill Erin."

"Who?" Melinda asked. She picked up the envelope to examine it.

There was nothing to see. It just had Ragnar's name and address on it. Otherwise it was empty.

"So the Tarot Slayer is threatening Erin if Ragnar doesn't back off?" Sippi said.

Delphine, her brow furrowed, stared at the photo with the tarot card on it. "How many photos were there?"

"Thirteen," Ragnar replied.

"What are you thinking, Delphine?" Melinda asked.

The manbo pursed her lips. "If we're sticking to The Tarot theme, the card labeled as the thirteenth step in the major arcana is Death."

"So that reinforces the threat," Roy replied.

Delphine nodded, the furrow in her brow deepening.

"Something doesn't sit right with you, does it?" Roy asked Delphine.

"It's just that I've never heard of the Tarot Slayer sending a threat to anyone. And it's…" She made a mildly disgusted sound. "It just seems a bit amateurish."

"What do you mean?" Ragnar folded his arms over his muscular chest.

"While Death seems like a scary card, it is more strongly tied to change and cycles. And The Fool card? Honestly using The Tower or The Devil might have been a more potent and accurate threat."

"Maybe they only had that many photos," José said.

Delphine carefully picked up a photo. "These look like your bog-standard stalker telephoto lens photographs. I'm sure whoever took these has plenty to spare." Setting down the photo, she spread out all thirteen images, maintaining them in the order they'd arrived in, in case it meant something. "Look. Different outfits, different locations. This wasn't a snap threat. They've stalked Erin long enough to have a variety of photographic evidence to show they can get to her anytime and anyplace."

Rage and nausea battled in Ragnar's gut and he clenched his fist tightly. His jaw hurt from grinding his teeth. If they didn't get to the end of this soon, he'd likely crack them.

"Well," Melinda said, "we're going to need to set up a rotation so that Erin is never left alone."

Delphine nodded. "I'll bring back some protection gris-gris for the house and your mom, and oils so we can anoint the house."

"But how long can we keep it up? The Tarot Slayer can afford patience." Ragnar turned his back on his friends. "We've got to find this bastard."

"I'll call my contacts again and see if we can get some more information." Delphine squeezed his shoulder. "And I'll also reach out to some of my magical contacts. See if we can look for something in the supernatural world to help us."

"We'll get to the bottom of this, Red. And we'll keep your mom safe," Melinda added.

Sippi nodded aggressively. "Damn right. Because that's what family does."

FORTY-TWO

Shouts and honking horns pulled him out of his sleep. He hadn't been asleep for very long. It was barely one a.m. Then the banging on the door and the ringing of the doorbell began.

Grumbling, he pulled on some clothes, dragged his fingers through his hair, and stumbled down the stairs in a tired stupor. Behind him, he heard the door to his mom's room open.

"Ragnar?"

"I'm on it, Mom. You stay there." He lumbered downstairs and found Roy sitting on the couch. It was his day for guard duty.

"What's going on, Uncle Roy?" Ragnar asked.

"Fuckin' press again. Not sure what's got them in a tizzy though." Someone pounded on the door again. "It's Bob. Let me in."

It had been a week since Ragnar had been to Bob's office—the day he'd received the threat against his mom. Bob had only been by a few times since then to visit with her, always arriving when Ragnar had snuck out to check in with his friends and see if anyone had any new leads. But everything had been quiet. Judging by the noise and Bob's appearance this late in the night, something must have happened.

Ragnar headed toward the door, but a firm hand on his shoulder stopped him.

"Wait. I want to slip out. I'm curious about something. Besides, Bob hasn't kept his disdain for my presence to himself."

"Right. I'll give you a few seconds to disappear."

Roy nodded at him, then jogged away. Ragnar looked around, spying the candles his mom liked. Quickly finding the lighter, he lit a few of them. He hated the smelly things. They bothered his sensitive nose, but she loved the scents, and it was her home. And if having smelly candles made her happy, this was no time to deny that to her.

And they'd serve to mask Roy's scent by irritating Bob's sensitive wolf nose.

Once he was ready, he pulled the door open and ushered in Bob, who looked impeccably dressed in a full suit and tie. It even looked like he'd showered recently, with his crisply combed and still slightly damp hair. The part looked like it had been made with a ruler.

"What's going on, Bob?" Ragnar asked, shutting the door.

"Took you long enough."

"I was asleep." Ragnar stuck his hand out, and Bob took it.

Bob inhaled, then cringed. "It wasn't me who woke you up; it was the press. I just sent them back out to the sidewalk."

"What stirred them up? Did the Tarot Slayer strike again?"

"No. The opposite." A grin spread across Bob's face.

"What's going on?" Ragnar's mom asked from the stairs.

A gleam flashed over Bob's eyes as he turned his head to the stairs. "They think the Tarot Slayer is dead. The man who killed your husband, Erin, they found his body in a dark alley a few hours ago."

Erin held her hand over her mouth as her jaw trembled. "What?"

"How do they know?" Ragnar asked.

"According to a leak in the police department, they found trophies from your dad and the other victim, and a weapon that matches some of the wounds."

Erin came into the living room and sank onto the couch, her eyes wide. Ragnar sat next to her and took her hand, squeezing it reassuringly. She squeezed back, but there was a tremble in her hand.

"It's over?" she asked.

"I think so. I'm sure there'll be more investigations, and you'll probably have to talk to the police." Bob squished in next to Ragnar's mom on the other side, despite there being not quite enough room, forcing everyone to shift down.

"Why?" Ragnar asked.

"This is just speculation, but probably to identify any items as having belonged to Gunnar."

"It might really be over…" Erin said quietly.

"Can you get rid of the press, Bob?" Ragnar asked.

If the killer was actually dead, then it would be nice if his mom could leave the house without an escort from his friends. She could start to deal with her grief. He sighed. Maybe he could do the same. With the killer lurking about town and the press harassing them about his father's death, it felt like he'd been forced into a stasis in which he had to exist in a world too close to the murder of his dad.

"It's almost hard to believe," she said.

"I'm not sure if I can get rid of the press, but if we promise them an official statement in a few days, they might take the bait and pack up and go home."

Ragnar nodded. "Let's go." He stood up and dragged his fingers through his hair again, trying to form it into some semblance of order.

"Alright," Bob said, standing up.

Together, they trooped out the door. Ragnar was nearly blasted off his feet from the sudden surge of noise and all the microphones shoved into his face.

"Mr. Magnusson! Have you heard the news? Do you have a statement on the death of the alleged Tarot Slayer?"

Ragnar couldn't tell who'd asked it. All he could see was lights and shadows. "I have no comment. The family will make a statement through our lawyer, Bob Sever."

Bob raised a hand and stepped forward. "I'm Bob Sever. At this time, the family is not prepared to make a statement. But I will reach out with a date and location where I will read the family's statement. There will be no other comments made until then. And if you don't vacate the premises and leave the neighborhood, I'll seek out an out-of-town news source and ensure they get exclusive access to the statement and any future comments from the family. Thank you."

Bob turned around and entered the house. Ragnar followed, leaving the press in stunned silence broken only by the occasional click of a camera shutter.

Once the door had been shut, Bob laughed. "That was enjoyable. Fucking vultures. Do you want me to take care of drafting a statement, Erin?"

She barely nodded. "I guess. I mean, yes, please."

"Send it over before the news conference. I'd like to review it first," Ragnar said.

A brief note of annoyance flashed over Bob's face before the affable and friendly expression returned. "Certainly." Bob pulled back the curtain from the narrow window next to the door. "Huh. Looks like they're actually going to listen this time. I guess threatening to give the story away to a competitor worked."

"Thanks, Bob. I'm going to return to bed." Erin stood up and headed upstairs.

"Good night, Erin." Bob watched her disappear.

Ragnar walked to the door. "I'll lock up after you go. Thanks, Bob. And don't forget to send the statement over, please."

"Sure." Bob stared upstairs for another moment then turned and left through the door Ragnar held open for him.

Ragnar lingered at the open door for minute and watched the news crews pack up. It was a deeply satisfying sight, but a couple brutal yawns reminded him he needed to go back to bed. He briefly thought about turning on the TV and checking the news but thought better of it. It would serve no purpose but to rev up his anxiety and rob him of a partial night's sleep.

The news wasn't going anywhere, except away from their house. Maybe he'd sleep in tomorrow.

FORTY-THREE

It had been a couple days since the news of the Tarot Slayer's death. Ragnar had avoided turning on the TV. No doubt the city was being swarmed with reporters covering the story. They loved serial killer news. It fed into their grubby obsession with sensationalism. But eventually, his mother had chivied him out of the house, claiming he needed fresh air.

And now as he sat on a bar patio with his friends, he had to agree with her.

"I'm surprised the press are leaving you alone," Melinda said.

"Me too, but they're probably more concerned with hounding the cops for details of his death," Sippi said, then snorted. "Good luck with that. They're more tight-lipped than a corpse."

José nodded along.

The only person missing—and Ragnar realized his presence had become one of comfort and strength—was his Uncle Roy. "Hey, have any of you seen Roy lately?"

"What do you mean?" Melinda's brow furrowed. "Isn't he staying at your place?"

"He was, but he ducked out when Bob showed up to tell us about the Slayer. Said he was curious about something." At first, Ragnar had just assumed he'd gone back to his motel so as not to disturb them when he came back. He wasn't needed for watch duty if the Slayer was actually dead. But when the second morning dawned, Ragnar grew more concerned.

"Huh. Interesting," she replied.

"I'm just wondering why we haven't heard from him." Ragnar pulled out his phone and shot off another quick text.

"I mean, maybe he disappeared again. He did leave all those years ago," Sippi said, waving down the server so he could order another round.

"Maybe, but that doesn't seem right. I still don't know what happened between him and my dad all those years ago and why he left town." He sighed. "And besides, it seemed like he was more interested in sticking around. I don't think he'd leave town without a proper goodbye."

"You're probably right."

Ragnar took an absentminded drink from his beer. "Maybe I'll swing by his motel to see if he decided to crash there."

"Couldn't hurt," Melinda replied.

"So how you doin'?" José asked him. "Now that... Well, you know."

"I don't know. It feels sort of...anticlimactic."

Melinda scoffed. "What do you mean? Did you expect to chase him through the city and have a standoff?"

"I don't know. Not really. But killed in some random altercation in Red City? The Slayer has been working for years, and the cops had no clue who they might be. Then a body is found with evidence from the other two murders? Just feels a bit too convenient."

"I don't know, Ragnar," José said. "Usually the simple answer is the correct one."

"I guess, but still..."

"Look, Ragnar, I think the Tarot Slayer has provided you with a focal point after your father's death. It gave you direction and purpose." Melinda set her beer down and leaned closer to him. "But now the Tarot Slayer is dead, you're back to being a guy who's unemployed, doesn't have a girlfriend, and is living with your mother. And the band is on hiatus without a drummer or plans."

He thought about what she'd said. He had been in a funk the last couple days since the news dropped. Perhaps she was right, and he'd been using the hunt for the Slayer as an excuse to avoid dealing with his life or lack thereof.

Melinda reached out and squeezed his forearm. "Once Roy turns up, let's make a trip to Colorado and get our gear and the money we had to leave behind when we went wolf. There's more than enough there to help you get into your own apartment. Plus, it'll be good for you to get out of town, and we can use the time to make some plans for the band."

"Fall is a lovely time to travel, with the leaves changing and all," José said.

The thought was appealing. He'd need to check in with his mother and make sure she'd be OK for a little while without him around, but she'd probably agree with Melinda about him moving forward with his life.

"Let me talk to Mom, but that does sound like a good idea. Some fresh mountain air would be nice." And he could shed the ugliness of Red City for a few days. The Rocky Mountains were exceptionally beautiful.

Once they finished and paid, they all went their separate ways. Now that the idea of a road trip had been raised, he was eager to plan it out, so he stopped by the motel Roy had been staying in. He didn't see Roy's pickup, but he parked in front of his room anyway.

Light peeked out from around the edges of the curtains. Someone was inside. He knocked and waited. Faint words sounding like a couple different voices drifted from the room, but he couldn't quite tell if it was Roy. And who would he be with?

A moment later the door cracked open and the partially obscured face of a white man appeared. "Who are you?"

"I'm looking for Roy. He's staying in this room."

"Don't know no Roy. We checked in here yesterday." He shut the door quickly.

"Well, fuck," Ragnar mumbled. If Roy hadn't come back to the motel, where had he gone?

Ragnar decided to check with the motel's office. He stepped through the door and stood out of the way while the clerk helped a man at the counter.

"Next," the clerk said, his tone and body language screaming his disinterest.

"I'm looking for the man in room 103."

"None of your business. Or mine."

"He's my Uncle, but I haven't seen him for a couple days."

The clerk rolled his eyes. "And why should I care?"

Pursing his lips, Ragnar pulled out his wallet and stared into the bill compartment. The stack of bills was entirely too thin. He pulled out a twenty and slid it across the counter to the clerk. "Does this inspire you to care a bit more?"

"Eh. Not really…" But his tone grew a touch livelier.

Sighing, Ragnar pulled out his last twenty and set it on top of the other. He hoped it was enough to get what he needed, because he doubted a pocketful of change and a couple wrinkly dollar bills would do much more.

The clerk snatched up the money. "I haven't seen him in days. When his weekly lease ran out and he didn't show up to pay for another, I cleaned out his room."

"Do you have his stuff? I'll take it to him."

The clerk's eyes narrowed as he stared at Ragnar for a moment. Then he shrugged. "Wait here." He returned a minute later with a small box and a brown shopping bag. "Here. Saves me having to trip over them."

The clerk walked out of the room, clearly done with the proceedings.

Ragnar picked up the box and bag and backed out the door. After he dropped Roy's belongings in the trunk, he sat behind the wheel wondering what to do next. First, he called his mom to make sure Roy hadn't turned up at the house. Nope. Then he checked the texts he'd sent. Still unanswered and unread.

He was starting to get worried.

Trying to think of any other connections the two of them might've shared, Ragnar was only left with one option — Bob.

FORTY-FOUR

Ragnar parked down the block from Bob's house. Roy and Bob weren't friends—Bob had made that abundantly clear. But perhaps Roy had gone to talk to him or maybe try to mend fences. Ragnar truly didn't know either man that well, but if Roy intended to stay in town and be part of Ragnar's and his mother's lives, making peace—or at least coming to a détente—with Bob would make everyone's lives less tense.

Before he left the car, he tried calling Roy. The phone rang and went to voicemail. Perhaps Roy had lost his phone, or it'd been stolen. He got out and walked toward Bob's house. Stopping on the sidewalk out front, he tried calling again.

He heard a ringing in his uncovered ear, so he lowered the phone and pressed it to his thigh. The ringing stopped. This time, he redialed and immediately lowered the phone so he could listen with both ears.

The ringing was faint and coming from the side of the house. He hung up and jogged around in the direction of the sound and called again. The ringing was louder. Focusing in with his enhanced hearing, he followed the sound to a window in a well at ground level. Ragnar dropped onto his stomach and peered into the window.

When the ringing stopped again, he redialed. The sound was definitely coming from the basement of Bob's house, which was concerning to say the least. Squinting, he looked into the basement but didn't see anything but the usual things one would see in such a place—boxes, tools, shelves, and work benches.

But when one of the metal shelves covered in boxes swung away from the wall, he gasped, his muscles tensing. Bob stepped out from a hidden door.

"Holy shit," Ragnar whispered, then pushed back quickly so he wouldn't be spotted through the dingy window.

A moment later, he heard cursing and the sound of a hammer smashing something. Well, that was the end of Roy's phone. But where was Roy?

Ragnar eased his way forward, keeping as low as possible. Bob chucked a hammer onto one of the workbenches and pushed the shelf back in place, sealing the door behind it. With a quick look around his basement, he left Ragnar's field of view. Next came the stomping feet of climbing the stairs until they faded to nothing.

Ragnar stared at the window, contemplating his next move. He couldn't ask Bob to show him the basement, and he doubted he'd manage to sneak downstairs if Bob knew he was in the house. The window wasn't terribly big, but maybe he could squeeze through it.

The window was newer and made from a single piece of glass, which meant it likely opened inward. Moving forward, he tentatively pushed the window. His luck wasn't that good—locked.

It appeared the window frame was made of some sort of metal, which was good news. If it had been made of plastic, his idea might not work. Reaching into his pocket, he pulled out his pocketknife and opened the blade.

He looked around to make sure he hadn't drawn anyone's atten-tion, but there were enough shrubs and trees in Bob's yard and the neighbor's yard to keep him reasonably concealed, as long as he didn't make a commotion. He closed his eyes and took a moment to center himself. Once he felt ready, he focused his intentions and carved the runes he wanted into the window frame. He felt something shift and a slight gap opened where the window met its frame. He pushed. The window moved.

Crawling forward, he poked his head inside the opening and shoved the window open enough to peek below the window on the inside. Some sort of heavy looking wood surface rose from the floor, likely a work bench or table. He couldn't go in headfirst and trust his landing, so he spun around and pushed his feet into the pane of glass, using them to lift it up. Then he shimmied backward, bending his legs into the window.

Grunting, he wiggled, trying to squeeze his tall, muscular frame down into the well and through the window. His body wasn't made for it, but he kept pushing backward. When his T-shirt was pulled up over his stomach, it exposed his skin, which got scraped by the metal wall of the well, the dirt in the well, and then the window ledge. Pausing, he fumbled around with his feet to find purchase.

Once he found the wooden surface, he resumed his descent into the basement, only pausing to readjust his feet. Tapping around with his toes, he heard a crunch, then his foot slipped and shot off the edge. The sudden drop of his feet shifted his weight and yanked him the rest of the way through the window.

Scrabbling at the windows ledge with his fingers, he tried to stop his fall but with nothing to wedge the window open, it fell and smacked into his fingers. He fell, slamming his stomach into the edge of the table. It knocked the wind out of him and added another layer of scrapes to his stomach.

He flailed his arms, trying to get hold of something to stop his fall. But everything his fingers met provided no hold. Just before his knees hit the floor, his head smacked into the edge of the hard, table and he slumped to ground, his vision dimming.

He sat immobilized, struggling to regain his movement but couldn't get his body to respond in a coherent manner. He vaguely heard feet tromping heavily down a set of stairs. He groaned, trying to force his body to move but only managed to flop to the side.

"Well, well, well. What do we have here?" an annoyed voice mumbled through the fog of Ragnar's brain.

And then something smashed into the back of Ragnar's head, and he knew nothing more.

FORTY-FIVE

The first thing crawling into Ragnar's awareness was a blinding headache. The next thing was dirt under his hands and back.

"Ragnar, don't move."

The voice sounded familiar and worried. He wasn't even sure he could move in the first place.

"I'm going to gently lift your head and give you some water, boy."

Boy? Who called him boy? He'd found Roy. As Roy slid his hand under Ragnar's skull, it rubbed where he'd been hit. Ragnar hissed and jerked.

"Sorry." Roy lifted his head and pushed a plastic cup against his lips.

Ragnar opened his mouth and let a little of the liquid fall onto his lips. When he didn't choke on it, Roy poured in more but took the cup away after only a few sips.

"That'll be enough for now."

Ragnar cracked his eyes open but slammed them shut against the sudden influx of light.

"Slowly now," Roy said.

Ragnar took his advice and eventually got his eyes open. It

wasn't actually that bright wherever they were, but the dull throb in his head magnified everything.

"How long?" he whispered.

"Not too long. But I don't know for sure. Ain't got my phone or a clock."

Ragnar's head had started to clear some, or he was getting used to it. But it was likely a bit of both. Being a wolf shifter had its advantages, and speedy healing was definitely top of the list.

"What happened?"

"To you? Don't know. Ol' Bobby dragged you in unconscious, pushed a gun against your head, and threatened to kill you if I didn't let him shove you in this cage with me. So I did."

Ragnar grunted. "And you?"

Roy shook his head, a look of disgust on his face. "Came over here to snoop around. Figured I'd have time while Bob was at your house. He caught me in the basement and whacked me a good one on the back of the noggin. Woke up in this cage. I always knew he was a sneaky one. Just didn't know he was a total snake bastard." He sighed. "I've got some bad news for you. I mean… You want to hear it?"

Chuckling, Ragnar cut himself off with a groan from the pain the effort had caused. "Worse than being attacked by a man I thought was a family friend?"

Roy nodded, his face slipping into a deep frown. "Worse than that, boy." He shook his head. "I think Bob killed your dad."

Ragnar lurched up into a sitting position, immediately regretting it. He slammed his eyes shut and gripped his head as it spun. Roy waited.

When his head stopped spinning and his stomach didn't feel like it was ready to hurl forth its contents, he asked, "How do you know?"

"I found some of your dad's things when I was snooping. Things that had no business being in Bob's basement. Then he basically admitted it without quite saying it. I don't think he's all there. He was mumbling about what to do with me. Said something about not being able to lay my death on the Tarot Slayer's doorstep since he'd taken care of him."

"What?" Ragnar asked, confused.

"I got to thinking how Bob heard about the Tarot Slayer's killing so fast. It's because he had a front row seat, if you will. He did it. Killed your dad. Then the poor homeless fellow to take care of a loose end. He tied it up all neat by killing some other poor bastard and leaving the things he'd collected as evidence."

"Bob?"

Roy nodded. "I don't know what his game is, but he killed your dad."

The pain in Ragnar's head continued to diminish. "Money."

"What?"

"The piece of shit did it for money." He clenched his jaw and squeezed his eyes shut as he tried to keep his anger in check. But the pressure on his teeth renewed the throbbing in his head, so he let his jaw drop open. "He told me Dad wanted to stop paying off the bikers and start a pack. Then one of Dad's friends came to me a few days ago and mentioned the price of peace had gone up steeply." Roy already knew these details, but Ragnar needed to say them out loud as he sorted through the thoughts careening around his skull.

"He killed Gunnar to keep the money flowing? Do you think he's working for the bikers?"

"Maybe. I don't know. But he's definitely in business for himself. Who knows how long he's been rigging the game, skimming off the top. Money?" He shook his head in disgust. "He killed the man he claimed was as close as a brother, all for dirty, stinking money."

Ragnar wanted to leap up and rip the bars of the cage they were trapped in apart.

Roy must have seen what he was looking at or guessed what he was thinking, because he said, "I've already tried escaping. He's got some powerful magic on this cage. I can't figure out how to break its hold or how to get out."

They were in a space with a dirt floor. It looked irregular, as if it had been carved out by hand instead of being part of the original construction of the house. It might have been a shallow crawlspace at one time, but now the floor dropped lower than the door, which looked to be the only exit. There were a few shelves against the wall near the door—too far to reach. He saw a few kitchen knives like the ones that had been stuck in his father's back stacked on one shelf. There were other things as well—perhaps trophies or other bits and pieces for Bob to use to frame someone else. A row of bars with barred door blocked off the back of the room and formed the cell he and Roy were trapped in. The side and back walls in their cell were naked, packed dirt. The room was illuminated by a single naked bulb dangling from the ceiling.

"Maybe the two of us can think of a way out," Roy said.

"Maybe. Give me a few more minutes to get my brain in order, then we'll see if we can figure out what Bob has going on for enchantments."

Roy handed him the plastic cup. "Here. A little more water won't go wrong."

After Ragnar drained the cup, he felt well enough to stand up. Roy shot up and caught Ragnar as he wobbled. Ragnar placed a hand against the wall to steady himself.

"Watch out. There's a piss bucket. Don't want to tip that over," Roy said.

Ragnar nodded and walked his way toward the bars, using the wall to steady himself. Once he got closer to the metal, he felt the power coursing through the vertical bars.

"Don't touch them. I made that mistake. Hurt like a sumbitch," Roy said.

Ragnar made an affirmative noise and extended his arm, aiming the back of his hand at the metal. As soon as his skin met the bar, he hissed and yanked his hand away. The touch had been the faintest of whispers, but it burned like a wasp sting and promised a whole lot more with prolonged contact. Whoever had enchanted the bars had done a thorough job. Another set of bars blocked the ceiling above.

"Can we dig through the floor or the walls?" Ragnar asked.

"I don't know. I tried, but it's hard as rock. I'm wondering if there's magic extending from the bars or something else. I'm not sure how deep it goes, but maybe the two of us could try it. Wolves are good burrowers."

Ragnar sighed. "Fuck. Let me sit down and think my way through this."

Roy helped him down.

Ragnar had no idea what Bob was doing at that moment, but it couldn't have been anything good. And even if he came back, he wouldn't let Ragnar and Roy go. No doubt their bodies would be found in some dark hole somewhere around Red City. Two more victims of the crime-ridden city.

Ragnar hoped his brain would calm down and heal so he could dig into problem, assuming there was a solution. This was a well-thought-out cage.

FORTY-SIX

"Shh, I think I hear something," Ragnar said.

Roy stood up and moved closer to the bars nearest the exit, turning his right ear at the room to the reinforced steel door. He nodded. "Me too. Tuck into the back corner. I'll take this one."

It wasn't like the back of the room was dark enough to camouflage them, but the single dangling bare lightbulb didn't reach the corners well. Ragnar tucked into the shadows and tried to squish his bulky form into the corner. It would be better if he could've shifted to his wolf. His dark gray hair would've blended in much better.

The scratching around the door grew louder. After a few seconds, it sounded like someone fumbling with a key in the lock.

"Stand clear!" a woman called out.

A moment later something slammed into the door and it bent inward.

"Fuck," she said.

This time, the door exploded as if rocketed by explosives. The light blinked out. Ragnar cringed as door slammed into the bars. In that instant, he was glad for their protection. After he peeled his eyes away from the door, which now looked like a broken hard taco shell or maybe a crumpled tissue, he found the source of the chaos. A shadow stood in the entrance, obscured by the dust commotion had made.

"Damn, that's a nifty little hammer right there," the woman said, spinning it so the head twirled on the axis of the handle. "Fuck, it's dark in here."

The voice and the silhouette sounded and looked familiar. It was Judy.

"You broke the lightbulb when you sent the door flying across the room," Roy said. "Now get us the fuck out of here."

"I can always leave you in the cell. Doesn't really matter to me that much," she replied, her voice dipping into a bored tone. "But that creep who lives here took his mom. If that matters to you at all."

"Mom?" Anger and urgency flooded through Ragnar. "No, we're grateful," he rushed to say before she walked away.

"Now just hold it there, boy," Roy said. "You yourself said she's showed up multiple times where the Tarot Slayer has been. She could be playing games with us like a serial killer would."

It was a fair point, though after being knocked out and stashed in a crawlspace prison by Bob, he was increasingly doubting her viability as a candidate for the Tarot Slayer.

"I don't need to be insulted." She turned around.

"Please. Judy. Help us out," Ragnar said. "Uncle Roy, just keep quiet for a moment."

"At least the young one has some sense. Now do you want out or not?"

"I want out," Ragnar replied.

Roy exhaled noisily. "As do I."

"Alright, wait here. I need to find some light. I ain't walking into some dark lair." She propped the hammer against the doorframe, head down, and disappeared back into the main part of the basement. A moment later, boxes thudded and objects clattered to the floor. She didn't sound like she was being too careful, and he didn't really care to correct her.

"Ah, that'll do," she said, reappearing in the doorway. She set down something that sounded like it was made of metal and disappeared again.

Light exploded from the floor light fixture and painfully slammed into Ragnar's eyes. "Damn it. Warn a guy next time."

Roy grunted in what sounded agreement.

"Tipping toward ungrateful again…" she said in a sing-song manner.

Ragnar bit off a retort, letting it fade into a grumble, and focused on getting his eyes used to the shop lights. "Mind adjusting the light so it's not shooting right at us? Please."

"That's more polite." She tipped up the lamp so it was aimed at the ceiling in center of the room.

Like the few times he'd seen her before, she wore motorcycle leathers.

"Well, shit. Ain't this just the cutest little serial killer pit." She looked around. "Is there a nice basket of lotion?"

"Why would you want serial killer lotion?" Roy asked.

"Good lotion is expensive," she replied, crossing the room.

"It's not exactly a pit and there's no hose. And he didn't provide much in the way of personal hygiene products." He looked down at the bucket sitting next to the back wall.

"What?" Ragnar asked, confused.

"*Silence of the Lambs*?" Judy raised an eyebrow. "Add it to your watch list."

She inspected the crumpled door—propped against the bars— she'd busted in, then squatted and tipped it away from the barred cell door with ease. Bending over, she looked over the section of the door that held the lock bolts. "Where's the keyhole?"

"If there was a keyhole, I could have picked it in a minute with a thumbnail," Roy said.

"It's electronic or magnetic or something," Ragnar said. "But I think the bottom is keyed as well. Who knows how Bob opens it."

"No problem." She strutted across the room and picked up the hammer. "I have a universal key right here."

Ragnar thrust his arm through the bars, being careful not to touch them. "Here."

She narrowed her eyes at him. "Nah, I got it. Now move away from the door." She drew back the large sledgehammer.

"Wait!" Roy held up a hand to wave her off, then snatched up the piss bucket off the floor and moved it into the back corner. "Probably best if we stand in the front corners."

Nodding, Ragnar tucked into the front corner against the bars and the wall. "I'm ready. Uncle Roy?"

"Yup."

Judy drew back the hammer again and brought it around and into the square where the locking mechanism held the bolts. This door blasted out of its frame on the first go and smashed into the back wall, sending hard dirt shards flying everywhere.

"I like this hammer," she said, admiring the head as the runes that had burst into light upon contact with the door faded back to inactivity. "I think I might keep this."

Ragnar stared at the damage his hammer had done, then shook himself out of his amazement. He wondered how she'd got it out of his mom's car. But if she'd broken a window to take it, it was a small price to pay for freedom. "I would prefer if you didn't. I need that. But if we get through this, I promise I'll make you something of your choice."

She nodded. "Let's go." She jogged out of the hidden room.

Ragnar looked over at Roy, who shrugged. If he didn't hurry after Judy, she might just keep his hammer. He ran out of the busted cell and into the basement. His assessment of her search had been right. She'd tossed around all kinds of stuff and knocked over a shelf. He wasn't sure if she'd needed to be that *thorough* but whatever. It wasn't like he was going to defend the sanctity of the Bob's basement. A bit of mess was the least the man who'd betrayed Ragnar's father and his family deserved.

They followed Judy out of Bob's house, hopping the fence into the neighbor's yard, and ended up out onto the street where they'd parked Roy's pickup truck. Her sport bike was parked behind the pickup.

"We have to get home," Ragnar said as he slowed down on his approach to the passenger door.

"She's not there," Judy said. "Bob took her somewhere."

"Fuck!" Ragnar yelled, pacing next to the truck.

"Don't worry your pretty little head," she said. "I know where they're going."

"How would you know?" Roy asked.

Ragnar stopped and stared at her, clenching his jaw.

"Well, I don't know specifically where they're going. But I can follow them." Her eyes flicked back and forth between Roy and Ragnar. "You're not the only one who can plant a GPS tag. I'm just better at it."

"What's your name?" Roy asked.

She gave the hammer another spin. "Hammer. Sarah Hammer." She lofted the sledge into the air, and it slammed into the bed of Roy's truck. Ragnar hoped it hadn't left too much of a dent.

"Sarah Hammer? What kind of bullshit name is that?" Ragnar asked.

"Don't follow Olympic medaling cyclists? That's on you. Call me whatever the fuck you want. But like Sarah Hammer, it's time to fucking roll." She climbed onto her Ducati and fired it up, revving it loudly to stifle any further arguments.

"Well, boy, get in. She's not going to wait for us."

Ragnar stalked back to the bed and yanked the hammer out of the bed. The sledge had left a dent, but without it being swung, it hadn't hit with any extra force. He wanted his weapon to be close to hand in the cab of the truck, but also it would be annoying as fuck sliding and thudding around in the bed of the truck. He yanked the door shut hard behind him, setting the head of the sledge on the floor and propping the handle against his knee.

"Leave the door attached next time," Roy grumbled.

"Go."

FORTY-SEVEN

Roy did his best to keep up with Judy or Sarah or whatever the fuck her name was, but the old beater pickup wasn't made for speed and maneuverability. Thankfully, she adjusted to let them keep pace and slowed down, though it looked like having to adhere a bit more to the rules of the road chafed her as she weaved back and forth and sped up and slowed down.

Ragnar wished his uncle had a better vehicle, but it beat not having one, if he discounted borrowing his mom's car. He really needed to get a new ride. As he gripped the handle of his sledgehammer, he was grateful for the solid feel in his hand and the enchantments reinforcing its strength, which prevented him from potentially crushing it. He didn't know if his wolf-enchanted strength could splinter wood, but as he tried to keep from exploding in rage at Bob's betrayal, the physical outlet of clinging to his weapon kept him somewhat grounded.

"Are you sure they're going to be able to meet us?" Roy asked.

Now that they'd climbed into the hills outside Red City and were winding up a narrow two-lane road that was rarely used except by the occasional camper or person taking the extra-scenic route, he had at least been able to give them a more specific and narrowed-down destination to aim for.

Ragnar checked his phone. "Melinda says they're on their way."

He sent a quick message to Melinda. *"Location check."*

A moment later, whoever was sending the messages on Melinda's phone—she was likely driving since she didn't trust Sippi to not go overboard and José was too reserved to really haul ass—replied with a geotagged map location.

"Looks like they're fifteen or twenty minutes behind," Ragnar said.

His friends had made good time, both getting ready and on the road and catching up to the slower pickup. He hadn't told them much other than it was an emergency and he needed them. They hadn't asked any questions, just saying they were on the way. With so much anger coursing through his veins, he hadn't been able to communicate much else other than the necessities, but they'd responded instantly. He'd have to savor that feeling of trust and support later when he was capable of it.

The pickup slowed down, forcing him to focus in on what was going on. "Why are we slowing?"

"Don't know. She's slowing," Roy said, rolling down the window. "Mind rolling down yours too?"

Ragnar rolled down the window and inhaled deeply as the cool, fresh breeze filled the cab of the pickup. He breathed in deeply again, letting it expand his chest. He'd been so tense, the muscles around his ribcage ached and expanding it was almost painful. But he worked through it, letting the pain center his mind as he tried to center himself.

Rage couldn't dominate his mind on this hunt. Ragnar needed to be the master of his feelings and use them to his benefit so he could save his mom. They found out a moment later why Judy had slowed as they turned onto an even narrower road. He pulled up his phone and opened the map app.

"We've got to be getting close," he said, sending the turn information to his friends.

After only a few minutes, the pavement ran out and they transitioned to a gravel road. The motorcycle in front of them disappeared in front of a cloud of dust. Coughing, Roy rolled the window back up. Ragnar rolled his up as well. The fresh air had been nice for a brief moment.

He checked the time. It would be getting dark soon.

"I hope she can keep her seat," Roy said. "Those fancy bikes ain't meant for roads like this, and I don't want to run over her."

Ragnar gave a neutral grunt. So far, she'd caused him mostly trouble but saving him and leading him out here might make up for it, assuming this wasn't an elaborate trap. Maybe she was working with Bob.

"Roy, keep an eye on her. I still don't trust her."

Roy nodded. "Me neither. But we'll see where this goes. She probably doesn't know you've got your pals coming, so that'll be a nice little surprise."

Ragnar agreed. She might be wily as fuck, but five-to-one or -two odds were pretty good. Especially where there were no witnesses and they could use all their supernatural powers against her. Assuming Bob didn't have a whole gang there, which was a distinct possibility if she was working with him or the bikers.

"Uncle Roy, slow down just a bit."

"How much?"

"Enough that we're not in her cloud of dust. I want to be able to see if anyone is waiting for us."

"Right." He backed off, slowly fading back from Judy and her Ducati. "Any messages from your friends?"

Rangar looked. "No signal. Shit. We'll have to hope they got my last message."

It was nervous work watching through the cloud of dust. He also hoped the decrease in speed would let Melinda, Sippi, and José catch up. Finally, they reached the end of the road as they entered a small, gravel parking lot. Judy parked along the far side, pulling her bike around so she was pointed back toward the road, probably in case she wanted to make a quick escape.

The only other vehicle in the lot besides the bike and the pickup was Bob's car, and it looked empty. Roy slowed even more as he followed her example and turned around and backed up. Ragnar scoped the surroundings and didn't see anything but trees. The woods might be empty or there might be an army hiding in a forested embrace.

"See anything?" Roy asked.

"No. But you stay behind the wheel and keep the engine running. I'm going to step out and take a look."

"Got it."

Ragnar grabbed the hammer and exited the pickup, leaving the door open. Keeping the truck between him and Judy, he took a deep inhale through his nose, trying to sort the smells out, but he mostly got dust and the typical aromas of the forest along with an undercurrent of engine exhaust. A sneeze jumped on him, triggered by the dust. He sneezed again.

"Gesundheit," Judy said quietly, surveying the woods.

The sound of tires crunching on gravel drew his attention to the road they'd just come down. Whoever it was, they still weren't within view. Making a snap decision, he jogged toward the edge of the parking lot and hid behind a wide-trunked pine tree. A moment later, Melinda's car pulled up and parked next to Roy's truck on the side opposite of Judy.

Melinda practically leapt out of the driver's seat and pointed at Judy. "What the fuck is she doing here?" she asked Roy.

Ragnar stepped out from behind the tree. "It's a long story."

"Make it fast, or I'm going to go fuck her up."

Judy snorted. "I'd like to see you try."

Sippi, who'd climbed out of the car in a more casual manner, grabbed Melinda's arm as she tried to bolt for the woman, who stood leaning against her motorcycle. Judy just folded her arms across her chest and chuckled.

"Make it short, Red," Melinda said once she collected her cool.

Ragnar inhaled, then blasted the air out, trying to set aside the simmering anger about ready to boil up again. "Long story short, Bob captured me and Roy. We found evidence that he's the Tarot Slayer—"

"He's not the real slayer. Just a fucking low-rent copycat," Judy said, spitting at the gravel in disgust.

"That's likely the case," Ragnar said. "But I think he did these killings."

"He killed his best friend?" Melinda asked, the blood draining from her face.

Ragnar nodded and clenched his jaw. "Yeah. Now he's taken my mom. Judy"—he chucked his chin over at the woman on the motor-cycle—"busted us out of the dungeon in his basement and led us up here."

"So he just dragged your mom up into the woods?" José asked.

"Seems like it. We haven't had a chance to look around though," Roy said, turning off the pickup. "Just got here."

Everyone took a step toward Bob's car, but Ragnar raised his hammer and said, "Everyone stop. Let me take a look first."

He walked confidently over to the car even though his gut prickled with anxiety. What if Bob had booby trapped the damned thing?

FORTY-EIGHT

Before Ragnar made it to Bob's car, the sound of an approaching vehicle drew his attention. Another round of adrenaline flooded into his system, and he signaled for everyone to spread out. Judy looked unfazed, casting only a mildly curious glance down the road.

Melinda, who had gone toward the edge of the lot and hidden behind a tree, stepped out from hiding and visibly relaxed. "We're good. I figured we could use a little help with tracking."

A moment later, the meaning of her begrudging-sounding statement became clear as a car pulled into the shadows of the tree. The glare from the setting sun reflecting off the window vanished, revealing Jamie Rodriguez. He hadn't considered asking the young woman for help, largely because he'd been too angry about Bob's betrayal and too scared for his mother. She wasn't really part of his inner circle so he'd forgotten she might be an option to help. But as the only wolf shifter they knew who had any skill with tracking, asking Jamie to come had been a smart move on Melinda's part.

Jamie pulled around and backed in between Melinda's car and Roy's pickup, reverse parking her car. After she turned the engine off, she stepped out and looked around. Her brow furrowed in anger when her eyes fell on Judy.

"What the fuck is she doing here?" Jamie asked.

"Don't worry, kid, I'm on your side at the moment," Judy replied before Ragnar could explain. "Now if you all want to get moving, your quarry is getting farther away from you."

"She's right," Ragnar said. "Jamie, can you shift over and sniff around this car carefully? We also want to check for traps. Then we'll follow the scents from here into the woods."

"I can do that." She stripped down behind her car, tossed her clothes into it, and shifted into her wolf. She shook out her fur and trotted over to Bob's luxury sedan and sniffed around, giving it a wide perimeter at first.

Ragnar stepped closer and looked into the car's interior, then got onto his hands and knees and looked under the vehicle while Jamie stuck her nose under the chassis and sniffed around. He didn't see anything. A moment later, Jamie shifted back from her wolf, covering her privates.

"I didn't smell any explosives. All I picked up was fear and anger and the scent of a man and a woman. The man is a shifter and the woman is…not." She sounded unsure about the last assessment.

"She's a normie human," Ragnar said. "My mom."

"Oh. Your mom? I'm sorry."

Melinda must not have told the young woman much about what was going on, but she'd showed up anyway to help out. It spoke to her character.

"Do you think you can track them?" he asked.

She nodded with confidence. "Yeah. No problem. The trail is fresh."

"OK. Everyone, shift over. Follow Jamie's lead and take your cue from her until we get close, then I'm the lead. José, do you mind staying here and watching the cars in case they circle back?"

"No problem, man," José replied.

"I got a scatter gun for you," Sippi said. "Melinda, pop the trunk."

She opened the trunk, and Sippi pulled out a sawed-off shotgun and a box of shells, then handed them over to José. "We should give him all our keys too."

"Mine's in my car," Jamie said, nodding toward the Toyota Corolla.

Ragnar stared at his hammer for a moment. He didn't have any way to carry it in his wolf form. That was a problem he'd need to come up with a solution for. Being a wolf came enhanced strength and sharp teeth, but he needed options if he was going to get more involved in fighting the bikers.

Striding across the lot, he tossed it Melinda's the trunk and looked over at Judy. "You coming with us?"

"I'm done here. I'm after the Tarot Slayer, not some incompetent copycat. I've done far more than I wanted to already." She pushed off from the bike and mounted it. "Good luck."

Ragnar's eyes narrowed as he looked her over. He couldn't quite tell what she might be, but she was intelligent, crafty, and strong. And if he allowed himself to think it, quite attractive. But she also might be just as or even more dangerous than the quarry they were hunting. He still wasn't a hundred percent sure she wasn't linked with the Tarot Slayer.

"Well, thank you for freeing us and tracking them this far. I do appreciate it." He gave a slight bow as a cautiously respectful gesture.

She clicked her tongue and winked at him. "Happy hunting." Then she fired up her Ducati and took off, leaving a rooster tail of gravel and a cloud of dust in her wake.

He watched her zip across the lot and disappear down the road.

"Red, eye on the prize here," Melinda said, nudging him with her elbow. She started stripping down, setting her clothes in the open trunk. Sippi did the same.

Sippi smirked. "That's what he was doing."

"Shut up, Sippi." He looked around at everyone. "Any last thoughts or suggestions before we go?"

"This would be a lot easier if we were a pack," Roy said, pulling off his clothes.

Ragnar sighed. "Yeah. It would be, but that's a discussion for another day. Alright. Everyone shift. José, be careful. Don't take any chances."

"You got it." José gave him a jaunty salute and a friendly smile.

Ragnar appreciated him. He was never terribly noisy like Sippi and Melinda could be, and he was always reliable.

Like Sippie and Melinda, Ragnar tossed his clothes in Melinda's trunk and shifted over. He jogged over to Bob's car. A moment later, Jamie joined him, snuffling the ground. Once Sippi, Roy, and Melinda joined him in their wolf forms, Jamie moved forward, weaving back and forth until she homed in on the trail. She looked back once, then took off at a jog.

FORTY-NINE

Jamie never wavered. Occasionally she slowed just enough to lower her nose for what was probably a quick check-in. If the need to find his mom and the man who'd murdered his father hadn't been so urgent, he'd have asked her to show him what she was doing. As it was, he tried on his own to find the scents that belonged to their quarry. He thought he picked them up well enough he could have followed the trail, but not as efficiently as the more experienced young woman leading them deep into the woods. They climbed higher into the remote hills outside of Red City.

Eventually she slowed, but he couldn't figure out why. Nothing had changed. All he smelled was the woods around them and his friends as the wind blew from behind them.

He yelped as a gunshot rang out and a branch in front of him exploded into bits.

"Y'all can stop right there, ya hear?" a voice carried toward them from the left.

Ragnar slowly moved forward in a low crouch until he got around the bush that blocked his view in that direction. Not far away stood a wooden shack. A white man in a ratty looking trucker cap and stained overalls sat on a chair on the shack's porch. A rifle rested in his lap, though his hands were placed in such a way that he could quickly lift and fire it if he wanted to.

Ragnar stopped and growled.

"Now just calm your tits, y'hear? If'n I wanted to, I coulda put a slug right through your ear." He raised his gun a little. "I ain't missing nothing I ain't wantin' ta hit. I coulda plugged ya right in the keister if I wanted to at thrice the distance."

Ragnar let the growl die in his throat and lowered his jowls to cover his upper teeth.

"That's betta. Now change over so I can have a word with ya," the man said.

Behind Ragnar one of his friends growled. It sounded like Melinda. He turned his head and gave it a little shake. A second later, he stood up on his two human legs and covered his crotch with his hands.

The old man laughed. "Chilly out."

Ragnar rolled his eyes. "What do you want, old man?"

The old man squinted at him, accentuating the wrinkles around his eyes, and moved forward in his chair. "You look familiar." His eyes opened wider. "Ah, you play down yonder at the Honky Tonk, dontcha?"

"Yeah."

The old man made an appreciative sound. "You're a mighty fine picker and singer. You legit? Like your songs?"

Ragnar wondered what he meant, then the wind shifted, bringing the smell of fire and distilling spirits. They'd stumbled on the old man's moonshining operation. He was clearly some sort of supernatural, since he'd immediately recognized them as more than mundane wolves. He probably wanted to know if they were going to create a problem for his little enterprise.

"Well, we aren't friends with the law, if that's what you mean. Definitely not the ones around Red City," Ragnar said.

The old man grunted. "What about them there bully boys they send around on two wheels?"

Ragnar snorted derisively. "Definitely not."

"Good on ya. One or the other always trying to scam a nickel out my still."

Ragnar chuckled, relaxing a little at the easy nature of the man's speech. "It ain't shining if you're paying taxes."

"Damn right!" The old man stared at Ragnar for a moment, then nodded. "Y'all are alright. You following some people through my woods? A man and a woman?"

"Yeah. The woman is my mother. The man abducted her."

The old man whistled and gripped his gun. "Well, sheee-it. I wish I'd been able to stop them then. But the still needed a-tending. You know. Delicate operation. I can tell ya you're not far behind 'em."

A bit of hope surged through Ragnar. They were close. "Were they alone? Did you see anyone with them or has anyone else come up this way recently?"

"Nah. Nobody but them. I been up here for a few days now. Nice to get outta the house and breathe some fresh air." He reached down and picked up a jug and took a swig, sighing happily. "I'd offer you a little toot, but I think you'll want to be movin' along."

"Thanks."

"If ya git yer bidness done, stop by and enjoy some shine with me."

"I appreciate the offer."

The old man took another drink. Ragnar caught a whiff of it on the wind and nearly cringed. Whatever the hell he'd made had to be one step under rocket fuel. If he decided to take up the old man on his offer, he'd have to be careful not to drink too much and get in serious trouble.

"Now you kids run along. And give my regards to the lady. She's a fine-lookin' gal. Tell her Pappy sends his regards."

Ragnar clamped his jaw shut before he could say anything stupid, instead choosing to shift into his wolf to avoid offending the man. He gave a signal to Jamie, who found the trail and resumed her jog.

FIFTY

Close was a relative term. They jogged along for another hour under the night sky before they got within range of their quarry. When Jamie slowed and dropped into a hunting crouch, the crew stopped.

"We're almost there," Bob barked. "Don't make me drag you."

They were close. Ragnar's mom whimpered, and the hackles on Ragnar's back rose. Melinda bumped into him, distracting him before he could let go of the growl building in his chest. Ahead of them, Jamie sat behind a bush, waiting.

Catching her eye, he signaled for her to come back to them. He led his little group of friends behind a large bush next to a huge pine tree and shifted back to his human form, and whispered, "No need for you to shift over, just listen. I want y'all to split up and fan out to surround him. I'll go up the middle. Try to stay hidden if you can. Our priority is protecting my mom and getting her out of here."

Jamie, standing next to Ragnar, shifted over quickly. "And try to keep the breeze in your face or hide behind something that'll block the wind. He won't have an extra-sensitive nose like he would in wolf form, but he'll still be able to pick up our scents." She shifted back.

"Thanks, Jamie. He's probably just as inexperienced with using his other senses as we are, Jamie excepted, but let's be extra careful. OK. Let's go." Ragnar returned to his wolf form.

Slinking out in front of his friends, he raised his nose and found the breeze. It was coming into his face, so he picked up his pace but ensured he didn't step on anything noisy or break cover as he moved from bush to bush, tree to tree.

"Bob, please. I need to rest," Erin said, her voice tight with fear and breathless from exertion.

"Fine. But we can't take too long. We're close to the cabin," he replied.

Ragnar was close. Bob and his mom were on the other side of the vegetation. He lowered himself and crept slowly around the tree trunk until he could hide behind a bush he could see under. Though most of his view was blocked by the branches and leaves, he saw two pairs of feet and lower legs. His mother was sitting on fallen tree, and Bob paced nearby.

"Why, Bob? Why'd you do it?"

"Because it was the right thing to do."

Erin gasped. "How was murdering your best friend the right thing to do?"

"He was going to get us all killed, Erin. Me, you, his precious little Ragnar. All of us. If he formed a pack, the Black Suns would've retaliated. They'd murder us all to make an example out of us."

A low growl formed in Ragnar's throat, and Bob stopped pacing to look around. Ragnar stifled his frustration. A moment later, Bob resumed his nervous pacing. "I had to protect you, Erin."

"By killing my husband?"

"If he'd loved you, he wouldn't have put you in danger. He would have collected the money and kept paying the Black Suns off. But he put his pride before you." Bob paused, facing away from Erin. "I'd never do that to you, Erin."

"Why?" Erin asked tentatively.

"I'd never do anything to cause you harm. If Gunnar loved you, he'd have never risked your life. If he'd loved you…like I love you."

Ragnar wasn't a hateful man, except when it came to the

racist and fascist bikers. Their violation of the social contract exempted them from the niceties of society. But a burning rage now flamed to life in his gut. Bob had murdered his father for money and to take his mother. Bob had betrayed Ragnar's whole family for his selfish desires for wealth and unrequited lust.

Ragnar raised himself off his stomach and peeled back his lips in a noiseless snarl.

Erin gaped and stood up. "What? Bob…"

Bob stared longingly at Ragnar's mother. "You'll come to love me, Erin. With time."

Erin backed away. "Bob…"

Bob matched her pace. "I can take care of you. Better than Gunnar. He was a sucker. You lived well, but he couldn't put his own pride aside."

Ragnar walked around the bush and growled loudly. Bob spun around, then darted to Ragnar's mom, snatching her upper arm.

She yelped in pain. "Bob, you're hurting me."

"Shut up." He backed away from Ragnar, dragging his mother with him. Looking over his shoulder for a moment, he grinned desperately at Ragnar and changed his angle until they approached the edge of a cliff they'd stopped near. "If you come any closer, we'll see if your mom can fly."

Tears rolled down Erin's frightened face. "Bob, please…"

"Ragnar, if you ever hope to see your mommy again, turn around and run away." Bob's eyes shifted around frantically looking for an escape route.

Ragnar stopped and shifted back to his human form, covering himself with his hands. "There's no escape, Bob. Let my mom go."

To emphasize the point, Melinda, Roy, and Sippi emerged from their various hiding spots and growled. The sound raised the hair on the back of Ragnar's neck. There was a deep level of aggression and anger in those growls, but he could match and top it with ease.

"He's been ripping off our people for years, Mom. And he murdered Dad to keep the money flowing," Ragnar spat out.

"Shut your idiot mouth, or I'll make sure you leave these woods an orphan, if I even let you live." Bob reached into his jacked and pulled out a gun.

The hand holding the gun was wrapped in a bandage. A mundane wound, such as from a simple letter opener, should have healed by now on a wolf shifter. Ragnar's mind flashed back to the simulacrum for the dagger's enchantment, which was in the pocket of his jeans in Melinda's trunk. The same jeans he'd worn when he and Roy had visited Bob a few days ago. It had worked. The proxy had marked the hand that had wielded the dagger. He'd have to tell Roy about it later, when a gun wasn't being pointed at him.

A malicious smirk spread across the murderer's face as he pulled back the hammer on the revolver. Ragnar would likely heal from a simple gunshot, unless he took one to the face or the heart. Or if it was one of those magic bullets the bikers had been using.

"You'll never get away with this, Bob. You might shoot me, but one of my friends will take you down and rip your throat out."

Bob scoffed. "Your coward friends? None of them have the guts to kill. They don't know the thrill of watching the life leave some-one's eyes. Knowing you have total power over them and that you took their most precious thing from them..." A vile gleam washed over his eyes. "I'd love to get the hat trick, Ragnar. Grandfather, Father, Son. The whole fucking lot of you noble bastards."

Ragnar's jaw dropped and his head spun. He'd thought it had been the bikers who'd killed his grandfather, Magnus. Had it really been Bob who'd claimed the life of the man he'd never met but admired? Had Bob been a tool of the Black Suns all those years ago? Ragnar's hands shook with rage, and he clenched his jaw and ground his teeth. Erin sobbed, her hand over her mouth.

FIFTY-ONE

The moment stretched out into an eternity as Bob breathed heavily, a hungry look smeared over his face. Out of the corner of Ragnar's eye, he saw a wolf creep out from hiding and slink on her belly toward Bob. Ragnar had wondered where Jamie was.

As long as Bob didn't turn his head too far in her direction, he wouldn't see her and she'd be able to take him from behind. But the plan failed when he looked in her direction. Whipping his gun around, he fired a shot at Jamie. She yelped and kept back as a puff of dirt rose from the ground where the bullet had narrowly missed her. He took another step back, dragging Erin with him.

"Bob, not another step!" Ragnar yelled.

"Or what?" He waved his gun around, stopping for a moment to aim at Ragnar and each of his friends.

Bob had to be doing the math. He'd just wasted one of his six bullets. He'd have to hit and disable each of his targets with only one shot apiece. He couldn't afford a single miss or poorly aimed shot. Ragnar doubted the accountant was that good with a gun, but he didn't want to risk his life and his friends. His mother was still the priority, and they needed to get her away from Bob before he threw her off the cliff.

Ragnar's eyes flicked around to his friends, who all stood still but were poised and ready to leap forward if an opportunity arose. But if they miscalculated their attacks, Bob might get knocked over the edge and take Ragnar's mom with him.

"Let my mom go, Bob, and you can walk away. None of us will follow you. You can just disappear and never come back." If Bob did take the offer, Ragnar hoped José would pop the murdering bastard in the face when he walked out of the woods alone. If José didn't, they'd track Bob to the ends of the earth to make sure he got what was coming to him. It might have been better if they'd left Roy to watch the vehicles. He wouldn't hesitate to pay Bob back for what he'd done.

Bob must have read the thoughts running through Ragnar's mind. "No deal." He put the gun to Erin's head. "Now back up. All of you!"

"Do it," Ragnar said, his voice tight. He took two steps back to join his friends. They all moved farther backward together.

Bob's shoulders relaxed slightly but hunched up again when a growl and a yowl shattered the momentary silence. Unable to stop himself, he spun around just as something large leapt up from the depths of the cliff and struck Erin in the back. Then the creature sprang off his mother's back toward Bob. It struck him in the side and sent him tumbling over the cliff with a short scream.

Ragnar's heart jumped into his throat as he surged forward. The creature landed nimbly, then sat and wrapped its long tail around its feet like a cat would. Ragnar scooped up his unmoving mom and carried her away from the creature as his wolf friends moved forward slowly, filling the air with a chorus of warning growls.

Once he was behind the nearest tree, he set his mom down and propped her up against the trunk. He lifted her head. When his mother groaned and her eyes fluttered open, he heaved a sigh of relief.

"Are you OK?" he asked.

She groaned again and raised her hand to touch her forehead, where a lump was rising. "I...I think so."

They'd have to get her checked out when they got back to town. She'd only been unconscious for maybe a few seconds though, so she'd probably be fine.

"OK. I'll be right back. Don't move."

She patted him on the cheek. "I'll be fine."

He nodded and stood up. Stepping around the bush, he folded his arms across his chest. A big black panther or jaguar sat prim and proper like a house cat. His friends had stopped about fifteen feet from the creature. And though their growls had stopped, their teeth were still out in snarls of warning. The cat tilted its head and blinked slowly as Ragnar approached him.

"Who are you?" Ragnar asked.

The cat just blinked at him again. Then its ears flattened in annoyance, and it twisted around toward the cliff. A faint groan of pain drifted on the wind.

Taking a wide berth around the panther, Ragnar walked to the edge of the cliff and looked over. On a ledge about fifty feet down lay Bob. He was still alive and moving. He rolled over onto his stomach and pushed himself onto his hands and knees.

He looked around him frantically, probably searching for a gun that wasn't there. It must have gone over the edge and fallen somewhere else.

"Hey, Bob. What are you doing down there?" Ragnar asked casually.

Bob glanced up and growled a human growl, a look of pure hatred on his face. He sat up and started stripping off his clothes.

Ragnar scanned the edge of the cliff, looking for a way down so he could go after Bob, but didn't see anything. "Damn it," he mumbled. "Uncle Roy, can you run back to that old moonshiner and see if he's got a rope?"

He yipped and took off. A moment after Roy disappeared, Bob shifted over to his wolf with a canine yelp of pain. He'd probably broken something when he'd fallen. Scrambling around the edge of the ledge, he leapt to another smaller ledge and worked his way down the mountain, sometimes jumping, sometimes carefully placing paws on outcroppings.

"Shit, he's getting away." Ragnar sidled closer to the edge of cliff, wondering if he could find a place to land above the bigger ledge Bob had fallen onto.

A hand rested on his shoulder. "Red, you can't go down there." Melinda, standing behind him, placed her other hand on his other shoulder and squeezed. "We'll get him. I promise. None of us will rest until we bring him to justice." She said the last word with heat and an invective that said she probablydidn't mean turning Bob over to the cops.

"Fuck!" he screamed, staring down at Bob.

The yell distracted Bob, and he misplaced a foot. Scrambling for a moment, he regained his balance, much to Ragnar's chagrin. He watched as Bob carefully moved down the cliff until he disappeared from sight.

When Ragnar looked to his right, he noticed the big cat, as well as his friends still in their wolf forms, had been watching Bob's descent as well. "OK, cat. Who the fuck are you?"

The cat tilted its head up to the sky and yawned, revealing massive, sharp fangs. Then it turned and walked away. Ragnar tensed until the cat altered its course to avoid both his friends and the spot where he'd stashed his mom.

Once it was far enough away that it probably felt safe, the cat shifted into the human woman who'd been haunting his steps this whole time.

"I thought you were done being involved," he said.

She shrugged. "Curiosity."

Behind him, one of his friends still in their wolf from chuffed in laughter — probably about her being a cat with curiosity.

"Who are you?"

She dragged her eyes over his body and winked. "I see the carpet matches the drapes."

Ragnar blushed, immediately covering his crotch with one hand while bring the other hand up to point into his eyes with his forefinger and middle finger. "My eyes are up here."

She laughed. It wasn't a pretty little tinkle of a bell, nor was it a deep guffaw. It felt like honest humor, and he kind of liked it.

"Judy…Sarah… Who are you?" he asked again, growing more determined to at least get one clear answer from her.

"Well, *Red*, if you insist… Ballou. Cat Ballou." She shifted into her giant black cat and bounded away, leaving a last laugh lingering in his ear as she disappeared into the woods.

Behind him, his friends chuckled and laughed, all now in their human voices.

Ragnar shook his head. "Fuck y'all." But he couldn't keep a humorous tone out of the curse.

A few minutes later, Roy trotted out of the woods with a coiled rope dangling from his mouth.

"I'll guess we'll have to drop that off on the way out," Ragnar said, grimacing. He wasn't ready for a mouthful of moonshine.

FIFTY-TWO

Ragnar couldn't wait to get out of the baggy overalls Pappy had lent him. They weren't exactly clean, and without underwear, they chafed in places he didn't want to have chafing. But it was cold, and he didn't want to have to walk his mom out of the woods wearing nothing but the suit he'd been born in.

He also couldn't wait to brush his teeth. The taste of moonshine lingered like hellfire and a cosmic practical joke. He'd barely managed two small swigs before having to pass it on. Though he didn't want to insult his host, he couldn't force down more than that. With all Pappy drank, Ragnar wondered how much of his liver was actually left. It was probably rock hard.

Roy and the rest of the gang—minus Jamie who'd gone home to get some sleep before work—had left in Melinda's car to head straight to Bob's house to ransack it before the villain could beat them to it. Unfortunately, they'd had to leave Bob's car up in the woods because the keys had gone over the cliff with him. But at least that meant he'd have to walk all the way back to Red City, giving them a head start.

Using Roy's pickup, Ragnar dropped his mother off at home to take nap. Owing to the urgency of searching for evidence in Bob's house, he'd called Delphine and asked her to take his mom to urgent car. After he scarfed down a sandwich and brushed his teeth, he changed clothes and climbed back into Roy's pickup.

Bob had been robbing a lot of the shifters and supernaturals of Red City. For a long time. If he'd actually killed Ragnar's grandfather at the behest of the bikers, then he'd been in their employ for decades. He'd likely been skimming off the top for ages, even before he tried to double the fees to pad his corrupt nest egg. Ragnar wasn't sure how it all had worked. That was one of the things they hoped to discover at Bob's house.

Ever cautious, Ragnar parked a few blocks away and used his shadow stick to sneak into Bob's house under the cover of the predawn darkness.

Melinda waited just inside the door. "Hey, Red. Did you get your mom home OK?"

"Yeah. She's resting now. Delphine will get her into urgent care later."

It had been long-ass day after another long day. He was bordering on passing out right where he stood. But this was too important. He'd catch a nap later, then crash out for a few days once they got things settled.

"We find anything?" Ragnar asked.

Melinda chucked her chin toward the coffee table. "His laptop. It's locked. But right now, they've split up and are scouring the basement and the office."

"Hmm. I'll have to find someone who can crack it. We need to find out where he's got all the money hidden and whatever other evidence he might have tucked away."

Melinda grunted, then yawned. "Fuck, I'm tired, Red."

"Yeah. I hear ya. That moonshine ain't helping."

She chuckled. "Ain't? Those overalls soaked in deep."

"Ha-ha."

She laughed harder. "You could've used those overalls when what's-her-butt started making jokes."

He rolled his eyes. "Well, at least we know she's a cat shifter."

"And rather impressive in her naked lady form, too. And she seems to have taken a shine to you."

He couldn't disagree with Melinda about Judy-Sarah-Cat's "naked lady form." Ragnar thought Cat or Judy or Sarah or whatever was indeed quite beautiful. But she was a total pain in the ass, and he still couldn't figure out why she kept showing up and how she was linked to the Tarot Slayer. "Hardly. She only exists to torment me and cause trouble."

"She did save your mom and knock Bob over the cliff. And she did it after she took us up into the woods and insisting she was done helping us."

"I guess. I still can't figure out what her game is. But she'll probably move on since the Tarot Slayer isn't here. If that's why she's really here."

Melinda raised a knowing eyebrow. "You could go look for trouble. She might just show up to make sure you get in more."

"I don't have room in my life for that kind of bullshit. Connie dumped me a couple months ago, and my dad was just murdered, and I need to take care of my mom." He sank onto the couch. "And I'm not looking for her kind of trouble."

"Red. You need to find some kind of trouble. You're not that old, and you're already trying to be an old man."

"Whatever." He hoisted himself off the couch. "It was a mistake to sit down. I'm going to go help them look around."

Melinda stopped him, placing both hands on his shoulders. "I'm glad you're OK and we got Erin to safety. I was worried when you disappeared. I thought the Tarot Slayer had taken you."

He snorted. "I guess he did, sort of. I honestly don't know how to feel. I'm glad he's not the real Tarot Slayer. With all the things going on in Red City, we don't need an infamous serial killer here too. But my dad is still dead."

"I mean, Bob was kind of a serial killer. In his own way. How many people has he killed over the years? Three in the last few weeks and a fourth if he was the one who got your grandpa."

He nodded, squeezing the bridge of his nose. "I guess we'll have to sort that out. Though it's going to have to wait until I have a few nights of sleep. I'm running on empty here."

"We'll get it figured out. Let's get this place stripped down so we can all go home and get to bed." She grabbed a couple kitchen towels from a nearby stack. "I grabbed these for us to use. Be sure to wipe down anything you touch. Let's not leave any tracks. I'm sure it's OK if some your prints are here, but not in every room. Better safe than sorry."

He grunted, then yawned. "Right."

He headed upstairs to begin his search. Roy was already working up there—he must have finished his previous location. Together, they were easily able to move furniture without dragging it and creating marks. He kept mostly silent, as did Roy, who wasn't much of a talker at the best of times.

It all felt very anticlimactic to Ragnar. They'd found the man who'd murdered his father and two other people to cover it up, but he'd slithered away like the snake he was. Ragnar sighed.

"You going to be OK, boy?" Roy asked quietly.

"I'll let you know after I get some sleep."

Roy set a reassuring hand on Ragnar's shoulder. "We'll get him. I promise."

"Thanks, Uncle Roy."

"I don't think there's anything up here. Let's go check in with everyone else."

Ragnar followed him downstairs and helped the rest of the crew finish their search. It was a good thing they had Roy's pickup, because the crew had found a couple safes. They'd load them up and crack them later.

When they thought they'd finished, they loaded up, putting everything in Roy's pickup truck. Ragnar would keep everything in the shed, which could easily be rune warded. It already had some basic security wards his father had set up, and between Roy and Ragnar, they could make it virtually impregnable…at least from the likes of Bob.

But figuring out all the dirty deeds Bob had done and tracking him down would be tasks for another day. As much as the escape stuck in Ragnar's craw, it didn't prevent him from passing out as his head hit the pillow.

EPILOGUE

Ragnar picked up the phone. "Hello?"

"Hey, Red. It's a beautiful sunny day, and we don't have too many of those left for the rain sets in. I'm coming to pick you up," Melinda said in a cheerful voice.

"I don't feel like going out." He hadn't gone out in the week since Bob had slipped through their fingers.

It had felt like the ultimate betrayal. Bob had been his father's best friend—almost like a brother—and he'd betrayed and murdered him in hopes of picking up the pieces of Ragnar's mother's shattered life. How Bob had decided to try to blame it on the Tarot Slayer, Ragnar had no idea. But once the news got out that the dead body the police had found wasn't the real Tarot Slayer—and it got out fast because of the media feeding frenzy Bob's well-timed leaks to the press created—the city fell back into its normal state of crime-ridden hellhole, just without a celebrity criminal.

"Don't make us physically drag you out," Sippi called in the background. "So you better make sure you're dressed and ready, or you're leaving in your Underoos."

"Yeah!" José yelled in the background. "But I bet he goes commando."

Ragnar laughed. "Fine. Whatever. How long before you're here?"

"Fifteen minutes," Melinda replied.

"Good. I've got time for a shower." He bent his nose toward his armpit and cringed. "Believe me, you don't want to hang out with me until I do."

"OK. I rescind the 'drag you out naked' dictate. Provisionally. See you shortly, Red." Melinda hung up.

He didn't doubt they'd drag him out, so he rolled off the bed and grabbed some clean clothes before crossing the hall to the bathroom. He made it a quick shower and was waiting outside by the time they rolled up in Melinda's car. José leaned across the backseat and opened the door for him.

"Where we going?" Ragnar asked after buckling himself in.

"It's a surprise," Melinda said.

"I've got a connection…" Sippi faded off before saying more once Melinda turned and scowled at him.

Ragnar chuckled. "Of course you do, Sippi. You always know a guy."

"He's even got a guy to find him new guys if he doesn't have a guy," José said.

He exhaled and relaxed into the seat. It did feel good to get out of his room. The general mirth of his friends helped raise his own spirits some. A little outing would be just what he needed to get out of his funk. Though he hadn't expected they'd end up in the business district, with its high rises and suit-clad businesspeople. He'd figured they'd go to the Honky Tonk Woman. But apparently Sippi had a "guy" with a connection downtown.

Melinda parked in a public garage, and they walked out into the beautiful day. It was just warm enough for a light jacket to perfectly handle the occasional stray breeze. Ragnar raised his face to the sun, letting the rays warm his skin.

Plucking out her phone, Melinda checked a message. "Good. They're already there."

Ragnar thought about asking but didn't feel like expending the energy to open his mouth. He'd find out what was going on shortly, and it would be a surprise. He could do with a good surprise for a change. They walked through downtown while José, Melinda, and Sippi chatted and he brought up the rear.

The crowds seemed unusually big for a random autumn day. Then he saw one of the banners announcing the big reveal of the new skyscraper.

"I didn't think you cared about architecture," Ragnar said.

"I don't," Melinda said. "But Sippi's friend got us a balcony table with a view of the festivities, and it's a glorious day for drinking in the sun."

"Fair enough."

A few minutes later, they disembarked from the elevator and were escorted through the bar and out onto the impressive balcony facing the new high rise, which had been covered in construction netting to protect workers and passersby while the building had been built. It had also effectively blocked the building from view. Melinda explained the owners had decided to make an event out of it—no doubt wishing to bring people downtown on a weekend day to fill the other businesses they probably had a hand in.

"Ragnar!" Delphine stood from the table as did his Uncle Roy. "So good to see you."

"You too." He hugged her.

"Boy," Roy said before giving Ragnar a back-patting hug. "Glad you got out of the house."

Once they were seated around their table, the server took care of their drink and appetizer orders, returning a few minutes later with a tray full of glasses. Ragnar's stomach growled, and he realized he hadn't had anything to eat for the day. He decided to put his glass down after taking the required drink after the cheers—he'd wait the few more minutes until the appetizers arrived before returning to the beer.

"OK. I'm putting a blanket ruling on the gathering," Melinda said. "No talking about recent events. This is just to have fun. Period."

Everyone agreed with another raised glass. Ragnar raised his glass and took another drink. He ran his eyes over the building across the street from their vantage point. It had to be over forty stories tall. He couldn't remember what the proposed design had been. He was sure he'd seen it on the news but hadn't cared enough to bother about remembering it.

After some appetizers and a second beer, Ragnar loosened up and joined in on the conversation. Even the normally laconic Roy participated and occasionally laughed at his friends' jokes. Ragnar even forgot about the building as he focused in on the table, until a nearby loudspeaker barked to life.

Everyone on the balcony shifted their gazes to the building, though most appeared to not care about the words being spoken, as they maintained their conversations. Once the talking was finished, fireworks exploded into the sky. The bright day dimmed the effect, but at least they were loud and smelly.

Then the construction netting slowly descended and the crowd quieted as the top of the building was revealed. It wasn't like the dropping of a sheet that instantly fell to the ground. The netting had been rigged up on poles and pulleys, so it required time to be lowered.

His friends hadn't come there to check out the building. It was just an excuse to gather and drink in the sun, so they returned to their conversation, though they had to speak a bit louder over the squeaks and grinds of the construction netting being lowered.

It wasn't until the screams started that he and his friends returned their attention to the surroundings.

The netting was about halfway down and had revealed something dangling against the side of the building. The yells and shouts of people mixed with the squeaking and grinding of the curtain still being lowered created a general cacophony that began to irate Ragnar.

"What is that?" Melinda asked, squinting up at whatever had drawn everyone's attention.

It looked vaguely person shaped. And there was a lot of red smeared against the shiny windows of the skyscraper.

"Oh my," Delphine said, a set of binoculars pressed to her eyes.

She must have brought them to check out festivities. "Ragnar." She lowered the binoculars and thrust them at him.

He took them and looked up. A body in a rough-cut tunic swung gently back and forth in the breeze, smearing more red around the window as it went. Flashes of silver caught his eye. Six swords—not kitchen knives, actual swords—had been stabbed into the body, three on each side, with the top pair pointing up at an angle, the middle pair pointing to the side, and the bottom pair pointing down at an angle.

"Fuck me," he hissed under his breath. He swept the binoculars up to the figure's head, and his jaw dropped. The surrounding noise faded to nothing in his ears. "Bob."

He stared at the dangling body of his father's murderer for a while until he couldn't look any more and lowered the binoculars. One of his friends took them from him, looked at the body, and gasped.

"I guess that solves the question of where he is," Roy said.

Delphine rummaged through her purse and pulled a deck of cards from its depths. She searched through them until she found what she wanted, setting it in the middle of the table. Ragnar drew his eyes away from the corpse of Bob and looked at the card she'd placed on the table.

"Seven of Swords," Delphine said, returning her gaze to the building and the body.

"But I only see six swords," Melinda said, peering through the binoculars.

"Cher, the name of the building is the Claymore Tower. It's the seventh sword." Her hand shook as she took a deep drink from her cocktail. "Apparently the Tarot Slayer doesn't like imposters."

THE RED CITY REAPER RIDES FOR THE FIRST TIME IN...

A SHOT FOR DEATH

CHAPTER ONE

Dax

Dax leaned against the scarred wooden bar top, looking over the sparse mid-morning crowd. Each time the front door opened, the knots between his shoulder blades clenched tighter. Until he'd become a human, he'd never known the annoyance and discomfort of physical responses to emotions. Something had felt off since he'd parked his motorcycle, something that was all too familiar. Something dark.

Death was present everywhere all the time, especially in a place like Red City. But today, something about the constant undercurrent niggled at the back of his mind. Every time someone came or went, a whiff of a frayed life thread entered, teasing him, taunting him.

He checked his watch. Tomi was late, which was unlike him. His bar manager and friend was one of the most reliable people he knew. Dax swallowed nervously and pulled in a deep breath through his nose, breathing slowly so as not to make noise. Even concentrating on every detail, he couldn't sort it out, he couldn't identify where the thread came from, went, or to whom it belonged. He figured that if it belonged to someone he knew well, it would be easier to find the owner. At least, that's what he hoped. He stopped a frustrated grunt from escaping his lips. Still nothing.

With a quick scan down the bar to distract himself, he pushed off and strolled to the balding white patron at the end of the bar. "Can I get you another round, Bill?"

"Yeah. I got one more in me," Bill replied, slugging down the last swallow before sliding the glass the short distance toward Dax.

Setting the glass by the sink, he grabbed a clean pint glass and filled it with Pabst before setting it in front of Bill. Four dollars were already waiting on the bar. Dax grabbed them, dropped one in the tip bucket, and deposited the other three into the till.

A gust of cold, moist air and another hit of impending darkness blasted through the freshly opened door. He whipped his head around to the front. Still no Tomi. Ginger, one of his morning regulars, shivered for a second then proceeded into the bar. He liked Ginger as much as any of his regulars, but the disappointment of not seeing his friend added to his discomfort.

Dax's worry compounded. His manager was never late. Well… rarely. But never forty-five minutes late, and certainly not without calling.

"I didn't expect to see you in today, Ginger," Dax said. "What can I get you?"

Ginger ran a hand through his shaggy, wet red hair, flinging away some of the accumulated rain. "Hadn't planned on it, but got home after work, and the heat's out in the fucking building. The super has no idea when it'll be back on." Ginger hung his coat up on the hook under the bar.

Dax pushed off the bar and turned toward the glassware. "That's unfortunate. The usual?"

"Yeah, the usual." Ginger turned toward Bill, running a hand through his damp hair again. "Hey, Bill."

Bill chucked his chin toward Ginger. "Yo, Ginger."

Dax grabbed a bucket glass and poured in a heavy shot of Jim Beam then filled a half pint for the beer back. After he set it down, he refilled his coffee from the carafe on the counter, cradling the cup in both hands to warm them as he leaned up against the back bar. After he felt it had cooled enough, he took a sip and made a face.

"Gack," he tossed the coffee into the sink then followed it with the rest from the carafe. He couldn't tell if it was just bad coffee or the increasingly bad mood he found himself in as he tried to home in on the sense of death. He couldn't even tell if it had happened or was only the potential of future events. He used to be so much more in tune with the threads of life and death—before his exile. Before being forced to live as a human.

Bill laughed. "You've got to get better coffee."

Dax scowled. "It's fine when it's fresh."

"Do your taste buds work, bro?" Ginger asked. "Even fresh, it tastes like shit."

Shaking his head, Dax shrugged. "If you want good hot beverages, I'll make you tea. Coffee is just wake up juice."

"You can keep your hot leaf juice," Ginger replied, with a coarse laugh.

Bill chuckled along, nodding at his friend down at the other end of the bar. "It's cold as fuck out there. Get some better coffee. I might want a Spanish coffee sometime."

Dax narrowed his eyes and looked between the two men. Coffee cocktails would be an up charge compared to their usual PBRs. He'd have to talk it over with Tomi, if he ever showed up. Looking up at the clock, the ball of tension in his gut tightened further. An hour late.

Movement out of the corner of his eye drew his attention. A tall, fat Black man stepped out of the hall leading from the back of the bar. He'd shucked his coat in the office already, but the black beanie he wore glistened with rain. Dax sighed in relief, his shoulders dropping but only fractionally.

"Sorry, boss. Had to help my mama with something this morning, and she insisted on making me breakfast." He shrugged. "You know you can't say no to her when she insists on offering food."

Dax nodded. "No worries. How is your mama?"

"The same. But when does she ever change?" Tomi washed his hands in the sink before drying them off. "Looks like I missed the morning rush."

"You didn't. This is it. If you can handle this unruly crowd, I'm going to head to the bank." He'd hoped Tomi's arrival would alleviate his sense of dread, but not only did it linger, it had intensified. Even with Tomi's presence, he couldn't discount him as a possibility. He still couldn't figure out why his sense of death was vibrating his awareness nor where it was intersecting his own life thread.

"Have fun. It's nasty out there."

Dax grunted and stepped into the hall and down to the office, pulling his keys from his pocket. After he threw on his black leather coat and a scarf, he opened the safe and pulled out the deposits from yesterday. His brow furrowed. The envelope was much thinner than he'd have preferred. Though this bar had never made a robust revenue in the years since he and Tomi opened it, he'd hoped things would pick up some. At least they kept enough money coming in to keep the employees paid, the bank off their backs, and enough left over to keep a roof over his head, barely. Stuffing the deposits into the custom zipper pocket inside his coat, he padlocked the pocket closed. He grabbed his helmet and pulled it over his shoulder-length black hair.

He pushed through the back door, shoving it closed, and paused under the awning in the alley. The rain had picked up since he'd opened this morning. It poured off the awning in rivers. Sticking his pale white hand out, he let the cold, late winter rain wash over it. An involuntarily shiver ran through him. At least it washed some of the stink of the alley away.

He sighed. "I need to get a car."

Inhaling deeply, he narrowed his eyes. The hint of death lingered. He shook his head, frustrated with his inability to track it. Being a human definitely hampered his former strength. About to close the visor of his helmet, he stopped when he thought he heard something. Looking down and to the left, he almost missed the movement in the shadows.

"Mew." A tiny kitten stepped out of a half-soaked box—the awning provided protection to part of it—but the rain was quickly winning the battle as it seeped into the rest of the cardboard.

In the dark gloom of the rainy day, the black kitten looked like a smudge. Pursing his lips, Dax squatted down. The kitten looked curious but stayed back. Holding out his hand, he left it hanging until the kitten approached and sniffed his fingers. He gave it a scratch under the chin. The kitten gave a half-hearted purr then shuffled back toward his box, looking over his shoulder before disappearing into its shadows. Was it the kitten's life thread?

Shrugging, he flipped down his visor and walked to the end of the long awning and mounted the big, custom chopper motorcycle. Kicking it to life, it rumbled loudly, adding its sound to the rain and the few cars moving down the street. He joined traffic and headed toward Redemption City First National Bank. Fortunately, they had a parking garage nearby, so he didn't have to park in the rain.

After he made his deposits, he slipped into a nearby coffee shop, picked up a proper cup, and sat down to warm up. Bill and Red were right. The coffee he served was shit. He'd have to get something better. When he finished, he tugged his helmet on and darted outside to run toward the parking garage. He really needed to get a car if he was going to make it another winter in Red City.

Join Dax in A Shot For Death, the first book in the Red City Reaper series.

ACKNOWLEDGMENTS

First, I'd like to acknowledge my lovely and talented partner Amy Cissell. She encouraged me to start working on my novels and supported me through the whole process, providing a sounding board and editing throughout the process. She really is awesome. You should check out her books.

Second, a big thanks to all my readers who have made it this far. We've gone on a journey together, and I hope you thought it was as fun as I did.

There are a lot of other people that contributed to this series, but I'd like to mention a few specific people. Dan—Thanks for your support and excitement about this series. You're the best friend and fan a person could have. Sue—you saw the first inklings of Luke in The Centurion Immortal and have provided top notch edits throughout the entire series. My ARC Team—Thanks for all the reviews! I hope you enjoyed the journey.

To my author friends in FAKA, your support and counsel have been invaluable. To my first writing group, you're a big part of who Luke has become.

To all the bars and coffee shops in North Portland, you have no idea how many words were laid down inside your walls. The Chill n Fill - Luke first drew breath on the page under your roof. I can't not include the others—Tiny Bubble Room, Leisure, Great North, Slim's, 45th Parallel—you've all been a home away from home when I needed to shake up the tedium of writing in the home office.

ABOUT THE AUTHOR

C. Thomas Lafollette is a student of history and a world traveler. He's dined with a Prime Minister, read poetry with Yevgeny Yevtushenko, and drank beer with monks. He's the author of the action-adventure urban fantasy series Luke Irontree & The Last Vampire War and the Red City Reaper series. Besides reading and writing, he loves a good action movie, be it a Hollywood blockbuster or a classic Samurai flick, as well as the occasional rom-com. He lives in Porto, Portugal with his partner – the devastatingly talented author Amy Cissell – his stepdaughter, and their three jerkface cats.

facebook.com/CThomasLafollette

bookbub.com/authors/c-thomas-lafollette

amazon.com/C-Thomas-Lafollette/e/B09JMTR7W7

goodreads.com/cthomaslafollette

threads.net/@cthomaslafollette

instagram.com/CThomasLafollette

tiktok.com/@cthomaslafollette

ALSO BY C. THOMAS LAFOLLETTE

Luke Irontree & The Last Vampire War

Book 0 - The Centurion Immortal

Book 1 - Dark Fangs Rising - March 22, 2022

Book 2 - Dark Fangs Raging - April 19, 2022

Book 3 - Dark Fangs Descending - May 17, 2022

Book 4 - Blood Empire Reborn - August 23, 2022

Book 5 - Blood Empire Avenged - September 20, 2022

Book 6 - Blood Empire Infiltrated - October 18, 2022

Book 7 - Blood Empire Burning - November 15, 2022

Book 8 - Ancient Sword Falling - March 21, 2023

Book 9 - Ancient Sword Unyielding - August 22, 2023

Book 10 - Ancient Sword Shattering - January 4, 2023

The Luke Irontree Historical Adventures

Rise of the Centurio Immortalis - April 5, 2022

Fall of the Centurio Immortalis - May 31, 2022

The Moonlight Centurion*

The Highway Centurion*

Red City Reaper - A Dark Urban Fantasy Adventure

Book 0 - Dead in Red City*

Book 1 - A Shot For Death - March 26, 2024

Book 1.5 - Death Uncaged - March 21, 2024

Book 2 - Death Orders a Double - July 23, 2024

Book 3 - Death With A Twist - November 7, 2024

Book 4 - Death On The Rocks* - February 25, 2025

Book 5 - A Fifth Of Death* - Fall 2025

Book 6 - A Dash Of Death*

Book 7 - A Chaser of Death*

Book 8 - A Nightcap of Death *

Red City Runesmith - A Wolf Shifter Urban Fantasy

Book 0 - Runing With The Wolves* - Summer 2025

Book 1 - Road to Rune - June 24, 2025

Book 2 - On The Rune Again* - 2025

Book 3 - Runing On Empty*

Book 4 - Runing Wild*

*Forthcoming

Titles and release dates may be subject to change.

www.ingramcontent.com/pod-product-compliance
Lightning Source LLC
Chambersburg PA
CBHW020746310726
48969CB00002B/440